Praise for
Double Booked for Death

"A fun mystery that kept me guessing to the end!"

—Rebecca M. Hale, *New York Times* bestselling author of
How to Wash a Cat

"Clever . . . Bibliophiles, ailurophiles, and mystery fans will
enjoy *Double Booked for Death*."

—*Richmond Times-Dispatch*

"A charming, cozy read, especially if cats are your cup of tea.
Make sure the new Black Cat Bookshop series is on your
bookshelf."

—Elaine Viets, national bestselling author of
the Dead-End Job Mysteries

"An engaging new series . . . Definitely the start of something
great."

—Sandra Balzo, award-winning author of
the Main Street Mysteries

"[An] outstanding debut to a very promising new series . . .
The characters are interesting and smart, the mystery is clever
and provides clues the reader will notice but [doesn't] let the
cat out of the bag prematurely . . . I had such fun reading
about Darla and her cohorts, and found Hamlet's antics made
me smile . . . If you enjoy a cozy mystery, a clever cat, a bookstore setting and smart, realistic characters you are sure to
enjoy *Double Booked for Death*." —MyShelf.com

continued . . .

Berkley Prime Crime titles by Ali Brandon

DOUBLE BOOKED FOR DEATH
A NOVEL WAY TO DIE

A NOVEL WAY

 TO DIE

ALI BRANDON

BERKLEY PRIME CRIME, NEW YORK

THE BERKLEY PUBLISHING GROUP
Published by the Penguin Group
Penguin Group (USA) Inc.
375 Hudson Street, New York, New York 10014, USA

Penguin Group (Canada), 90 Eglinton Avenue East, Suite 700, Toronto, Ontario M4P 2Y3, Canada
(a division of Pearson Penguin Canada Inc.) • Penguin Books Ltd., 80 Strand, London WC2R 0RL,
England • Penguin Group Ireland, 25 St. Stephen's Green, Dublin 2, Ireland (a division of Penguin
Books Ltd.) • Penguin Group (Australia), 250 Camberwell Road, Camberwell, Victoria 3124, Australia
(a division of Pearson Australia Group Pty. Ltd.) • Penguin Books India Pvt. Ltd., 11 Community
Centre, Panchsheel Park, New Delhi—110 017, India • Penguin Group (NZ), 67 Apollo Drive,
Rosedale, Auckland 0632, New Zealand (a division of Pearson New Zealand Ltd.) • Penguin Books
(South Africa) (Pty.) Ltd., 24 Sturdee Avenue, Rosebank, Johannesburg 2196, South Africa

Penguin Books Ltd., Registered Offices: 80 Strand, London WC2R 0RL, England

This is a work of fiction. Names, characters, places, and incidents either are the product of the author's
imagination or are used fictitiously, and any resemblance to actual persons, living or dead, business
establishments, events, or locales is entirely coincidental. The publisher does not have any control over
and does not assume any responsibility for author or third-party websites or their content.

A NOVEL WAY TO DIE

A Berkley Prime Crime Book / published by arrangement with Tekno Books

PUBLISHING HISTORY
Berkley Prime Crime mass-market edition / November 2012

Copyright © 2012 by Tekno Books.
Cover illustration by Ross Jones.
Cover design by Annette Fiore Defex.
Interior text design by Kristin del Rosario.

ISBN: 978-0-425-25169-0

BERKLEY® PRIME CRIME
Berkley Prime Crime Books are published by The Berkley Publishing Group,
a division of Penguin Group (USA) Inc.,
375 Hudson Street, New York, New York 10014.
BERKLEY® PRIME CRIME and the PRIME CRIME logo are trademarks of
Penguin Group (USA) Inc.

PRINTED IN THE UNITED STATES OF AMERICA

10 9 8 7 6 5 4 3

ALWAYS LEARNING   **PEARSON**

*To my mom, Helen Smart,
and her cat, Chloe. Love you!*

ACKNOWLEDGMENTS

Thanks to my editor at Tekno Books, Larry Segriff, who kindly took me under his wing and always has an encouraging word. And special thanks to my editor at Berkley Prime Crime, Shannon Jamieson Vazquez, who makes me write the very best book that I can. Love as always to my husband, Gerry, who has been unflagging in his encouragement. And a big "paws up" to the many readers who have written to tell me how much they enjoy Hamlet and Darla's adventures. Hamlet says, *Meow!*

ONE

"MADISON, THIS IS A GREAT RESUME."

Darla Pettistone tossed her single auburn braid over her shoulder and scanned the page again. "Not only do you have a brand-new degree in English literature, but you spent all your holidays and summers working at one of the major book chains. You've got retail, and you know the classics. But you do realize that this is a part-time position that you're interviewing for, right?"

"Part-time would be awesome," the plump blonde declared and gave an eager smile. "I live with my parents, so there's no rent to worry about. And in addition to working at the local women's shelter, I do spend a lot of time involved in community organizing. If there's a protest in town, I'm there! So I really can't fit a full-time job into my schedule."

"Well, I can certainly understand that," Darla replied, managing not to roll her eyes.

When Darla was Madison's age—a dozen years ago—she'd

locked down a full-time job with a major corporation a good six months before graduating with a business degree. She had paid her own rent on a furnished duplex during most of her college time, managing to also pay off a little compact car a year earlier than her loan schedule. The full scholarship had helped her make ends meet.

And, like Madison, she had worked part-time at a bookstore . . . though Darla's hours had been after classes and weekends, leaving her scant time to save the red-tailed chipmunks or protest for the universal right to tip jars. Later, she'd kept busy enough at the marketing firm where she worked that her charity efforts had been limited to the annual walks sponsored by her company.

Of course, that had been back home in Dallas. Maybe it was a generational quirk, or maybe things in Brooklyn simply were different. She'd found many such disparities in the eight months since she had inherited the restored brownstone, which housed two apartments as well as her bookstore, Pettistone's Fine Books.

"All right," Darla went on, determined not to hold the girl's off-hours activities against her, "let's see about your stock knowledge. Suppose I'm a customer looking for that famous book about the girl in overalls, but I can't remember the author or title. What do you give me?"

"To Kill a Mockingbird?"

"Bingo! What if I want the controversial new novel that my book club is reading?"

"Fifty Shades of Grey," she replied, her faintly disapproving tone indicating she did not consider it book club material.

Darla nodded. "Very good. Now, the one with a tiger on the cover?"

"The Jungle Book. Oh, wait, no . . . *Life of Pi."*

"Last one. How about the book about the guy who fights all the time?"

"*The Art of War*, by Sun Tzu," Madison answered with a triumphant smile.

Darla smiled back. "I have to say, I'm pretty impressed. You seem to be just what we're looking for."

Then she sobered and added, "There's just one thing more. We have a shop cat, and he'd have to approve you first before I could consider hiring you. His name is Hamlet."

Hamlet.

Darla shook her head. If someone composed a soundtrack to her life at the shop, then every mention of Hamlet would be accompanied by shrieking violins and an ominous *dum-dum-DUM* stinger. A stereotypical bookstore feline would curl picturesquely in a wicker basket near the front door and greet customers with a purr. But Hamlet stalked the shelves like a miniature Genghis Cat, black fur gleaming and green eyes as cold and sparkling as emeralds. The store's regulars all knew the drill—knew, as well, where they stood in his feline rankings—while first-time shoppers quickly learned their places in the hierarchy.

Big spenders, once-a-week customers, and those who read classic literature got the paw print of approval, meaning they were allowed to fawn over him and occasionally scratch his chin. Genre fiction readers (unless they fell into the big-spend, once-weekly category) were not allowed to touch him, though he would condescend to send a small *meow-rmph* their way in appreciation for their business. Customers who shopped once a month made up the next lower tier, meaning they were tolerated, and nothing more (though, on days when he was in a particularly good feline mood, he might deign to give them a whisker flick). Those who attempted to return their purchases got his patented Cat Stare of Death and moved down a notch from whatever rank they'd previously held.

Unabashed browsers and magazine-only customers were

treated to his kiss-off treatment: a flop on the floor followed by one hind leg flung over his shoulder and a lick to the base of his tail.

Madison, of course, knew nothing of this. No doubt she'd already conjured the cat-in-the-basket image in her mind.

"Oooh, a kitty!" the girl squealed. "When I was little, I had a white Persian named Mr. Cuddles. Mommy got allergies, so we had to give him away to my uncle and aunt, but I've always loved cats."

"Well, that's important, but what's more important is that Hamlet loves you back," Darla replied. Though, given Hamlet's persnickety nature, "love" was something of a stretch. "Tolerate" would be more appropriate.

Bad enough that she had to hire a new part-time employee. She never would have suspected that the true challenge lay in finding someone who could get along with Hamlet, the official black cat mascot of Pettistone's Fine Books. Darla had been shocked earlier that year to learn that she had inherited Hamlet along with the building and business from her late Great-Aunt Dee. It wasn't as if she'd been close to the old woman. They'd actually interacted only a handful of times over the years; still, Great-Aunt Dee was the original Darla Pettistone, for whom Darla had been named.

They had shared similarly round faces and snub noses, though the old woman's red hair had come courtesy of Miss Clairol, while Darla's wavy auburn mane was strictly her own. The octogenarian had also originally hailed from Texas, just like Darla. However, about sixty years earlier, the then twenty-five-year-old had fled north, renaming herself Dee to put distance between her new life and her country roots. Despite the twangy Texas accent that she could never quite lose, Dee had apparently settled in surprisingly well in Brooklyn. Perhaps it was due to her three native–New Yorker husbands—all of whom had been wealthy and had thoughtfully predeceased her—that she'd sequentially married over the years.

Hamlet had appeared on the scene long after, coming to the store as an abandoned kitten. He'd been named for the tragic Shakespearean character . . . or, rather, for the copy of the play that he'd pulled down off the bookshelf and made into his personal little kitten bed.

Hamlet had split his time between apartment and bookstore for almost ten years now. And since Dee had been Hamlet's caretaker (Darla never thought of the cat as being owned), this meant that Darla technically was as close to a blood relation to Hamlet as a human could be. It also meant that they—feline and woman—were pretty much stuck with each other. And given that Darla had never been much of a cat person, her learning curve in this relationship had been steep. Still, she had grudgingly concluded she could only hire an employee that Hamlet liked . . . or, at least, one that he wouldn't feel compelled to systematically terrorize out of a job. Unfortunately, he'd already ix-nayed the first few candidates she had interviewed.

"Let's get this over with," Darla told the girl. "Go ahead and bring your things"—she'd learned not to let a potential hiree leave behind anything they'd have to come back for later—"and we'll go down to the main store to find him. While we're looking, I'll show you around the place a bit."

She had been conducting the interview with Madison on the shop's two-room second floor. The front area, which overlooked the street, was designed as a lounge. In this space, Darla hosted the occasional writers' groups and book clubs, though the rest of the time the area served as a reading room and employee break area. In one corner, a small galley kitchen lurked behind an Asian-inspired screen, allowing for a bit of cooking and washup.

The shop's storeroom was housed in the rear room, where

packing materials vied with cartons of books awaiting shelving. Housing her storeroom on the second floor was not the most convenient of arrangements, but Darla found that bribery (in the form of coffee and pastries) usually worked well enough on the delivery drivers to get them to haul one or two hand trucks' worth of books upstairs. And if her baked goods didn't suffice, well, there was an old-fashioned dumbwaiter that went between floors. Though slow, it was sturdy enough to accommodate a case of hardcovers—or, as she'd discovered as a child, objects quite a bit larger!

As they made their way down the steps, Madison clutched her pink iPad case to her ample chest and gave an exaggerated sigh. "I think your shop is wonderful! It's nothing like a chain store at all. It's, well, quaint . . . just like your accent, Ms. Pettistone. Where did you say you were from?"

"I'm from Dallas. A Texan born and bred."

"Well, I think it's adorable," the girl confided, as if she were the elder of them. "The accent, I mean. Boys just love girls who talk all cute like that."

"Good to know," Darla replied, trying to keep the sarcasm from her tone.

She wasn't exactly in the market for a "boy." A couple of years ago, she'd finally gathered the gumption to divorce the inferior specimen she had married and was presently enjoying her independence.

Turning the subject back to the shop, Darla said, "Our main room started life as the brownstone's parlor. See on that wall, how we still have the original mahogany-mantled fireplace? Now, if you go through that broad arch there"— she pointed toward the rear of the store—"you'll see what was once the dining room. That's where most of the classics and reference books are stocked. We keep the fast movers and the gift items up here so we can keep an eye out, if you know what I mean."

The girl nodded wisely. Having worked in retail, she'd probably seen her share of shoplifters.

Darla continued her quick tour, Madison on her heels. Beyond the old dining room lay the back door, which in turn led to a tiny courtyard where Darla and her staff often took lunch when the weather permitted. She pointed out to Madison how all the doors lined up. In fact, the floor plan reminded Darla of what they called a "shotgun shack" back home in Texas, meaning one could walk a straight line—or fire a shotgun—from front door to back without hitting anything in between.

Or, rather, one could've if the shop's rooms had been empty.

Instead, a maze of oak bookshelves filled the place, the tangle practically requiring a map to negotiate and technically defeating the single-shotgun-blast-traveling-from-door-to-door concept. Great-Aunt Dee had eschewed the concept of optimum use of the available space, choosing instead to make clever little alcoves of the shelves. The old woman also had left most of the rooms' original ornately carved wooden built-ins intact, so that they served as additional shelves for both books and an eclectic collection of vintage miscellany.

"That's the nickel tour," Darla ended with a smile. "Now, about Hamlet—"

"There he is." Madison cut her short, smiling and pointing to the nearest bookshelf. There, beneath a garland of orange jack-o'-lanterns that Darla had draped in anticipation of Halloween, the cat was stretched at full length, snoozing. But Hamlet was not the stereotypical scrawny Halloween scaredy-cat.

Cliché as the notion was, Darla had always thought of Hamlet as a scaled-down panther. He was large for a domestic shorthair and solid black save for a tiny diamond of white on his belly. His paws when fully splayed were the size of a small child's hand, though far more lethally equipped, since Great-Aunt Dee had not subscribed to the idea of declawing indoor cats. And he was all muscle, as Darla was reminded of every time she tried to dislodge him from somewhere that he didn't belong.

Before Darla could warn her, the girl hurried over to the cat. She put out one French-manicured hand in his direction, as if to pet him. "What a cute—"

"No!" Darla shrieked, seeing a glimmer of emerald as Hamlet opened one eye a slit. Rushing to the shelf, she all but bodychecked the girl, and just in time. Barely was Madison out of claws' reach than Hamlet sprang to his feet and swiped.

Darla dodged the claws but managed to step on the girl's foot in the process. Madison, who had just caught her breath after being elbowed, gave a little cry of pain. Grabbing at her crushed toes and hopping on one foot, she dropped her iPad, which gave a couple of bounces of its own.

"Well, really," she huffed once she'd regained her balance. Bending to retrieve the fallen tablet, she added in a peeved tone, "If you didn't want me to pet the darned cat, you could have said—"

She broke off with a gasp as she found herself nose-to-nose with Hamlet, who had lapsed into ninja-cat mode and slipped unnoticed off the shelf. Suddenly he was on the floor, standing between the girl and her property. Green eyes cold and unblinking, the throaty *meowrmph* that emanated from him dared her to make a grab for the bright pink case.

"Don't do it," Darla hastily warned as the girl huffed again and made as if to reach around him. "Let's walk back to the cash register and give him a chance to leave, and then we can come back for it."

"And let a cat get the better of me?"

Madison planted her fists on her hips and shot the feline

an evil look of her own, earning a bit of admiration from Darla. She'd dismissed the girl as a cream puff—particularly after her Mr. Cuddles reference—but it seemed she was made of sterner stuff. Darla allowed herself a small flicker of hope. Maybe this was a test, and all Hamlet was looking for in an employee was someone who would stand up to him.

Or not.

Hamlet had defeated far more formidable foes than blondes with liberal arts degrees, and it appeared he wasn't about to let a challenge go unanswered. He walked over to the pink case and plopped atop it, front paws tucked neatly under his chest. Despite her irritation with the feline, Darla found herself smothering a grin. If this had been a chess game, then this had been Hamlet's official "check."

Madison's glare dissolved into a look of pleading. "This isn't funny. Please make him move, Ms. Pettistone."

"Hamlet, give it up."

The cat blinked but remained firmly settled on his prize. Cautiously, Darla edged a foot in his direction, intent on nudging him off. He raised a warning paw, claws fully extended, and she prudently pulled her foot back out of reach again. She'd seen those claws go through shoe leather before. *Check, again.*

"Hang on, Madison," she said with a sigh of resignation. "I'll get the squirt gun."

She'd bought the toy a couple of weeks into her tenure at the bookstore as a last-ditch cat disciplinary tool . . . say, for times that he stole gizmos worth six hundred dollars plus from would-be employees. The cat version of water boarding never failed to work. The problem was that Hamlet always exacted his own revenge for such tactics—last time, she'd found her store keys buried in his cat box—so she employed this method of persuasion only when she had no other choice.

She headed to the register and returned with the plastic

gun firmly clutched in hand. She checked the water level and gave the gun a quick pump. "Last chance," she warned him, then pulled the trigger.

The instant the first drop of water hit his sleek black fur, Hamlet gave a vertical leap that would have done an Olympic athlete proud. Then, with a hiss that sounded like a combination of a cobra on steroids and a semitruck's air brakes, he made a beeline for the next aisle, leaving the iPad behind.

Darla bent and scooped it up. "Here you go," she told the girl and handed over the tablet.

Madison hugged the pink case like a prodigal child returned and managed a smile. "I guess he doesn't like me much, does he?"

"Maybe he just had a bad day," Darla assured her. "Should I put you down on the list for a second interview?"

"Well, I—"

She broke off with a look of horror, staring at something beyond Darla. Darla swung about to see that Hamlet had returned, green eyes narrowed to slits as he stood behind her.

"Uh, maybe I'd better go," the girl declared, taking one step back. Hamlet took a step forward. She took another step back, and Hamlet moved forward again. Slowly, she backed up, with Hamlet smoothly pacing her step for step. She froze . . . and he did, too.

That was enough for Madison. With a squeal of horror, she turned and ran. Darla heard the discordant jangle of bells as the front door flew open, and winced as it slammed shut with a glass-rattling *thud*.

Darla turned to glare at Hamlet. He sat calmly in the middle of the aisle, unconcernedly licking his paw and swabbing it over one black velvet ear.

"Great, another one bites the dust," she told him. "I hope you're proud."

Hamlet looked up from his toilette and gave an innocent blink. Then, with a flick of his whiskers as if to say, *My work here is done*, he turned and calmly padded toward the children's section.

"Great," Darla repeated, this time adding a Madison-esque huff.

Still, she did have one more interview after lunch. Maybe this candidate would appeal to Hamlet, since the ornery feline obviously hadn't cared for Madison. Of course, he hadn't cared for any of the other previous and equally qualified candidates, either. All of them—the grandmotherly retired teacher; the middle-aged gay writer; the fortyish female former editor— had suffered one variation or another on the treatment that Madison had just received.

The bells jangled again, and Darla hurried toward the front to see if Madison had perhaps decided to come back for another round. But instead it was her neighbor, Mary Ann Plinski, stepping through the doorway.

The sprightly septuagenarian and her brother, Mr. Plinski (Darla had yet to learn the elderly gentleman's first name) owned the matching brownstone next door. Like Darla's building, theirs had long since been converted to apartments above and retail space below. In their case, the shop was Bygone Days Antiques, specializing in nineteenth- and early-twentieth-century fixtures and furnishings, along with period jewelry, clothing, and other collectibles.

"Hi, Mary Ann," Darla called to her and waved her in. "I've been meaning to stop by. What was with the moving van in front of your place yesterday?"

"Hello, Darla. I'm afraid that was our garden apartment tenant, Mrs. Gallagher. She was a snowbird"—Darla knew that fanciful term referred to a northerner who lived in the South during the winter months—"and she finally got tired of shuttling back and forth between two homes. She decided she wanted to live in Florida permanently, so off she went."

"Oh no. I'm sorry to hear that. I only met her a time or two in passing, but she seemed a pleasant enough lady."

"Actually, she was an obnoxious old biddy," Mary Ann replied with a polite sniff, "but she paid her rent on time and kept to herself mostly. What's upsetting is that we have to find a new tenant now. The whole interview process is so taxing!"

"Tell me about it," Darla said with a wry grin. "But don't worry, I'll be glad to keep my eyes open for someone who's looking for a place."

"Thank you, dear. But that's not why I'm here. I wanted to tell you that I think I saw Hamlet outside of the building last night."

"Hamlet was outside? I never let him out."

"I know, but these buildings are old. He must have found a way to sneak out."

"The little devil," Darla fumed. "Why couldn't Great-Aunt Dee have had a nice little orange tabby, the kind that would sit on your lap and purr contentedly?"

"Well, to be fair, I did see Hamlet sitting on Dee's lap many a time, and he's cuddled on my lap a time or two."

"He's never sat on mine yet," Darla replied, wondering why she felt offended by the slight. "But this slipping-outside thing has me worried. Especially with Halloween coming. You know how the animal shelters always warn people to keep their black cats inside around the holiday in case some weirdo is out looking for a live decoration or something."

"Maybe he found a spot somewhere in Jake's place to sneak out," the old woman suggested, referring to Darla's own garden apartment tenant.

Darla nodded. "That makes sense. I'm meeting Jake for

lunch in a little bit. I'll be sure to ask her to keep an eye out for any AWOL cats wandering through her place. Thanks for the heads-up."

Mary Ann smiled. "My pleasure, dear. Oh, and good luck with your interviews for the part-time position. I believe that I may know one of your candidates."

She left on that cryptic note, but Darla let the comment fly past her. She was more concerned with her warning about Hamlet's nocturnal wanderings. Of course, it was always possible that the old woman had seen another black cat on the street, but Darla doubted it. Prior to becoming a cat owner, she'd always believed that all black cats looked alike. Since taking custody of Hamlet, however, she had discovered that aside from their fur color, the difference between one black feline and the other was as great as . . . well, day and night. If Mary Ann thought she'd seen Hamlet, it was likely that she had.

Darla shook her head. Bad enough that the feline was playing havoc with her hiring attempts. The last thing she needed was Mr. Hell on Paws loose on the streets. She'd have to put a stop to this, and soon. Otherwise, who knew what sort of mayhem the cantankerous cat might cause?

TWO

"HE TOOK OUT ANOTHER ONE?"

Jake Martelli put down her half-eaten turkey Reuben and leaned forward in her chair, her expression incredulous. Lowering her voice, as if she were worried that someone else in the crowded deli might overhear her, she went on, "How did he do it this time?"

"iPad kidnapping, followed by a full-frontal fake out. I swear the little so-and-so is back at the store laughing up his cat sleeve at his cleverness."

Darla took an angry bite of her own sandwich, chewing miserably. Even the mile-high stack of juicy white turkey breast piled on pumpernickel and topped with sauerkraut, Swiss, and dressing wasn't enough to restore her to something resembling a good mood.

Jake nodded sagely and reached for her own sandwich. Through a mouthful big enough to choke a linebacker, she mumbled something that sounded like, "Any blood?"

"Not this time. But the screams were pretty darned awful."

"Look, kid, why don't you just stick Hamlet in a carrier or something while you're interviewing?" Jake suggested in a reasonable tone. "Keep the applicants out of claws' reach, at least until after they've filled out the paperwork and you've asked all your questions. Once you've hired someone, well, it's survival of the fittest."

Darla considered the notion a moment and then shook her head.

"Unfortunately, I know who's going to come out on top in that battle. And I don't have time to train a series of people. It's mid-October, which means the holiday buying season is only a month away. I need someone I can depend on to help me and James, and I need them trained before the big rush starts."

Darla took another bite.

"I've got another applicant coming in after lunch," she told her friend. "Maybe I'll luck out with him. Of course, with the job market like it is, it's not like Hamlet will run out of potential hires to torment anytime soon."

"Well, speaking of the job market . . ." Jake swallowed the last of her sandwich and reached into the pocket of her brown corduroy jacket to withdraw a business card. Tossing it onto the table in front of Darla, she gave a casual shake of her curly black mop and said, "Check it out."

"Does this mean what I think it does?"

Jake nodded, her strong features glowing with a proud smile. Darla hurriedly wiped a bit of errant dressing from her fingers and snatched up the card to read it aloud.

"Martelli Private Investigations, Inc., Jacqueline 'Jake' Martelli, President. Oh, and you even have a website!" Darla's smile matched her friend's as she added, "I can't believe you finally did it. Congratulations!"

"Well, I figured sitting on my butt for two years was enough," Jake replied. "Those occasional security jobs along with the disability settlement might pay the rent, but I can only watch so much cable television when I'm not hanging out in your store. I missed being in the thick of things."

"Once a cop, always a cop, right?

"Pretty much. Besides, fifty is too damn young to retire."

"So is forty-nine," Darla said, knowing that her friend wouldn't actually be turning fifty until January, when she'd officially start collecting her retirement. This still gave Darla a couple of months to plan the surprise birthday party she intended to throw. And since Darla's own next major milestone birthday wouldn't be for almost five years, when she hit forty, she was pretty confident that she was safe from any similar birthday revenge for a long time.

Aloud, she merely said, "Actually, as soon as you started talking about going into business, I checked into the zoning laws here. There's no issue if you want to go ahead and run your office out of your apartment."

"I was hoping you'd say that, since I already ordered the signs to hang on the fence and doors," Jake confessed, her grin now a bit sheepish.

Darla had inherited Jake as her garden apartment tenant—Darla always had to correct herself from calling it a basement—in much the same way she'd ended up with Hamlet and the bookstore. The aforementioned fence was a sturdy, wrought iron barrier to the short series of steps that led down to the apartment, which was partially below sidewalk level. Jake had moved into Dee's brownstone soon after the on-duty shooting that had left her with a permanent limp and hastened her retirement from her police detective career. Viewing Jake as her personal on-site security force, Darla's great-aunt had in return offered Jake a rent well below the going rate.

Darla had also inherited the subsidized lease, but she

agreed with Dee that it was rather cool to have her own personal cop—or rather, ex-cop—keeping an eye on things. Besides, she and Jake had become fast friends.

Now, Darla laughed. "Actually, I think there's a certain cachet to having a private investigator in the same building as an independent bookstore. Maybe I need to expand my mystery section, take advantage of the atmosphere."

"Don't go wild until I see if things really take off or not. I'm hoping for walk-in business, to start . . . you know, the old word-of-mouth thing. God knows how many PIs in town I'm competing against. I figure if I keep it in the neighborhood, I'll have an advantage."

"So, you going to be skulking around with a camera taking pictures of cheating spouses?"

Jake snorted. "Not if I can help it. I've got plenty of corporate contacts, so I'm looking at narrowing the field. Corporate espionage, insurance fraud, surveillance—"

"Mystery shopping," Darla supplied with a grin, earning an eye roll from her friend. "Let me know if you need any help with that. I can spend other people's money with the best of them."

"Maybe I'll hire Hamlet. He proved himself a pretty good little sleuth with that whole Valerie Baylor business."

Jake's tone was rueful, but Darla had to concede that she was right. Valerie Baylor, the YA author famous for her *Haunted High* series, had made a well-publicized stop at Darla's store—drawing hundreds of fervent fans, and one pitiless murderer. In the aftermath, Hamlet had demonstrated an uncanny knack for what Darla began to call "book snagging": knocking seemingly random books off the store shelves, books that had proved, in retrospect, to have bearing on Valerie's murder and the killer's true identity. And though Hamlet didn't get any credit, the feline had definitely had a paw in solving the crime.

Then her frown deepened. "Actually, I should hire you to tail the little beggar. It's bad enough that he's got some secret cat tunnel where he can go back and forth between the shop and the apartment. Now I think he's found a way to sneak out of the building at night."

"What makes you say that? Did you see him out on the sidewalk or something?"

Darla shook her head. "He's too smart to tip his hand—er, paw—like that. But Mary Ann said she saw him outside last night. And, come to think of it, the other morning when I went to feed him, I saw what looked like grease or oil on his fur, like he'd crawled under a car. I'm afraid he's out prowling the neighborhood looking for trouble."

"Not good," Jake agreed.

Darla took another determined bite of sandwich. "Mary Ann thinks he might be getting out through your place, so keep an eye out, okay? And let me know if you stumble across a cat-sized GPS we can stick around his neck." Then, with a glance at her watch, Darla added, "Time to get back to the shop. James will be waiting, and I've got a few things to do before the next interview."

They gathered their now-empty plates and dropped them off in the overflowing dish bin before heading for the door. Jake paused by the community bulletin board near the exit long enough to pin up a few of her new business cards.

"Half the neighborhood eats here," she reminded Darla. "You never know who might need a private investigator."

Darla pulled her olive-colored hip-length sweater more tightly around her as they made the two-block walk back to her store. The temperature was barely above fifty. It made for a perfect day for New Yorkers, but was pretty darn cold for a Texas girl used to battling summertime weather this time of year. She definitely wasn't looking forward to winter in New York.

Jake must have seen her reflexive shiver, for she laughed. "Toughen up, kid. In another month or two you'll be wading through snow up to your waist."

Which meant said nasty white stuff would come up only to Jake's thigh, Darla thought with an inner snort. Her friend was a good six inches taller than Darla's own five-foot-four-inch height, and in the stacked Doc Marten boots that were part of her personal uniform, Jake easily topped six feet.

Halfway down the block from the corner deli, they both halted before the lace-curtained windows of one of Crawford Avenue's many brownstones. This building, like Darla's elegant, three-story Federal and several other brownstones on the surrounding blocks, had been converted to retail on its ground floor and apartments above.

The shop in question was a bath-and-body boutique that had become a favorite guilty pleasure of theirs. Aptly named Great Scentsations, the store was designed for indulgence, offering custom perfume, handmade soaps, and organic makeup, among other alluring merchandise.

"Wanna do a little retail therapy?" Jake suggested, her expression one of longing as she gazed at a genie-bottle-shaped vial of body lotion displayed amid a tiny desert oasis scene.

Darla gave her head a reluctant shake, even as she moved to the next window.

"I really need to get back to the bookstore. But Hilda is so talented with her window designs that I always like to take mental notes every time she puts up a new display."

"Hilda" was Hilda Aguilar, the impeccably coiffed and dressed owner of the boutique. The petite Cuban woman was in her fifties, and bore a faint resemblance to the late Princess Grace of Monaco. She exuded an air of class and good taste that, to Darla's mind, one had to be born with, though Hilda constantly asserted that she used no beauty products other than what could be found at Great Scent-sations. Which gave her customers hope that they could attain similar class and good taste simply by shopping there.

"Not that I can ever come up with anything half as clever," Darla added on a note of admiring regret. "I thought I was doing pretty good hanging my store with black crepe and jack-o'-lanterns. But next to Hilda, I'm a rank amateur. Isn't that cute how she made that little Halloween graveyard with soaps for tombstones and those net poufs for ghosts?"

"Yeah, cute," Jake agreed with a quick look at the phantom scrubbies, though her gaze quickly returned to the genie bottle. Then, with a sigh, she added, "I really shouldn't be spending anything until I pull in a client or two. But once I cash my first check, a-shopping I will go."

"All right, but in the meantime, let's get you out of temptation's way." Grabbing her friend by the arm, Darla dragged her back to their brownstone.

They arrived at the bookstore a few minutes later. While Jake headed down to her apartment, Darla trotted up half a dozen balustraded concrete steps to her shop's door.

She paused as she reached the top to glance over at a second, smaller set of steps that lay to the right of the bookstore's stairway. At the top of those steps was a modest glass door. This was Darla's private entrance to a hallway where a long flight of stairs led up to her third-floor apartment. It was a handy arrangement. She didn't need to cut through the store to go home; instead, an inner door connected that hallway to the shop, which meant she could travel from home to store at any time of day or night without ever leaving her building. She had a feeling that, come winter's snowy weather, she'd be doubly grateful for this convenience.

For the moment, though, she was looking for cat-sized exits and entrances. She saw no gaps in the bricks, however, which meant Hamlet must be pulling his Houdini trick around the back of the building. Sparing a few choice words for the little beast, she reached for the doorknob. Gilded letters on the door's wavery glass above it proclaimed "Pettistone's Fine Books." As always, the sight gave Darla a small thrill.

Once inside, she headed straight for the counter. Sections of the parlor's original mahogany wainscoting had been cleverly repurposed to build a narrow, U-shaped counter near the front window where the register was located. Darla fondly regarded this area as her control center, her personal literary cockpit. For the moment, however, her store manager had assumed command and was planted there behind the register.

Dressed in his usual cable-knit vest, handmade Oxford shirt, and sharp-creased wool trousers, James looked more like a model for an upscale gentlemen's emporium than a clerk in a neighborhood bookstore. A former English professor at one of the area's more prestigious universities, Professor James T. James was, to put it mildly, terminally stuffy.

James—*You may call me Professor James, or you may address me by my Christian name, James. You may not, however, ever call me by my surname sans any honorific. And trust me, I will know the difference*—had taken early retirement from the academic world ten years previously. He had been working full-time at the bookstore ever since, both to supplement his pension and, as he put it, to keep him off the streets. While his area of expertise was nineteenth-century American literature, he also was an expert in rare volumes in general. In that capacity, he brought in a nice revenue stream for the store by catering to collectors—one more reason that Darla tolerated his often supercilious air.

The other reason was that she actually quite liked the man. Besides, he and Hamlet, while not exactly bosom chums, got along well together. This alone was worth the price of his salary.

"Ah, the prodigal returns," was his wry greeting as Darla stepped into the shop and headed in his direction. With a deliberate glance at his watch, he added, "I was beginning to fear that you and Ms. Martelli had been abducted by aliens—or, even worse, by one of those Russian gangs I have been reading about in the newspapers."

"One of the perks of being the owner," Darla cheerfully replied. "I can drag my butt in a few minutes late, and no one can fire me."

"That may well be, but such disregard for scheduled break times does set a poor example for the other employees."

Since James was, for the moment, her only employee, Darla shrugged off the criticism. Instead, she asked, "Were you able to work out the price with Mr. Sanderson on that signed Hemingway while I was gone?"

"A thousand here, a thousand there, and we finally came to an agreement," he replied with a casual wave, going on to name a dollar amount that made her gulp. While she mentally tallied their profit, James added, "As soon as we have confirmation of his bank transfer, I will have the book couriered to him."

Darla nodded. Book lover though she was, she still could never see paying five figures for a volume to stick on the shelf, no matter that it was rare or that it had been autographed by a long-deceased popular author. And it took every bit of effort she could muster to put up a similar cash outlay on speculative rare book purchases, even knowing that James had never failed to resell any such purchase for a respectable profit. But in a down economy, Darla felt it her duty to take advantage of those wealthier sorts who weren't feeling the pinch like the rest of the common folk, and wouldn't let a thing like pesky double-digit unemployment hold them back from making luxury purchases.

"Good work," she said sincerely, adding with a rueful smile, "At least we won't have to sell the china to pay the electric bill this month. What else did I miss?"

"Your one-thirty interview arrived a bit early. I took the liberty of sending the young man upstairs to fill out the application and told him to stay put until his appointed time."

"You left him upstairs? Alone?" Faint tingles of alarm began racing up her spine. "What about Hamlet?"

"I saw no sign of him in the lounge, or down here, for that matter. Besides, you assured me before you left that he was safely secured in your apartment."

"I did, and he was," Darla replied, grabbing up the folder that held resumes and her notes on the various candidates. "But you know Hamlet. I'm coming to believe that he has all sorts of secret little cat passages throughout the building that let him sneak around wherever he wants to go."

Leaving James to hold down the fort downstairs, Darla rushed up the steps to the second floor, keeping in mind another of Hamlet's tricks: flying up the stairs and zipping between some unwitting climber's feet—usually, Darla's. Agile as he was, and lucky as Darla apparently was, he'd never yet tripped her; still, she was waiting for the day when his impeccable feline timing was off a second or two. The result would not be pretty.

But her greater concern at the moment was that Mr. Fur-covered Land Shark might have decided to seek out yet another hapless would-be employee to terrorize. No way could she let this happen. She'd had enough cat mayhem for one day.

Panting slightly, she reached the top step and discovered to her relief that the lounge area was free of marauding felines. At the round table that usually held a pile of advance reader copies for employee perusal, a young man was bent over a clipboard, scribbling away at an awkward angle. An empty candy wrapper lay on the table in front of him; obviously, filling out forms was hunger-inducing work.

From what she could see of the youth, huddled as he was over his paperwork, he couldn't be much older than eighteen or nineteen. Younger than she'd hoped to find, but at that age he'd be more likely to accept the salary she could offer. Besides, it would be useful to have a strong young man to haul boxes around the store. James was nearing retirement age, and she felt guilty every time he wrestled cartons on delivery days. Heck, her own back had developed a twinge or two in recent weeks.

Crossing mental fingers that the boy was as good as the resume that he'd emailed her, and that Hamlet might find him acceptable, Darla headed in his direction.

"Hi, I'm Darla Pettistone, store owner," she said with a bright smile, holding out her hand. With a quick glance at the paperwork in her other hand, she added, "You must be Robert Gilmore."

He looked up and unfolded himself from the overstuffed chair, and then grunted what she took to be an affirmation. The handshake he gave her in return was unenthusiastic, at best. Darla, who had taken her share of motivational workshops in the past, reminded herself: *Not always a negative trait, particularly in teenagers.* Still, her own enthusiasm flagged as she took swift stock of him.

Up close, Robert looked vaguely familiar. Her fleeting confusion faded, however, when she realized he simply resembled any number of young men his age that she'd seen about the neighborhood. The one difference was that, while he was dressed all in black, his shirt was tucked in and his pants did not sag unduly.

Neatly groomed. For that, she mentally gave him credit points; this despite the fact that his posture needed work.

If he stood up straight, he'd be almost as tall as Jake. Unfortunately, his slouch and his unsmiling visage lent him an air of teen surliness that even the undeniable spark of intelligence in his bright blue eyes couldn't quite counteract.

Definite problems in the customer service area, she predicted, picturing him interacting with the portion of her customer base that was Social Security age. Still, he'd made the effort to send a resume and come in for an interview. The least she could do was hold up her end of the deal and grill him over his qualifications.

"All right, let's talk about your work experience," she began, determined to give it the old college try. "It says here you've done the fast-food thing summers and weekends, you graduated high school back in June, and up until last week you worked at Bill's Books and Stuff."

But barely had Darla gestured him back to his chair and taken a seat opposite him than she knew why he'd appeared familiar to her.

"Robert!" she exclaimed, her red brows knitting into a thunderous frown. "You've got a girlfriend named Sunny, right?"

Not waiting for his reply, she shoved back in her chair and stood. "You've chopped off that silly lock of hair and gotten rid of your piercings, but I know who you are. You're that kid who accused me of murder!"

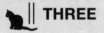 **THREE**

DARLA STARED ACCUSINGLY AT THE YOUNG MAN SLOUCHED in the chair in front of her. No doubt about it, this was the same sullen teenager who, along with his girlfriend, had issued some not-so-veiled threats against her following Valerie Baylor's death. Then, he'd sported all manner of piercings and chains, while his dyed black hair had been limited to a single luxuriant lock that hung in his face. Now, while still favoring the same hue of shoe-polish black, he'd removed the hardware and cut off the dangling tail of hair while letting the rest grow back in. It had been an effective disguise-in-reverse, she conceded. It might even have worked if he'd managed to lose the 'tude along with the metal bits and the rest.

She slapped the paperwork onto the table in disgust, the sound making the youth jump.

"So why are you really here?" she demanded. Robert stared at Darla in what appeared to be genuine alarm. "Were you planning some weird sort of undercover espionage while you pretended to work? Or were you and Sunny going to start up that whole online protest thing again?"

"Uh, me and Sunny, we're not dating anymore. And, I-I wasn't planning anything," he managed. "We knew what happened that night wasn't your fault. We were all just bummed about Valerie dying like that. It was, like, a real trauma."

His words held a note of honesty that dialed down Darla's stereotypical redheaded temper just a notch. To be fair, the original online protest against Pettistone's Fine Books had never really gotten off the virtual ground . . . still, it was the principle of the thing! And now, the kid had the nerve to show up in her store as a potential employee? If she were smart, she'd show him the door now and be done with it.

Her intention must have been obvious, for Robert dropped his gaze to his fingernails, which had been bitten to their quicks. "I'm, like, sorry we took it out on you. Honest, I came here about the job. I even have a letter of recommendation from Ms. Plinski."

Ms. Plinski? Darla raised her brows in surprise. Robert was the candidate Mary Ann had said she'd known?

Darla did know that the older woman had a soft spot for customers of the goth and steampunk persuasion. Robert and his girlfriend had fit into the former category and, according to Mary Ann, were among her regulars. But she hadn't realized that Mary Ann apparently had an acquaintanceship with the youth beyond that of buyer and seller.

Before she could comment, Robert reached into the backpack at his feet and withdrew a heavy, cream-colored envelope. Gingerly, he slid it across the small table toward her. Darla suppressed a sigh as, with an unwilling sense of obligation, she picked up the letter.

To Whom It May Concern, the letter began, written on

matching cream-colored stationery in the old woman's spidery yet elegant hand. *I have known Robert Gilmore for approximately three years and have found him to be of exemplary character. He has provided seasonal help at my establishment, Bygone Days Antiques, performing such tasks as packing and unpacking furniture, running errands, and tidying the store. He has always been honest and polite in his dealings, and I wholeheartedly recommend him to any employer.*

Darla studied the signature an extra moment, just to make sure it was indeed Mary Ann's; then, folding the letter back into its envelope, she handed it back to the youth.

"It seems Ms. Plinski thinks quite highly of you," she conceded. "But your resume doesn't say anything about your having ever worked for her."

"I helped out the last couple of Christmases, and the time Mr. Plinski broke his leg. Mostly, I did it for free, so I didn't put it on my resume," he added, answering her unspoken question.

His gaze flickered toward Darla again, the sullen expression brightening. "It was pretty easy, hauling things around and making some deliveries. And Mr. Plinski showed me things like, you know, how to tell a fake antique. Him and Ms. Plinski, they're pretty sick for being so old."

Which expression, Darla knew from some of her teen customers, meant the elderly brother and sister were what she would have called "cool."

She suppressed a reflexive smile, as her earlier irritation began to fade. Maybe the kid had potential after all. Moreover, she was impressed that he'd actually dealt with the reclusive Mr. Plinski in person. Even though he lived and worked next door, Darla had caught only glimpses of the old man and had never actually spoken to him herself. In fact, at one point she had even theorized to Jake that perhaps "Mr."

Plinski was actually Mary Ann dressing up like a male and pretending to be her own brother!

"Fine, let's start over. You've got stocking and delivery experience. So tell me what you did at Bill's Books and Stuff," she urged him, returning her attention to his resume. "Is this a full-fledged bookstore, or do they sell gifts, too?"

"It's, um, not exactly a regular bookstore. It's more like magazines and videos and, well, you know, stuff."

"Stuff," Darla echoed, confused now. "What kind of stuff?"

"You know, stuff."

To Darla's surprise, the boy's cheeks reddened, making him look even younger than his eighteen years. His gaze dropping to his chewed fingers again, and he mumbled, "Like, X-rated stuff."

"You worked in an adult bookstore?" Darla squeaked, dropping his resume as if it were contaminated with porn-shop cooties by association.

Robert gave a defiant nod, though he still wouldn't look her in the eye.

"It paid good, and the hours were after school if I decided to take some classes. It's not like I did anything, you know, kinky. I just ran the register and stocked the shelves and helped the customers."

"So, why did you quit?"

"I didn't exactly quit. I kind of, you know, got fired."

This time, he met her gaze squarely. Darla stared back at him in surprise. How in the heck did someone get fired from a place like that? Too much time spent perusing the stock, maybe? But something in his expression kept her from speaking that snarky thought aloud. Instead, in as neutral a tone as she could muster, she asked, "Why don't you tell me what happened."

"It was a few days ago. This customer came into the store

around midnight. You know the type . . . sunglasses at night, wearing gold chains, that kinda thing."

He paused and snorted. "He was old—at least, like, thirty—and he had this underage girl with him. A lot of the girls that hang with guys like that dress like kids on purpose, but I recognized her. She was one of Sunny's friends. Fifteen, sixteen, tops."

He hesitated again, but this time his expression hardened, making him look more adult than teen. "So I'm like, bro, she's a minor, you've got to leave. And he was like, pal, mind your business. Then he grabbed her arm and dragged her back toward where the video booths are."

Darla flinched. Not that she'd ever been inside a porn shop before, but she was pretty sure she knew what went on in those booths. It wasn't politely watching classic movies.

Robert, meanwhile, was continuing, "Anyhow, I went down one of the side aisles and, you know, jumped out to block the way. And I'm like, bro, I already told you she's not allowed in the store. And he goes, yeah, well she's my daughter, so F-you, pal. I knew he was lying, but we're not supposed to argue with the customers. So I was going to let them go, but then the girl—her name is Fancy—did one of those things you see in the movies. You know, while he was busy being all tough guy with me, she mouthed the words, *help me.*"

"What did you do?" Darla asked, drawn into this drama despite herself.

The youth shrugged.

"I stood there and told him he had to get the hell out, but that Fancy was staying with me. He starts poking me in the chest"—Robert pantomimed fingers stabbing at an invisible sternum—"and cussing me out, and Fancy starts crying, like she's real scared now. So I knock his hand away and tell him if he doesn't leave, I'm going to make a call. And then he's all, go ahead and call the cops, and I'll tell them you assaulted me. And I'm like, I'm not going to call the cops. I'm going to call my friend, Alex Putin."

Alex Putin? The name rang a faint bell, but Darla wasn't sure where she'd heard it before. Maybe Jake or Reese had mentioned the man in passing. Whatever the source, however, she found herself recalling James's comment about Russian gangs.

She didn't have time to pursue that line of thought, however, for Robert was saying, "So the dude, he was all, no way a kid like you knows Alex Putin. And I go, yeah, I know him, and I also know Alex's got a couple of daughters Fancy's age. You should have seen Mr. Gold Chain Dude's face when I said that. I thought he was going to puke right there.

"Anyhow, I grab my cell and start punching in numbers. He doesn't stick around to find out if I'm telling the truth or not, he just runs out of the store. So I call Sunny, and she and some of her friends come to the store and take Fancy home to her parents. Fancy acted like I was some kind of hero, but I just told her I'd kick her butt if I ever saw her hanging with some old guy like that again."

"Wow, some story," Darla said, deliberately overlooking the fact that, in Robert's world, she also fell into the *old* category. "But how did you end up getting fired?"

Robert's smile faded.

"I guess Mr. Gold Chain Dude got a little braver since, you know, Alex didn't stop by his house or anything. So he comes back to the store that next night before I get there and yells at Bill. He tells Bill that I cussed him out and hit him for no reason, and that he's thinking of suing. So by the time I got to work later, he was boiling mad. He didn't want to hear my side of the story or even look at the security tape."

The youth glanced down at his hands again.

"Bill was always kind of a jerk to us guys who worked at

the store, and he kinda looks like that big monkey in those dumb Clint Eastwood movies I watched when I was a kid. So when he wasn't around, I started calling him the Not-So-Great Ape." He paused and looked up at Darla, trying for a grin. "Get it?"

When Darla nodded that she did, indeed, get it, he went on, "Anyhow, Frankie—he's one of the guys—told me I'd better not make fun of him, because Bill once attacked a guy with a hammer for making wisecracks like that. So I learned to keep my mouth shut. But this whole thing with the gold chain dude, it wasn't, you know, fair. I tried to tell him that."

"So what happened?" Darla urged him on.

Robert shrugged. "Not much. He just yelled at me that the customer is always right, and paid me out of the cash register for the week before, and that was it. No more job."

"Wow," Darla repeated, frowning as the youth subsided into silence again. Then, with another look at his resume, she told him, "That whole thing about the customer always being right? Well, it's not true. But what is true is that they always *think* that they're right. So no matter your personal opinion, you have to suck it up and pretend you agree. It's the first law of retail. I can't hire someone who doesn't understand that."

Robert gave a glum nod and had just started to rise when Darla put out a restraining hand.

"But, on the other hand, I can't hire someone who won't stand up for what's morally right. I'd rather lose a sale any day than compromise my principles—or someone else's safety—for a few dollars. And it sounds like you're on that same page with me."

"So, like, maybe you'll consider giving me the job?" he asked, a look of hope momentarily lighting his features as he sat back down again. "I really would like to work here."

"It's only part-time," she reminded him. She gave him a

quick rundown of the expected duties and then told him the hourly rate. "Over the holidays, you might be able to go full-time for a while, but no guarantees that would be permanent."

"Hey, it's all good. I also do a little construction work on the side for Alex, er, Mr. Putin, so that'll make up the difference. And I'd get an employee discount on books, right?"

"Twenty percent," Darla confirmed with a nod, "but I thought all you kids preferred the electronic readers to the real thing."

"No way," he replied. "I mean, those things are sick and all, but a real book's got, you know, a soul. It's not the same, reading a bunch of electrons. Anyone knows that."

"Hey, real books are what keep us in business," she agreed, pleased to find a kindred spirit in that matter. "Of course, I have to do a background check first, but so long as you pass it . . ."

She trailed off, feeling her smile falter as she recalled the final requirement for employment at Pettistone's Fine Books. "One more thing, Robert. Anyone who works here has to be able to get along with—*Hamlet!*"

That last word morphed into a shriek as Darla spied a large black furry shape racing in their direction. Before she could turn exclamation into action, the beast in question made a single graceful leap and landed on silent paws upon the table.

With the reflexes of youth, Robert had shoved back his chair from the table at the same instant Hamlet came in for his four-point landing. Now, seeing what appeared to be nothing more innocuous than a rather large black feline sitting there before him, he grinned.

"Hey, little goth cat bro," he exclaimed, apparently appreciative of Hamlet's inky coat. "Where did you come from?"

Normally, Darla would have given a snarky answer on

Hamlet's behalf—*the bowels of Hell*, for example, or *Satan's School for Cats*—but with the feline only a paw's length away from her potential new employee, she didn't dare try for humor.

Instead, feeling like she was in one of those nature specials where the host unexpectedly stumbles into the path of a deadly beast, she said in a soft voice, "Just back away from the table slowly, Robert, and everything will be fine."

But barely had the words left her lips than Hamlet raised a large black paw in the teen's direction. Darla didn't have time for a warning. She could only wait for the carnage she was sure would follow.

Don't let Robert be like Mr. Gold Chain Dude and want to sue, was her one frantic thought as she watched the teen reach out a hand in return. But rather than trying to pet him, he lightly touched knuckles with Hamlet's raised front foot.

"Yo, fist bump, little guy," he said, still grinning.

Darla held her breath and winced. To her astonishment, however, no claws ensued. Instead, Hamlet gave a quick *meowrmph* and, to her even greater amazement, appeared to return the gesture. Then the feline turned tail and hopped off the table, padding in the direction of the stairs.

"Epic cat," Robert said. "Does he hang out here in the store all the time?"

"Y-yes," Darla choked out, unable to believe what had just happened. Hamlet actually seemed to *like* someone she was considering hiring? Surely that had to be an indication that she was making the right choice . . . that, or a sign that the End Times were near.

Robert, meanwhile, was nodding his approval. "I like cats. If I lived in a place where they were allowed, I'd adopt one. So, what's the one more thing you were talking about?"

"Actually, that was it. Just let me make sure I have your

correct phone number, and I'll get back to you as soon as I check your references."

"I can, you know, start right away." His tone was neutral, but Darla could see the excitement in his eyes, and she abruptly hoped that everything *would* be okay. Despite his past rush to judgment about her, he had the makings of a reliable employee. And the fact that Hamlet seemingly agreed with that assessment was a miracle that she hadn't expected.

"Let me walk you back downstairs," she said with a smile, "and then I'll get the paperwork going. Assuming everything checks out okay, you can expect to hear from me tomorrow sometime."

She saw in approval that he gathered up his empty candy wrapper and stuffed it in his backpack before following her down the steps, his earlier sullen attitude long gone. As he passed the register, he gave James a comradely nod and called out, "Yo, hoss, see you later," before heading out the door.

James waited until the door jangled shut behind the youth before turning to Darla.

"Yo, hoss?" he repeated in precise tones, his expression sharp as the crease in his trousers. "Please do not tell me that this young man will be working here at the store."

"Actually, he will, assuming he passes the background check," Darla replied, doing her best to suppress her amusement. James and Robert would make for an interesting pairing, indeed . . . though surely, during his career as a college professor, James must have dealt with more than his share of irreverent young men. In a conciliatory tone, she added, "But don't worry, Hamlet actually likes him."

"Hamlet approves?"

"You bet. He and Hamlet, they're like bros. They fist bumped and everything."

James's peeved expression immediately settled into a look of genteel relief, and he gave his vest a tug back into place. "Well, then. If Hamlet has given his nod, so to speak, regarding this youth, I am content with your choice."

With those words, the manager returned to the special order he was boxing up for one of their mail-order customers. Darla smiled. The relationship between James and Hamlet was also quite an interesting pairing. While James had been the one to insist that Hamlet remain as the bookstore mascot after Darla inherited the place, she rarely saw the two of them together. It was as if they had a gentleman's—or gentlecat's?—agreement to coexist peacefully without actually crossing paths.

Of course, there was that one time when neither of them knew she was watching that she'd actually seen James petting the ornery feline. Both had seemed to enjoy the interaction, though she suspected each would deny it should she mention the incident.

Then her smiled faded. From what she'd observed, Hamlet was indeed a capable judge of human character. But no way could she make a hiring decision based solely on the feline's instincts. The only way to go these days was with a battery of references and drug-screening tests and Google searches . . . heck, even a look at a potential employee's Facebook page was now considered de rigueur. Because when it came to an employee's character, she'd already learned a valuable lesson as store owner: one never knew what lurked in a person's past.

And, even more important, one never knew when that past might rear its ugly head and bite an unsuspecting bystander in the hindquarters. Which was why she intended to trot said hindquarters down to Jake's place that minute and hire the newly minted private investigator to put Hamlet's new buddy under a microscope.

*   *   *

JAKE HAD BEEN BUSY SINCE LUNCH, IT SEEMED. THE PROMISED SIGN
for "Martelli Private Investigations" was now hung on the
wrought iron railing outside the garden apartment. A discrete
arrow pointed downward to Jake's door, where a similar sign
minus the arrow had been screwed on beneath the peephole.
Feeling rather like a character in one of the thriller novels that
she sold, Darla hurried down the steps and gave a quick knock.

"Come in," came Jake's shout in return.

Darla entered. The apartment had an open floor plan similar to Darla's on the third floor, with a single large space serving as a combination living room, dining room, and galley
kitchen . . . and now, apparently, as Jake's detective agency
office. She nodded approvingly as she found her friend seated
at a rectangular 1950s-style chrome dinette table, a gleaming
new laptop and a neat stack of paperwork before her.

Since Darla's last visit, Jake had rearranged the furniture
so that a folding screen blocked the kitchen from view, while
what had been her dining table now was flanked by a file
cabinet and bookshelf. The table's matching set of chrome-
framed, red vinyl-cushioned chairs had been replaced by the
sort of oversized office chair that Mickey Spillane might
have used, with two small tweed wing chairs for client seating. The laptop looked more out of place than the vintage
furnishings, since Jake's entire apartment was decorated
with a distinct mid-twentieth-century vibe.

Some of the pieces, like the table, had come from the
previous tenant; the rest, Jake had scrounged from various
thrift shops and flea markets. Darla's favorite of Jake's finds
was the mod floor-to-ceiling lamp with its three shades that
looked like melted red plastic bowls, though the trio of
gaudy plaster mermaids swimming across Jake's bathroom
wall came in a close second.

Darla settled in one of the wingbacks and gave her friend a mock-stern look. "I can't believe you, of all people, would let someone waltz into your place like I just did. What if I'd been a mad killer or something?"

"Eh, I saw you through the window coming down the stairs. And don't forget, I'm operating a business here. Can't leave the clients standing out in the street." Jake shook her curly head in amused dismay. "Besides, you're the only one I know who does that old shave-and-a-haircut knock. Seriously, kid, you need to update your image."

"There's nothing wrong with my image," Darla shot back, only slightly offended. Sure, she might dress a tad on the conservative side, but that didn't mean she didn't at least have a passing knowledge of the latest trends. With a meaningful look at her friend's décor, she added, "Talk about being behind the times."

"I'm retro, not old-fashioned. There's a difference."

"Well, maybe I can get a few pointers from my new employee," Darla replied with a triumphant smile. Setting the folder on the table, she went on, "I'll be your first client. I need a background check run on a Robert Gilmore, age eighteen. Lives in walking distance of the store. Last place of employment, Bill's Books and Stuff."

"The porn shop?" Before Darla could ask how Jake happened to know what Bill actually peddled, the ex-cop went on, "That was pretty quick. An hour ago you thought you'd never find anyone who wouldn't end up as kibble for Hamlet."

"He and Hamlet are officially BFFs," Darla replied, glad for the chance to show off that she at least knew the texting term that meant *best friends forever.* "Besides, Mary Ann next door gave him a letter of recommendation."

Jake flipped through the folder before nodding and tossing it on top of her stack. "I'll have this back to you this afternoon. But sorry to disappoint you, kid. You're not my first client. Hilda Aguilar is."

"Hilda?"

"Right after we got back from lunch, she called and said she wanted to hire me. She must have seen the business cards I left on the bulletin board at the deli." Jake glanced at her watch. "She'll be here in about half an hour to discuss her case."

"What could she want with a private detective?"

"Beats me, but I'll find out soon enough . . . not that I'm going to tell you anything once I do," she added when Darla gave her an eager look. "Client confidentiality, and all that."

"Yeah, right, I understand." And she did; still, she was a bit disappointed to lose this hot source of gossip.

Jake paused and looked at her watch again. "Sorry, but I'd better kick you out. I need to print up some forms and contracts before Hilda gets here. I'll bring you the results on your hire in a few hours."

"Perfect," Darla said as she rose. "Just try not to find out anything bad about him, okay? I really need a new part-timer, and so far our boy Robert is my best shot."

🐈‖ FOUR

IT WAS ALMOST CLOSING TIME WHEN JAKE STROLLED INTO the bookstore, folder in hand. "Good news, kid," she announced. "Your boy Robert is clean. Hire away."

"Fantastic! I'll give him a call and make him a formal offer."

Darla took back her folder plus a second neatly bound sheaf of papers—the background check—from Jake, glancing as she did so at an invoice clipped to its front. She frowned as she saw the total.

"Jake, that's way too cheap," she declared, pointing to the dollar figure. "It would have cost me more for one of those online services, and I trust you a heck of a lot more."

"Eh, just call it the introductory friend rate. I haven't done backgrounds in a while, so this was good practice for me."

Still, Darla felt a bit guilty as she unlocked the company checkbook from a drawer beneath the counter and paid the bill. As the owner of her own small business, she knew how hard it was to earn every penny. Which reminded her . . .

"How did it go with Hilda? No, no, don't worry," she hurried to add as Jake gave her a look that would have made Hamlet proud. "I'm not going to try to make you break your confidentiality vows, or whatever they're called. I just want to know if everything is all right with her."

"Strictly routine," Jake assured her, grinning a little as she got a look at the check Darla had handed her.

Tired of the boring banker's green that Great-Aunt Dee had always used, Darla had splurged when it came time to order new checks. Now, in addition to the store name and address, a faint trail of black paw prints ran across every check in homage to Hamlet.

Jake tucked the check into her shirt pocket and gave a satisfied nod.

"Feels good to be earning an honest living again, kid," she declared, and Darla realized just how frustrating the past couple of years of forced inaction must have been for the other woman. "So, you want to stop by my place for a little celebratory toast after you close up? I'm going to ask Reese and Mary Ann and James to stop in, too."

"I'd love to. Give me about thirty minutes."

Though, actually, it was closer to an hour by the time she had closed up the place and, having first sent James on his way to the impromptu party, made her call to Robert. Even though she was the one doing the hiring, she found her fingers shaking a bit as she dialed the number. What if he didn't want the job, after all? Would she ever find anyone else qualified who could win over Hamlet the way Robert seemingly had?

To her relief, the youth seemed just as eager to accept her offer as she was to hire him. "Sure, I can, you know, be there as soon as you open tomorrow . . . or earlier, if you want."

Smiling a little at his enthusiasm, she suggested that he hold off until ten a.m. when she unlocked the doors. Then, recalling his affinity for the goth lifestyle, she added, "And the all-black wardrobe is fine for work, but don't put on any facial jewelry or eyeliner, okay? Our clientele is a bit on the conservative side."

She heard what might have been a snicker through the receiver before he replied. "No problem, boss. That's, like, why I cut my lock. I figured I'd get stuck working for the man, so I wanted to be, you know, mainstream."

Mainstream is something I doubt Robert will ever be, Darla thought with a smile as she hung up a few moments later and then headed upstairs for a final check of the upper level. Still, it would probably do both her and James good to be shaken up a little. Things had been pretty quiet of late, with the only excitement being Hamlet's recent midnight escape. With that in mind, she paused for a glance through the wavy glass of the uncurtained window, which overlooked Crawford Avenue below. Though the busy daytime traffic slowed considerably in the evenings, enough vehicles prowled the streets in the wee hours to pose a real hazard to any bookshop cat who decided to take in the nightlife. Maybe Robert could help her look for whatever cat escape hatch Hamlet had apparently uncovered.

Darla turned to head back downstairs again, only to almost stumble over the feline in question. Hamlet was sitting silently at attention, his green eyes narrowed in seeming disapproval as he stared up at her. Biting back a couple of bad words over her near fall, she met his glare with an equally stern look.

"Eavesdroppers never hear anything good about themselves," she warned him, "not that anyone was talking about you. That was your new BFF on the phone. He starts working here at the store tomorrow."

Hamlet's emerald eyes widened, and he gave a small *meowrmph*. Darla laughed. "Oh, so you approve? Maybe you'll listen to him, then, if *he* tells you that it's dangerous for cats to be out after dark."

Hamlet had no comment on that last. Instead, he rose and turned tail, spilling down the stairway like a small oil slick. Darla shook her head. With trouble like Hamlet roaming the store, she suspected that Robert joining their ranks could only be a good thing.

AS PROMISED, ROBERT SHOWED UP RIGHT ON TIME THE NEXT MORNING. Darla quickly got him settled in and put him to work. To her pleased relief, he picked up on the routine immediately, and by the end of his shift had even waited on a couple of customers. Things were progressing so smoothly, in fact, that she should have known it was only a matter of time before something went wrong. And so Darla was distressed but not unduly surprised when, a couple of days later, something did.

"I got a beef with you," a belligerent voice rasped, the harsh sound an unpleasant counterpoint to the pleasant tinkling of bells that always announced someone entering the bookstore. Startled, Darla glanced up to see an unknown man heading toward the counter where she was busy reconciling the morning's paperwork.

Fell off the ugly tree and hit every branch on the way down, was her first reflexive thought.

He was squat rather than simply short. His bullet-shaped head jutted well past his rounded shoulders, giving him the familiar Neanderthal hunch common to men who'd long since forgotten their mothers' admonitions to stand up straight. Oversized hands that dangled from longer-than-normal arms contributed to his cavemanlike bearing. The man's wardrobe didn't help matters. He was dressed in a faded blue-striped T-shirt emblazoned with the FCC's favorite four-letter word, while his baggy jeans were less a deliberate fashion statement than a case of belly out-sizing butt.

Had his pale blue eyes been filled with friendliness rather than disdain, his physical features might have appeared less unsavory. As it was, from his doughy, pockmarked face only slightly camouflaged by a patchy red-gray goatee, to the stringy tonsure of matching hair, he exuded an angry, unkempt air that made her want to break out the hand sanitizer. She'd never met the man before; that much was certain. So what possible beef, as he'd put it, could he have with her?

"I'm sorry, I didn't get your name," she replied, deliberately assuming her most polite shopkeeper manner in an attempt to stave him off.

He bared small, tobacco-stained teeth, but the gesture fell far short of a smile.

"Name's Bill. You stole my best employee from me."

"You're Porn Shop Bill?" she blurted before she could catch herself.

Remembering Robert's nickname for the man—"the Not-So-Great Ape"—she was surprised it had taken her as long as it had to connect those dots. The man *did* bear more than a passing resemblance to the orangutan from those old Clint Eastwood movies. Though she doubted that the simian in question had ever viewed his surroundings with as much jaded malevolence as this man did, surveying her store.

Now, he snapped the bullet head back around to look at her, and the pale blue eyes narrowed. "Hey, lady, don't get all high and mighty. You and me, we're in the same business. My customers just happen to be a bit more freethinking in their choice of"—he paused and assumed a deliberately effete accent—"literature."

"Literature, my . . . foot." She'd almost ended that retort with another body part, but the thought of possibly being overheard by the pregnant stay-at-home mom in the reference section made her purposely temper her word choice.

"And I don't steal employees," she went on in the same deliberately calm voice. "They apply, they meet my requirements, I hire. So unless you want to buy a book that has an actual plot, why don't you leave before I call security?"

His reply was a variation of his T-shirt slogan. Darla's temper flared, and she snatched her cell phone from under the counter, hitting the speed dial for Jake.

"You. Out. Now," she demanded in a voice that trembled only a little, pointing at the door while she listened to Jake's phone ringing.

Pick up, pick up, pick up, she silently urged her friend, and then bit her lip in dismay when she heard Jake's voicemail message kick in. James wouldn't be in for another hour, so it was just Robert and the pregnant lady for backup. She'd have to handle Porn Shop Bill on her own.

"Hey, Jake, it's Darla," she told Jake's mailbox, doing her best to sound as if she was talking to the real thing. "No, not so good. We have a situation up here. Can you come up right away? Great."

Hanging up, she said to the man before her, "Security will be here in a minute. If you're not already gone by then, I'll see that you're arrested for trespassing."

"Yeah? Well I'll slap you with a civil suit for unfair business practices," the porn shop owner threatened right back, stabbing a bony, nicotine-stained finger in her direction. "Tell ya what. Let me talk to the kid a minute, and I'll be on my way. No harm, no foul."

Before Darla could whip out another bluff, she heard Robert call from behind the stacks, "Hey boss, can you, like, tell me where to find—"

The teen's question broke off abruptly as he poked his head around the edge of the reference section and caught sight of his old employer. Bill, meanwhile, had swiveled in the direction of Robert's voice. Spying the youth, he bared his teeth again.

"You, kid, c'mon out. You and me, we gotta talk."

"Robert, you can go right back to helping your customer," Darla countered. "This . . . gentleman . . . was on his way out the door."

"It's okay," Robert said, looking equal parts frightened and defiant as he started toward them. "I'll talk to him."

"If you're sure," she reluctantly agreed, phone tightly clutched in one hand and ready to step between the two if the situation warranted it. "But I'm staying right here. If things get out of hand, I'm dialing 9-1-1."

The teen shot her a grateful look before turning to his former employer. His voice small, he asked, "How did you find out I was working here?"

"Them teenage girls, they gossip about everything. I stopped one of your little friends outside the shop, and she told me." Now, the bony finger was thrust in Robert's direction. "So where you been the past week? I've been short-handed for three nights running. I should fire your butt."

"Don't you remember? You, like, already fired me a few days ago."

Bill gave a rusty chuckle, though Darla spied no matching humor in the pale eyes. "Naw, I was just in a bad mood. I didn't expect you to off and take another job. C'mon back to the shop, and we'll forget all that nonsense."

Robert shook his head, his confidence seemingly returning. "No way, dude. I work for Ms. Pettistone now."

"Yeah, well I need someone tonight. So have your butt at the store seven thirty sharp," the man told him. "Besides, I paid you for two days you didn't work. You owe me."

"I figured that was severance," the teen replied, and then turned an uncertain look on Darla. "I wouldn't have taken it if I didn't think he wanted me to have it. I'd give it back, but I already spent it. Do I really have to go work for him again?"

"Certainly not," Darla declared before Bill could reply. To the porn shop owner, she said, "If you overpaid Robert in error, I'll advance him the money to repay you so you two can call it even. How much are we talking?"

"Give or take a few cents, a hundred bucks."

Darla looked over at Robert, who nodded. Slipping her phone into her pants pocket, she punched in the code to open the register and then withdrew five twenty-dollar bills, which she handed over to the teen.

"There you go, Robert, an advance on your first check. Go ahead and repay the man . . . and be sure you count it out so there's no question later."

While Robert obediently laid out the money on the counter one bill at a time, Darla pulled out a receipt book from beneath the register drawer. Swiftly, she filled out the top copy and handed the pad to the teen. "I suggest you have Bill sign a statement that he received the money from you, and that it repays him in full."

"I'm not signing nothing. Now give me my—"

Bill broke off abruptly, eyes widening as a sleek black shadow spilled across the line of twenties. *Hamlet, coming to the defense of his new "bro,"* Darla thought in surprise as the feline abruptly sat atop the money.

"Get that cat outta the way," the man demanded and made as if to shove Hamlet aside. Hamlet, with a deep-throated growl that sounded more Doberman pinscher than domestic shorthair, raised a large paw to display a set of formidable, needle-sharp claws.

"I think he, you know, wants you to sign first," Robert replied, a hint of a grin on his lips as he held out the pen and receipt pad. The cat seemingly confirmed the teen's words with another Baskerville-ian rumble.

With a cold look that encompassed all three of them, the man scrawled his name on the pad and ripped off the top copy, then slapped the pad back on the counter. Hamlet obligingly rose and padded to the far end of the counter, where he sat and surveyed the man with cold disapproval.

"You two think you're smart," he snarled, reaching for the bills, "but I won't forget this. Mess with me, and I'll—"

Whatever his threat might be, Darla wasn't to learn. The shop door jingled, and a jovial voice boomed, "Hiya. Anyone home?"

FIVE

"COME ON IN, CURT," DARLA GRATEFULLY REPLIED, recognizing the irony that, for the first time since she'd met him, she was thrilled to see one of her most annoying customers walk in the door.

In his late forties, with slicked-back black hair and a handsome if florid face, Curt Benedetto was a new regular customer at Pettistone's . . . nice, since he had no compunction about whipping out his credit card and buying a book or two each visit. And he'd also placed a couple of expensive special orders, stopping by promptly to pick them up as soon as they arrived. All in all, he should have been on Hamlet's official approved list.

Unfortunately, Curt tended to be both boisterous and flashy—*Hey, I'm a born salesman*, was the line he often used on her to excuse himself—which rated a *fail* in Hamlet's cynical green eyes. Darla, for once, was in total agreement with Hamlet's assessment. Part of that dislike, she realized, was that he reminded her a bit too much of her slimeball ex, Curt's New York accent notwithstanding. Not that she ever was anything but friendly, in keeping with her previous philosophizing to Robert about the first law of retail.

Besides, there was also Curt's business partner, Barry Eisen, to consider. A pleasant-looking balding guy with brown eyes and an affable smile, Barry had given all signs that he was interested in Darla as more than simply his neighborhood bookseller. And, if she were to be totally honest, Darla had found herself looking at Barry as more than just another customer. Unfortunately, it had been a week since she'd last seen Barry.

Any other time, she would have thought it too bad that she couldn't say the same for his partner. For the moment, however, she welcomed Curt's beefy, obnoxious presence as a secondary backup in case pervy Bill had more than just a verbal threat in mind.

Curt strutted on in, toothpaste-commercial grin at full brilliance. He'd apparently come from the brownstone that he and Barry were remodeling, for his khaki pants and red polo under a bright blue Windbreaker had a faint coating of white plaster dust. The project, Darla knew from past discussion with the pair, was an extensive one, but the two men expected to make a sizeable profit once they finished work and put the refurbished building back on the market. They'd already recouped their investments on a couple of similar properties, Barry had previously told her, and despite the down economy their construction partnership was inching into the black.

"Hello, fine people," Curt called, waving at her and Robert as he headed toward the register. Then, catching a glimpse of Porn Shop Bill, he stopped short and added in a dumbfounded tone, "What the—?"

"Benedetto," the man snarled in return. "Hell, this is the last place I expected to see you. I had no idea you even knew how to read."

"Real funny, pal," Curt retorted, his florid face growing even redder. "I'll have you know I'm a regular customer here."

"What, my selections aren't good enough for you anymore?"

Bill leered as he said it, and Darla saw Curt's fists clench in response. *Where the heck is Jake?* she frantically wondered. Apparently, the two men knew each other, and the relationship wasn't a cordial one. The last thing she needed was a bookstore brawl, and it looked like the pair was headed that way, fast. She exchanged a glance with Robert, giving a nod in the direction of the reference section where the pregnant customer still browsed. Eyes wide, he gave a return nod of comprehension and trotted off in that direction. If Darla couldn't defuse the situation, at least no innocent bystanders would walk into the melee.

Darla reached into her pocket again for her phone; then, with an air of authority that she didn't quite feel, she held up the cell so both men could see. "If you gentlemen have an issue with each other, take it outside, now. Otherwise, I'm calling the police."

A few seconds ticked by, both men's angry gazes still locked. Then Curt took a deep breath and with seeming effort managed a halfhearted smile for her. "No worries, Darla. I don't want any trouble. I'm just here to pick up my special order."

"Yeah, yeah, I'm outta here. I got a store to run," the other man retorted, stuffing the cash into his back pocket. "But in case you forgot, Benedetto, you and me, we got some unfinished business. I'll be seeing you later."

Long arms swinging, he shuffled to the door and slammed it shut behind him, leaving behind an unpleasant atmosphere that was equal parts anger and poor hygiene. Darla reached under the counter for the organic gardenia air freshener she'd purchased from Hilda's shop the previous week. She gave a few defiant spritzes in the direction that the porn shop owner had gone; then, aware that she was shaking in reaction, she settled on the stool behind the register and heaved a deep breath of her own.

"Hey, Darla, I'm really sorry about all that," Curt ventured, his expression contrite. "That Bill, he's a class-A jerk. I never figured I'd run into him in a nice place like yours. Uh, not that I hang out at his store or anything."

"Of course not," Darla agreed, politely accepting that bit of fiction. "Unfortunately, he came looking for one of his ex-employees who happens to work for me now. He was trying to threaten me and Robert, and doing a pretty good job of it. At least you distracted him."

"Yeah, well, the guy holds a grudge."

Darla knew from Curt's dour tone he was referring not so much to Robert's situation as to whatever "unfinished business" the porn shop owner had alluded to before leaving. Not that she planned to pursue the subject. The less she knew about Curt's dealings, the better!

Nodding, she said, "I think that situation is all settled, but if he ever sets foot in my store again, I'll have him arrested for trespassing."

"Good plan." Then, literally brushing off the earlier unpleasantness—and sprinkling a bit of plaster dust on her clean floor, in the process—Curt resummoned his flashy grin. "So, is my book in yet?"

Darla took a look under the counter where special orders were staged, and then shook her head. "Sorry, it doesn't look like your book on vintage trims and moldings has arrived yet."

"No problemo. We still have the last bit of wiring to finish before the new plaster goes up." Curt glanced about the shop. "Where's that big cat of yours hiding?"

"Hamlet? Oh, he's somewhere around."

"Are you sure?"

Darla smothered a smile. The feline in question had slipped away during the confrontation between Bill and Curt. Now he reappeared, silently padding his way out of the children's section and beyond Curt's line of sight. Spying the man, Hamlet halted and shot him the same look of green-eyed contempt he gave Curt every time the man entered the store. Darla did a silent countdown—*three, two, one*—and nearly laughed aloud when, right on cue, Hamlet flopped on the floor to give Curt his patented kiss-off treatment.

Unfortunately for insults, Curt chose the same moment to pause in front of one of the barrister-style bookshelves that housed their first editions. While Hamlet was busy flinging hind leg over shoulder, Curt was using the glass front as a makeshift mirror while he dislodged a bit of leftover breakfast from between two back teeth; thus, he missed the demonstration. Hamlet paused in midlick as he realized his dissing was going unnoticed. Scrambling upright again, he hissed in Curt's direction before stalking off.

"Oops, you just missed him," Darla said with a smile, pointing at the cat's retreating form. "Maybe next time."

The man shrugged. "Well, I seen a big black cat that looked just like him running out of my brownstone this morning when I got there."

"Really?" Recalling her suspicion that the crafty beast was making nighttime forays, she cautiously replied, "He runs back and forth between the store and my apartment, but he's an indoor cat. Or, at least, he's supposed to be."

"I dunno. It sure looked like your guy. Had to be around six, six thirty in the a.m. Scared the crap out of me. I thought it was a giant rat or something at first."

Then he gave a wise nod. "Cat's gotta be careful around a construction site. I seen a stray end up in a bucket of plaster someone left open one time. Wasn't a pretty sight the next day when the tape-bed man showed up. Know what I mean?"

"I can imagine," Darla replied with a reflexive shudder. "I'll be sure to keep a good eye on him." Then, eager to change the subject, she pointed to the nearby display table marked "Just Arrived." "Since your special order isn't in, what about some new true crime instead?"

She knew from previous purchases that both Curt and Barry were suckers for real-life blood and gore. But this time, Curt shook his head, his megawatt grin dimming.

"Actually, that whole crime thing is kind of why I'm here. Barry sent me over to warn you."

"Warn me?" Darla echoed, a frisson of worry sweeping her at his dour tone. "About what?"

"Eh, those damn scrap thieves are back. We got hit last night. They made off with a roll of copper pipe we had chained to a joist. Hell, they used our own saw to cut the damn two-by-ten so they could steal it."

"Curt, I'm so sorry."

Her momentary panic was replaced by relief that his news was nothing disastrous, and then supplanted by a flash of anger on their behalf. "I can guess how maddening that has to be. I swear, I can't believe they haven't been caught yet."

The "they" in question had been a scourge in the surrounding blocks for several weeks now. Working in the wee hours, the thieves' usual targets were construction sites or vacant buildings, but they'd been bold enough to hit a few occupied places as well. Searching for copper or aluminum, or any other metal they could conceivably sell for scrap, they'd left an equal amount of damage in their wake. So far, the police had been unable to catch them in the act, even with stepped-up patrols. And, despite the reward offered by the neighborhood association, no one had come forward to identify any of the parties responsible.

"Rumor I hear, the cops think it's a couple of kids looking for quick cash so they can party. They found candy bar and cupcake wrappers at a couple of the crime scenes, all that junk them kids like to eat. I'm considering staying overnight in the building for the next few days in case those punks come back again. I catch them trying to make off with anything, and I'll introduce them to Mr. Crowbar," Curt threatened, waving a phantom bludgeon for emphasis.

Darla gave a sympathetic nod, even as she hoped that he and Barry would leave the derring-do to the police. While chances were that the thieves weren't armed with anything more dangerous than brass Spaldings, as Jake would put it, one never knew.

"And you're not home free," he added, shaking a thick finger in Darla's direction. "You got some nice fixtures outside—them brass numbers, and that fancy new knob on your door. Them punks, they wouldn't think twice about pryin' them off even with you right here in the store."

Before Darla could reply to that, she heard a sudden blast of cha-cha rhythm, and the lyrics of a late-1990s megahit emanated from the vicinity of Curt's chest. *"Gimme your heart, make it real. Or else forget about it . . ."*

Darla suppressed a grin as she mentally sang along to the familiar lyrics—though, in Curt's case, those last few words should probably be "fuhgeddaboudit." "Smooth," with Rob Thomas's soulful vocals and Carlos Santana's signature guitar wails and trills, had been one of her favorite songs during the tag-end of her misspent youth before her marriage. She suspected, however, that Curt had chosen that ring tone less in tribute to a special lady and more as a paean to himself.

He plucked the phone from his shirt pocket, frowned a

little as he checked the caller ID, and then hit the "Ignore" button. "Now, back to what I was tellin' you—"

"Don't worry, Curt, I've got security cameras at the front and back doors. And I've got Jake downstairs, just for good measure."

"Oh, yeah, the lady cop." Curt's grin returned as, seemingly forgetting his outrage, he wagged his eyebrows meaningfully. "She looks pretty good for a broad her age. You think she might be interested in a date with yours truly?"

"Ex-cop," Darla hurriedly clarified. "And I think she's, er, already seeing someone."

A small falsehood Jake would owe her for, Darla thought with an inner grin. Jake had met Curt once in the store and had been distinctly underwhelmed by the man—though, of course, the "older" woman (Jake barely had a couple of years on Curt) had been a bit earthier in her recap of the encounter. Then came a more sobering thought, and Darla added with a frown, "Besides, Curt, I thought you were already dating someone. Haven't you been going out with Tera Aguilar?"

The daughter of Great Scentsations owner Hilda Aguilar, Tera was barely twenty-one. In face and figure, she closely resembled her petite, elegant mother, but unlike Hilda, Tera favored revealing clothing and exaggerated makeup, which, in Darla's opinion, masked the girl's genuine beauty. What she saw in Curt, who was twice her age and pretty far down the scale from Prince Charming, Darla couldn't guess. But even if Darla didn't think much of the matchup, she still didn't like seeing the girl played for a fool.

Curt, however, displayed no embarrassment at being called out.

"Sure, me and Tera, we have a few laughs together, but, hey, I like to play the field," he replied, smoothing back his hair in a preening gesture.

The move shifted the open collar of his polo shirt,

revealing a glimpse of gold chain against hairy chest and reminding her of Robert's Mr. Gold Chain Dude. Darla suppressed a grimace. What *was* it with these middle-aged guys pursuing girls half their ages? Well, she knew what it was; she just couldn't believe that the girls in question fell for it every time.

To Curt, she simply said, "I'd watch my step if I were you. Hilda Aguilar might look all sugar and spice, but I have a feeling that she could kick the butt of any man she thought was two-timing her daughter."

"Hey, who's to say I didn't already put the moves on Mama, too?" Curt countered with a wink. "I like 'em young, I like 'em old." Then, when Darla shot him a sharp look of disapproval, he puffed his cheeks in an exaggerated sigh. "What? I was kiddin'. You women, you got no sense of humor."

"Guess not," Darla agreed in a cheerful tone, though she wasn't smiling. Odd how, with just a few words, the man could use up his store of goodwill that he'd banked with her only a few minutes before. "Anyhow, thanks for the warning about the scrap thieves. We'll keep our eyes open. Tell Barry I said hi."

Curt raised his blunt hands in mock surrender. "Okay, I know when I'm not wanted. Call me when that book comes in, will ya?"

"Sure thing, Curt. Have a nice day, now."

The door closed behind him, and Darla felt a bit of serenity return. Just for good measure, though, she spritzed again with the organic gardenia scent. Robert, meanwhile, poked his head from around the reference shelf again, then, seeing Darla's "all clear" nod, he led his customer toward the register. The mom-to-be was busily perusing one of the short stack of volumes she clutched, seemingly unaware of the unpleasantness that had just occurred.

Darla stepped aside to let Robert handle things, watching

in approval as he zipped through the transaction like a pro. One of the advantages of his having grown up in an era when Baby's First Toy was, more often than not, something electronic, she supposed. Her own favorite electronic toy took that opportunity to ring. A glance at the caller ID confirmed her guess that it was Jake on the line.

"Hey, kid, I was in the middle of a client conference call, so I just got your SOS," came her friend's concerned voice before Darla could get out a hello. "Hang tight. I'm headed up there right now."

"Don't worry, the crisis is over," Darla assured her. "I'll tell you about it later."

"Go ahead and tell me about it now," Jake replied, her voice in stereo as she stepped into the store.

Darla gave a wry smile as she hung up her cell. "A day late and a dollar short, as my dad always says," she told her friend as Jake strode toward her. Darla glanced over at Robert, who was bagging up his customer's purchase, and waited until the woman had started for the door before saying to him, "I need to chat with Jake for a minute. Will you be all right alone?"

"Yeah, I'm good," he said with an exaggerated nod. "And thanks for, like, sticking up for me with Bill."

"No problem. And we can spread out that loan over a few paychecks," she added, earning another grateful nod.

"So what was that all about?" Jake asked as they settled into the twin wing chairs tucked behind the self-help area, the weather being a bit too chilly for sitting outside in the tiny courtyard for more than a minute or two. "Something to do with your distress call?"

"Unfortunately, yes."

Darla quickly recapped for Jake the unpleasant encounter with Porn Shop Bill, including his unfinished threat against her and Robert. Jake listened, her expression grim, though she smiled a little when Darla described Hamlet's strong-arm—or, rather, strong-paw—tactics to convince Bill to sign the receipt. But her expression darkened again when Darla explained how Curt had appeared just as things were getting tense.

"Yeah, that Curt Benedetto gets around, doesn't he?" the older woman remarked, whipping out a small notebook and one of those half-sized pens Darla remembered using when she was in grade school. "Speaking of which, I'm conducting interviews for my investigation for Hilda Aguilar. Maybe you wouldn't mind answering a few questions?"

What did Curt have to do with Hilda's case? And what could she possibly know that had anything to do with it? Curious, Darla shrugged and nodded. "Sure, if you think I can help."

"Our friend Mr. Benedetto has been a customer at your store for about a month now. Can you tell me what you know about him . . . I mean, outside the fact that he's a class-A jerk?"

Which had been what Curt had called Porn Shop Bill, Darla thought with a flash of amusement. Maybe Jake should be told about that situation. But first, she gave her friend the rundown as she knew it, including Curt's admission that he played the field while dating Tera Aguilar. And, unable to resist temptation, she also recounted the man's question regarding Jake's own relationship status.

Jake snorted, and her bland expression sharpened just a little.

"Man lives in a dreamworld," she retorted, lips curling as if she'd accidentally taken a bite of seafood past its prime. Then, in what sounded to Darla like an exaggeratedly casual tone, she asked, "I don't suppose Curt ever mentioned if he was married, did he? Or maybe talk about any ex-wives?"

Now it was Darla's turn to snort, even as she eyed Jake in

surprise. "He never mentioned anything about being married. Though I could pretty well guarantee that if he ever was, there's at least one bitter ex-wife wandering around."

"What about kids? Legitimate or not?"

"None that he's ever talked about. Sorry, we just haven't gotten that personal in our conversations, thank goodness."

By now, Darla's curiosity had bypassed overdrive and shot straight into redline, though it wasn't hard to put together the puzzle pieces. If Hilda was Jake's client, and Jake was asking questions about Curt, then it stood to reason that Hilda was worried about the man's relationship with her daughter. But hiring a private detective? It did seem like overkill. Then again, for helicopter parents like Hilda, such coddling was pretty much the norm these days.

"There's something else you probably should know," she added. "I told you how Curt happened by just as Porn Shop Bill was threatening us. Well, it seems like there's some sort of feud going between those two. They almost came to blows right here in the store."

"Do tell," Jake murmured, scribbling notes. "Any clue what this feud is about?"

"Bill just called it unfinished business, and later on Curt told me that the man holds a grudge. They didn't part friends, but at least there wasn't any blood spilled."

"Yeah, well, the two of them deserve each other," Jake replied and snapped her notebook shut. "You've been a big help, kid. You think of anything else, you let me know. And I'll mention to Reese about the threats. If it happens again, don't wait on me. Call him."

But the mention of Reese reminded Darla of her other conversation with Curt about the scrap thieves.

"Curt actually did have a good reason for stopping by," she told Jake. "He wanted to warn me that the same people who've been stealing copper and aluminum are back in the neighborhood. He had a whole roll of copper pipe stolen out of his building."

"Well, I guess it sucks to be Curt, doesn't it?" was Jake's glib reply.

Darla nodded. "Maybe, but he was nice enough to point out that they're stealing stuff from occupied buildings, too. He was concerned because of those antique brass fixtures I bought from the Plinskis' store last week." A bit defensively, she added, "And it's not just Curt taking the hit. It's Barry, too."

Jake's expression brightened. "Yeah, what's up with you and geeky Mr. Chrome Dome? He seems like a nice enough guy, even though his partner is a jerk. You two hooking up yet?"

"Jake!" Darla protested in embarrassment, glancing around to make sure Robert wasn't suddenly in earshot. Lowering her voice, she went on, "Really, I hardly know the man. But I can tell you he's not a geek. He and Curt both were jocks in high school . . . Curt was a running back on the varsity team, and Barry ran track and pitched two years for their school's baseball team. And he's not bald; he simply has a receding hairline."

When her friend grinned knowingly at her instinctive defense of the man, Darla blushed and conceded, "All right, I admit it, I like him, but—"

"Like?" her friend cut her short with a shake of her curly head. "What, are you two in junior high? Next thing, you'll be asking me to call him up and ask him if he likes you, too. Quit playing coy, kid. If he won't make the first move, you do it. Ask him out on a date already. You've got his phone number, don't you?"

"Well, no. He hasn't offered it, and I'd feel kind of weird

asking for it." Of course, she did happen to have Curt's number, since he was the one who usually picked up their special orders from the store.

Jake, meanwhile, was giving her a pitying look. "You could tell him you're updating the bookstore mailing list and you want his contact info. Or you could just say you're thinking of asking him out and need a way to get hold of him."

"How about I compromise and offer to spring for lunch at the deli the next time he stops by, instead?"

"Perfect. And then spill the gory details to me afterward."

"Only if you promise to spill about Hilda's case."

Which would never happen. No way would Jake breach client confidentiality, not even for the prospect of good gossip. Darla allowed herself a smug grin, knowing she'd won this particular skirmish.

Jake must have agreed, for she gave Darla a rueful smile in return.

"Fair point. But I warn you, don't run back asking me for advice when you've got old Barry on the line and can't close the deal," she declared, mixing metaphors in a manner that would have given James fits. "When it comes to your love life, you're on your own, kid."

SIX

"TELL CURT I'M SORRY IT TOOK ANOTHER WEEK FOR HIS book to finally show up," Darla said with an apologetic smile, handing over the long-awaited book on historically accurate woodwork and trim. "I swear, I sometimes think they send those special orders by mule train."

"No problem. This book is worth the wait."

Brown eyes alight, Barry Eisen flipped through the pages and then stabbed an enthusiastic finger at one of the full-color photos. A faint cloud of plaster dust wafted from the sleeve of his gray hooded sweatshirt and onto the page. "Take a look. We're not talking about your basic home improvement store wainscoting here."

Darla smiled but took a prudent step back to avoid a similar dusting. Apparently, Barry had worn this garment on the job site recently. The flannel shirt in shades of black and yellow under it, however, appeared freshly laundered, and his jeans were crisp enough that they probably had come starched from the dry cleaner's the day before. Obviously he hadn't been by the brownstone yet that morning.

"This is pretty close to what Curt and I had in mind for the first floor," he went on, "and it's authentic to the brownstone's original décor. Sure, the wood itself might be oak, but you've got your classic hand-carved egg-and-dart panel moldings, and those inlays are mahogany. I'm not sure I like the wreath design for the inlays, though. Maybe a nice rosette motif instead."

Then he flipped back a few pages to another photo. "But this works, too. See, the raised panels are simple, but that's okay. The denticulated chair rail along the top really classes it up, and it won't overwhelm the other architectural detail in the rooms."

"Either one would be beautiful," Darla assured him, wondering if she should brush up on her interior design vocabulary if she was going to hang around the man.

While she'd learned a little about typical brownstone styles simply by living in a prime example of same, Darla couldn't describe most of its features beyond basic color and texture. But the fact that Barry and Curt intended to replicate the period-style paneling and other woodwork and plaster, themselves, impressed her almost as much as Barry's easy familiarity with such terms as "denticulated."

"We've still got a little more time to decide," he replied with careless shrug, shaking off a bit more dust. "We're starting the plastering tomorrow, and that will take us a while."

Then, closing the oversized volume with an almost reverential gentleness, he gave Darla a hopeful smile and added, "If you can spare an hour or so, why don't you come back to the brownstone with me so you can get a final 'before' look at the place, and then we can grab some lunch at the deli?"

A date! He'd beat her to it! Smiling a little, she began, "I'd like to, but—"

She paused for a look at Robert, who was busy straightening stock near the back of the store. The youth had been working part-time for a little more than a week now and was already proficient in the store's main protocols. Even better, despite the first "yo, hoss" incident, Robert had managed to ingratiate himself with the eternally stodgy James. The crowning touch had come yesterday, when the teen had engaged the former professor in debate on some theory Robert had developed regarding Charles Dickens and what he'd decided was the metaphorical use of orphans in his writing. James had vigorously argued a counterpoint, but Darla had heard the pleasure in his voice at discussing his specialty with someone equally as interested in that time period.

But James would not arrive for his shift until after lunch, and Darla still felt uneasy leaving Robert to mind the store alone after the confrontation with Porn Shop Bill the week before. So far as she knew, the issue between Robert and Bill was settled, but on the off chance that the man returned, she didn't want to leave the teen alone to deal with such a volatile situation. Then again, Jake was just a cell call away downstairs. After all, what could happen in an hour or so on a Thursday?

"—but next meal is on me," she finished, making the quick decision that the teen had the smarts to work on his own for a bit.

"Robert," she called, "I'm going to step out for an early lunch. Do you feel comfortable handling things alone until James gets here?"

Not that he'd be totally alone, she reminded herself. He'd have Hamlet for company.

Or would he? Darla looked around. The cat had spent most of the last hour stretched across one end of the counter, recovering from a strenuous morning of watching her and Robert unpack shipping cartons. Apparently, however, he had regained his strength in the few minutes she'd been chatting with Barry, for he was nowhere to be seen now.

Robert, however, did not seem to share her concerns. "Take all the time you need, boss. I'm, like, good," he replied and gave an exaggerated "okay" sign in case she didn't believe him.

He wore his usual black jeans and black shirt, but today he'd topped the outfit with a black knit vest in apparent emulation of James's personal uniform. She wasn't quite sure if the fashion statement was genuine or simply a subtle bit of tongue-in-cheek ribbing at the older man's expense. She rather suspected the latter explanation, but if James was offended, he was perfectly capable of taking the youth down a peg or two.

"All right, then," she told him. "Hold down the fort until I get back. If you have an emergency, call me on my cell, or else call Jake. The numbers are taped to the register."

Robert gave her a snappy salute in return, and she sighed. Apparently, she'd forgotten what it was like to be that young and impulse-control challenged, for the cheeky gesture wasn't as amusing as Robert surely thought it was. "Quick, let's get out of here before I change my mind," she told Barry and grabbed her phone and familiar olive sweater from underneath the counter.

The air outside had a distinct nip to it despite the fact it was already after eleven o'clock. She hurriedly pulled on the sweater, feeling a small tingle of pleasure when Barry helped adjust its collar. It had been a while since she'd had a man pay her that sort of small courtesy. Maybe Jake had had a point about her hooking up with him.

Darla glanced over at Barry, who was now expounding on plastering techniques. At five-ten and with even features, and minus the beer gut many men pushing fifty sported, he was more than acceptable in the looks department. True, he wasn't the muscle-bound, young blond hunk like Jake's cop buddy, Reese . . . but then, most men weren't.

She smiled a little as she pictured the burly police detective. She had briefly—as in, for about ten minutes—considered exploring a possible relationship with him after their first meeting, and had even sensed a few vibes that indicated he might be open to said exploration. Then common sense had kicked in, and she had decided they were better suited as friends. Besides, Darla had learned the hard way that good looks alone weren't a strong enough basis for a lasting romance. Sighing just a little, she turned her attention back to Barry and listened to his plastering homily.

They reached the brownstone a few minutes later. "What happened?" was Darla's first comment as she took in the scene before her. Then, realizing that might sound critical, she hurriedly amended, "I mean, uh . . . that is . . ."

In its glory days, the building would have been a prime example of what Barry had told her on her first visit was Greek Revival style. Not technically a brownstone, the three-story house was red brick and fronted with what he had explained was called a "Grecian doorway": fluted columns atop a short stoop supporting a flat porch roof. And typical of the style, the simple windowsills and lintels—the "eyebrows" of the windows—barely protruded from the surrounding brick, giving the place a sleeker look than its neighbors. Those architectural touches were enhanced, quite appropriately, by Greek key designs worked into the stone.

But what gave the property its greatest value was the fact that it was set back slightly from the street and had a tiny slip of what once had been green lawn, though the grass had since been trampled into the dirt. A tree pit to one side of the yard held what appeared to Darla's untrained eye to be some sort of large oak whose leaves had turned a mottled yellow and orange for the season. But with some decent landscaping and an updated facade, the men would be able to turn an enviable profit on their investment even with only the most basic remodeling being done to the interior.

While she struggled for something encouraging to say about the building's current state, however, Barry laughed. "Yeah, it looks kinda rough right now, but I promise we're making progress."

"Rough," Darla privately thought, was putting a charitable spin on the situation. Indeed, rough was the shape the place had been the last time she'd seen it. The first-floor windows had been partially boarded up, and net-style orange barrier fencing had taken the place of the wrought iron fencing with a Greek key design that had surrounded the handkerchief-sized yard.

Now, the place appeared more demolition than renovation. A construction Dumpster had been squeezed into a narrow gap between that building and the one beside it, while a pile of brick surrounded by more of the orange netting spilled alongside the barred windows of the basement. One of the porch columns had been removed and replaced by several sturdy wooden posts, while the pieces of the missing column were propped against the building's corner like an afterthought.

"I guess I should have brought my hard hat," she replied. "I'm sure it looks better on the inside."

"Ha, not by much," a man's unfamiliar nasal voice behind them proclaimed with a sniggering laugh.

Startled, Darla swung around to see a tall, thin man about Barry's age standing on the sidewalk clutching a clipboard. He was dressed in baggy brown trousers and a white buttoned shirt topped by a bomber-style cloth jacket with a fake shearling collar. The jacket hung open, and Darla spied what appeared to be an official photo ID hanging from a lanyard around his neck. A city worker of some sort?

From Barry's expression, Darla guessed that he knew the man, and that he was not terribly pleased to see him. "What are you doing here, Toby?" he demanded, his usual affable tone sharp now with irritation.

Toby waved his clipboard, the untidy sheaf of multipart forms fastened to it flapping like a paper hen. "We got a little inspection business here to take care of, pal. Or did you forget?"

"I didn't forget anything. You're not supposed to be here until next week." Barry took a few steps toward the man, his stance challenging. "You'd better not have been wandering on my property without my permission."

"Relax, I just got here. But I need to move up the schedule, know what I mean?"

"I've got someone with me right now. It's not a good time. Understand?"

Darla glanced from an obviously ticked-off Barry to the glib newcomer, who bore an uncanny likeness to one of those artist renditions of an alien. His small, pinched features appeared to have slid south toward his receding chin, leaving a broad expanse of forehead to fend for itself. The lopsided effect was enhanced by the way he'd scraped back his collar-length, surfer-blond hair—a home-bleach job if Darla had ever seen one—into a single frizzy tail that looked more porcupine than equine. As for his personality, Darla had known him for less than a minute and already found his company distasteful.

Unfortunately, if the man was indeed a city inspector, then Barry likely had to put up with his rudeness in order to keep his job site running.

"Tell you what, pal," came Toby's nasal reply. "I'll give you until Monday. Fair enough?"

"Monday," Barry agreed, his expression stiff. "Until then, stay the hell off my property."

"That's what I get for being a pushover," the man complained with a grin, giving Darla a wink. "You'd think I'd get a thank-you every so often, but no . . ."

Tucking his clipboard under his armpit, the man sauntered his way to a battered white two-door parked quite illegally and on the wrong side of the road. He climbed inside; then, with mocking wave, he pulled out into traffic accompanied by the blare of horns from those drivers he'd just cut off.

"And I thought retail was a tough business," Darla observed in an ironic tone that, per her intent, earned a reluctant smile from her companion.

"Yeah, dealing with the city is always a good time. But if we want a certificate of occupancy, we're stuck with him." Then, in an obvious effort to recapture the earlier bantering mood, he added, "But don't let Toby scare you off about taking the nickel tour inside."

He gestured Darla up the steps. After fiddling with his key in the knob, Barry pried open the front door and, to the accompaniment of squealing hinges, ushered her inside. Darla halted a few steps past the threshold and gazed about her in bemused disbelief.

This is better?

On her last visit, the rooms had stood empty, forlornly stripped to their plaster, with fixtures removed and wires hanging like pointy tentacles from open outlets. Now, large sections of plaster were missing, revealing the original studs and wood supports and what appeared to be new electrical wiring running through the recesses. A pile of two-by-fours temporarily blocked the only other door, located beyond the foyer and at the end of a short hall. Not that this last inconvenience particularly mattered, for she knew from her previous visit that the rear door opened onto a miniscule enclosed courtyard. And, unlike the brownstones on her block, the homes on this street had no alley behind them, an alley being something of a rarity in Brooklyn, as Darla had been surprised to learn.

As for the stained carpeting and torn linoleum—doubtless courtesy of previous remodels that had gone for practicality rather than aesthetics—that floor covering had been ripped up to reveal the original wood beneath. In some areas, all that remained was the subflooring, or nothing at all.

She recalled Barry previously telling her that they'd turned off the electricity at the box while they were redoing the wiring. As a result, heavy black extension cords snaked along the floors and up the stairway, posing tripping hazards for the unwary. To make up for the missing light fixtures, a scattering of portable lights—some heavy-duty contractor floor lamps, and others the cheap clamp-on style with the big aluminum shades—sat in corners or clung to exposed studs. At the moment, however, none were turned on, so the only illumination inside the place came from the open door and the man-sized gaps in the ceiling where portions of the second-story flooring had been sawed out.

Barry, however, seemed concerned with something other than her lack of enthusiasm. His earlier expression of amusement had been replaced by a frown. "Is something wrong?" she asked in concern.

He shook his head. "I'm not sure. But I know I locked the front door when I left here yesterday, and it wasn't locked just now when I stuck the key in."

"Maybe Curt is already here?" Darla suggested, recalling how the man had mentioned being at the brownstone at six in the morning the day he'd claimed to have seen Hamlet wandering loose.

But Barry was eyeing the area with suspicion. "If he was here, he'd have heard us and come out already, even if he was down in the basement. You can't sneak into this place, not with those rusty hinges. That's one reason we never oiled them. Kind of like a homemade alarm system."

Darla smiled at what she assumed was a small joke. When she saw he was deadly serious, however, she instinctively edged closer to him.

"Should we call the police or something?" she asked, her fingers tightening around the cell phone in her sweater pocket.

Barry made no immediate reply as he reached for a bulky silver flashlight that had been left on one of the stairs. Clicking it on, he took a few steps and shined its beam through the open arch to their left that led into the next room. Gray shadows danced behind the flashlight's broad yellow swath of light, but they concealed nothing more incriminating than a row of five-gallon buckets and a neatly folded drop cloth. Then he shook his head.

"There's nothing to call about. For all we know, Curt stopped by earlier and then decided to run out for a cup of coffee without bothering to lock up. It wouldn't be the first time he's done that."

She heard a flicker of irritation in his tone, but he managed a strained smile for her and added, "Why don't you wait here while I take a look around?"

"No, I'll come with you."

She thought for a moment from his expression that he'd protest her decision, but then he nodded. "Okay, but stick close," was his doubtful reply. "With everything torn all the hell up, I don't want you smacking your head on something or twisting an ankle."

Neither did she, but no way was she waiting there alone while Barry checked out the place. After all, how many times in the movies did the character that remained behind in the supposedly safe spot fall victim to the mad killer? Not that there was any killer lurking about in your basic distressed brownstone, she reassured herself. Like Barry said, maybe Curt had simply been careless. Heck, he'd probably show up in another couple of minutes with a double latte in one hand and a cruller in the other while swearing that he'd locked the place before he left.

Darla trailed Barry down the short hall to what was now the kitchen. She pulled her sweater more closely about her, all too aware there was no heat source in the house. Come winter, the place would be an icebox if they didn't set up some of those big portable heaters while they worked.

But the cool temperature was less on her mind than Curt's warning to her the week before about the salvage thieves. What if they had come back, breaking in to the place in search of more spoils? Worse, what if they were still somewhere in the building?

"Curt," Barry abruptly called, the sound echoing through the open rooms and making Darla jump. "You in here, buddy? Darla and I are here on the first floor, looking for you."

That seemingly innocuous statement, she knew, translated to, *If someone's here who doesn't belong, you've still got time to hop out one of the windows before we stumble across you and things get all nasty.*

"Nothing here," Barry said a moment later when they'd taken a look at the other two rooms on the first floor. His voice louder than necessary, he added in the direction of the stairway, "Hey, Darla, why don't I show you what's on the second floor."

Which meant, *Last chance, suckers. Get out now while the getting's good.*

When no stampede of fleeing footsteps sounded overhead, Barry shrugged and gestured for her to follow him toward the stairs. Darla complied. By the time she'd taken four or five steps up, however, she was rethinking that whole victim-in-the-safe-spot theory and wondering with a fleeting sense of panic if it wasn't too late to stay downstairs, after all. She wasn't particularly concerned now about their stumbling across any intruders up there. It was the stairway itself that was doing her in.

Not that the steps were all that narrow or rickety—in fact, the staircase seemed the sturdiest structure in the place—but the balustrade had been removed, and only a ribbon of yellow caution tape now drooped from newel to newel in place of the handrail. She didn't have much of a head for heights, and that open side did bad things to her sense of balance.

Climbing the open staircase was a test of nerves for her in the low light. To make matters worse, the dim lighting combined with Barry's moving flashlight beam added a distinct fun-house effect to the whole stairwell. By the time they reached the landing, Darla was sweating despite the house's chill, while bits of plaster were lodged beneath her fingernails from where she'd been gripping the wall for moral support.

At least the balustrade at the top was intact, she saw in relief. She reached out to take hold while she regained her bearings . . . only to feel herself grabbed by her free arm and pulled back to the middle of the landing.

"Sorry, I should have warned you, it's a bit wobbly," Barry said with an apologetic smile. He demonstrated by giving the handrail a gentle shake that caused it to sway, and Darla's stomach to pitch. "That's actually on today's list to repair."

"Great," Darla replied. "Any other death traps I should know about?"

"Just the holes in the floor." He aimed the flashlight toward a pair of sawhorses near the end of the short hallway. They were set across one of the cutouts in the subfloor that she'd seen earlier from her vantage point on the lower level.

"Don't worry, the rest of the floor is sound. Stay clear of the spots we've blocked off and you're perfectly fine."

"Uh, maybe I'll wait here while you finish checking out these rooms," she suggested, earning a sympathetic nod in return.

"Probably a good idea. It won't take me more than a minute."

While Barry made his way down the short hall, Darla gave a cautious poke at the wall behind her. When it neither crumbled nor swayed, she figured it was safe to lean against it. She'd end up with plaster dust on the back of her sweater, but that was a small price to pay for regaining her equilibrium.

She shoved her hands into her sweater pockets and felt the slim weight of her cell phone beneath her fingers. It occurred to her then that they were doing this all wrong. Why not simply try to get hold of Curt first and see if he'd been by the brownstone? If, as Barry had suggested, he was simply down the street grabbing a late breakfast, that would eliminate the other more unsettling possible scenarios regarding the unlocked door.

She pulled out her cell and swiftly scrolled through her contacts. She often used her personal phone for business when James was tying up the landline with his negotiations. Sure enough, Curt Benedetto was there under the "B's." She pressed the dial key and listened while the phone rang on his end.

But while she waited for him to pick up, she abruptly heard a faint but unmistakable cha-cha rhythm coming from somewhere below her. It took her a moment to realize what that meant. By then, Barry had finished his exploration of the surrounding rooms, and the last tinny notes of Santana's "Smooth" had already faded. The sound of Curt's recorded voice—*"Yeah, too bad, I'm not here, leave a message"*—was now playing in Darla's ear.

"What?" Barry asked as she pushed the "End" button and stared at him in dismay. "Who are you calling?"

"Curt," she choked out. "I forgot until a moment ago that I had his number programmed in my cell phone. I called it to see if I could find out where he was, and I heard his phone ringing."

"Well, did he answer?" he replied with a frown, apparently not understanding her meaning.

She swallowed hard and clarified, "I meant I heard his phone ringing here . . . somewhere downstairs."

A look of seeming shock passed over Barry's face, and he swiveled to look over the railing. Then, turning back to her, he snapped, "Quick, call the number again."

Fingers trembling, Darla hit the redial button and then strained her ears. Sure enough, she could hear Rob Thomas singing his heart out and Carlos Santana strumming away somewhere in the distance.

"Dial it again," Barry demanded and rushed toward the stairs, flashlight bobbing as he started down. "Keep calling it until we find out where the sound is coming from."

Darla hit redial once more and then hurried after him, taking the stairs as swiftly as she dared and pausing midway down to dial yet again. The familiar tune was far louder now, and Barry, who had already reached the ground floor, was looking about wildly. Darla joined him a moment later and redialed Curt's number yet again. The rhythm started up once more, and Barry pointed his flashlight at a closed door she hadn't noticed earlier.

"The basement," he declared. "He must be down there. But why isn't he answering?"

Maybe because he can't, Darla thought as her stomach did a small flip-flop. From the grim expression on Barry's face as made his way in that direction, he obviously was thinking the same thing as she.

He yanked open the door, revealing a large area of gloom lit only by what daylight was let in by the narrow exterior windows. A workmanlike set of open wooden stairs with railings on either side led down into the darkness, where she could make out the vague shapes of stacked boxes. Shining his flashlight into the shadows, Barry headed down a couple of steps and called, "Curt? Buddy? You down there?"

When he got no reply, he turned back to Darla. "Call him one more time, would you?"

She nodded wordlessly and edged her way to the door while pressing the redial. This time, it sounded like a concert was happening almost at their feet. Barry swung his light down the stairs, searching . . . and then burst into laughter as his beam caught and held on a slim metallic shape lying several steps down from them. Glancing back up at Darla, Barry gave his head a rueful shake.

"The idiot, he must have come down here for some reason and then dropped his phone," he declared, his expression relieved. He turned again and started down the steps, adding over his shoulder, "He's probably wandering all over the neighborhood right now trying to figure out where he lost it."

"Hey, it happens to the best of us," Darla observed a bit breathlessly as she heaved her own sigh of relief. She'd truly feared something bad had happened to Curt. Now that she knew it was nothing worse than a dropped phone, she and Barry could have their lunch as planned. As for Curt, he likely could survive awhile without his smartphone.

While Barry bent to retrieve the errant device, Darla squinted into the dimness to look around the basement. The requisite old-fashioned coal boiler was to one side, along with storage boxes and a couple of old chairs. The floor appeared to be its original brick, although sections of plywood had been laid near the stairs to give a more stable storage surface. She hadn't noticed any unusual exterior access other than the windows. Her practical side kicked in. If Barry could convert the space into a garden apartment like Jake's, that would add even greater value—

She paused in midthought as the wavering flashlight beam momentarily revealed a flash of blue as Barry pocketed the phone and started back up the steps toward Darla. A chill swept her, and she gripped the doorjamb.

"Wait," she choked out. "Shine your light all the way down the steps, and to the right. I thought I saw . . ."

She trailed off, and Barry stared at her in seeming confusion for a moment. Gathering her wits, she leaned past the doorway and pointed downward into the shadows. "It's probably nothing, just a blue rag, but you'd better take a look."

Obediently he swung around and began moving the flashlight beam back and forth in wide arcs toward the area she'd indicated. "Tell me when you—"

"There!"

Shaking now, so that she didn't dare let go of the doorjamb, Darla stared down at the spot where Barry's flashlight beam had paused. It could be a blue tarp, she tried to tell herself. But as Barry slowly moved down the stairs, the pool of light around the fabric widened. *No, not a tarp.* It was a blue Windbreaker . . . the same jacket that Curt had been wearing last time he had stopped by the bookstore.

And as the flashlight beam zeroed in on it even more closely, she now could see what appeared to be a human hand protruding from the jacket's sleeve.

▌SEVEN

"CURT!" BARRY YELLED AND WENT STUMBLING DOWN THE steps toward the still figure lying on the basement floor.

Darla rushed after him as fast as she could, given the spotty light. Surely Curt was simply unconscious, she frantically told herself. No doubt he had tripped on the steps and hit his head when he landed. A tumble could explain why his phone had been lying on the stairway rather than in his pocket. Frankly, she was surprised that neither of the men had injured themselves before today. The brownstone was nothing short of a disaster site.

By now, Barry was already kneeling beside his friend. Darla could see by the flashlight's yellow beam that Curt was lying on his belly a few feet away and to one side of the bottom step. What looked like a crowbar lay across his back, reminding Darla of Curt's previous threats to lay in wait for the salvage thieves in case they made a return visit.

A chilling thought came to her: had Curt tried to wield

the bar against an intruder only to come out on the losing side of the encounter?

She barely had time to consider that possibility before Barry grabbed the crowbar and tossed it aside, and then leaned over his friend's prone form.

"Curt, can you hear me?" he demanded as Darla breathlessly knelt beside him on the dusty concrete floor.

For the space of a heartbeat, she held out hope that Curt would groan and then begin to move. That optimism lasted only until the flashlight beam illuminated both the bloody gash across the back of his skull and his wide-open, sightless eyes. Darla bit back another gasp. Curt couldn't hear them . . . wasn't ever going to hear anything ever again.

"Son of a bitch," Barry choked out, and made as if to turn his friend over. Hastily, Darla grabbed his arm.

"Leave him alone, Barry . . . there's nothing we can do. Besides, the police won't want us touching anything."

"The police?" He rose and rubbed a frantic hand over his thinning hair. "Yeah, you're right. Call 9-1-1, while I get some more light in here."

It took her two tries to punch in the right sequence of numbers, for her hands were shaking. Barry, meanwhile, had rushed back up the steps and plugged in a pair of the clamp lights so that they shone like faint headlights down the wooden stairway. The additional illumination made Darla blink and gave Curt's unnaturally still form an even more unreal appearance. She promptly scooted several feet away from the corpse, preferring the relative darkness of the rest of the basement to being right next to the dead man as she made her call.

Why couldn't this have happened upstairs? She already had something of an aversion to dark basements. She suspected she would end up with a full-blown basement phobia now that she'd managed to find a dead body lying in one.

After what seemed an interminable wait, though surely it had been but a matter of seconds, the emergency operator came on the line. In a strained voice she barely recognized as her own, Darla gave her name and explained the situation.

"It could have been an accident, but we don't really know. An ambulance?" she answered the dispatcher's question. "You can send one, but I'm pretty sure he's been dead awhile. Address? Barry," she called to the man, who now sat silently beside his friend, "what's the street number of the building?"

Barry stirred from his reverie long enough to give her the address, which she hurriedly repeated into the phone, along with a few more details about the body's location in the building. The dispatcher instructed her to remain on scene and not touch anything in the vicinity of the dead man . . . too late, as Darla recalled how Barry had moved the crowbar off Curt's body.

"They're sending the police and an ambulance right out," Darla told him once she'd hung up. Then, carefully avoiding looking at Curt again, she suggested, "Maybe we should wait upstairs until they get here."

"But I don't want to just leave him here like this," Barry countered with a miserable shake of his head. "I should find a blanket or something to put over him."

"The dispatcher said not to touch anything," she reminded him. "We don't know what actually happened to him, so we don't want to accidentally destroy any evidence." *Like picking up the pry bar*, she told herself, though she probably would have reflexively done the same thing had she been first to reach Curt.

Barry gave a grim nod and gestured her toward the stairs. "I guess I should take a look around while we're waiting on the cops to see if any wire or tools are missing. Curt's been worried about those bastards who stole our copper last week paying another visit."

Darla had come to much the same conclusion. Bad enough that since Curt's warning the week before, she'd worried over the possible loss of her street numbers to the scrap thieves. Now she had to fear the possibility of falling victim to criminals who were bold enough to commit murder if they were crossed?

They retreated upstairs to the main floor again, leaving the body alone in the basement. *The body.* Darla felt uncomfortable referring to someone whom she'd personally known in such a manner, but she found it hard to reconcile the ghastly corpse sprawled beneath the stairs with her boisterous if obnoxious customer Curt. To be sure, she had tolerated the man rather than liked him, but never would she have wished such a fate on him. And of course, the situation was far different for Barry, who had been both a friend and a business partner to Curt for more than half their lives.

She glanced Barry's way. Once he had determined that nothing seemed to be missing from the work area, he had joined her in the parlor. Now, he sat slumped against the wall, hands limply propped on his knees as he stared at a gaping hole in the plaster opposite him. She couldn't think of an appropriate platitude for this particular situation, and so she simply sat with him in what she hoped he'd view as sympathetic silence, though the truth was that she was guiltily wishing she'd turned down his lunch invitation and thus avoided the whole unpleasantness.

She remembered abruptly that Robert was alone at the bookstore. She'd better let him know she was going to be delayed.

Robert answered on the second ring, his "Pettistone's Fine Books, this is Robert, and how may I assist you today?" greeting enunciated in respectable imitation of James's precise tones.

Feeling rather like she was breaching some major etiquette rule by making her call, she murmured, "Robert, this is Darla. Yes, your boss," she clarified before he could ask for further identification. "There's been a bit of trouble here at Barry's place. I-I might be later than I thought. Will you be all right until James gets in?"

"Under control," he replied. "It's a bit slow, so I'm working on a window display for those new political autobiographies from last week. You know, the ones that turned out to be, like, real dogs."

Momentarily returning to retailer mode, Darla winced, knowing to which ones he referred. Nothing worse than moving only a half dozen copies in a week of what was supposedly a blazing *New York Times* best seller. "A window display, huh? Do you know how to do that?"

"Sure," was his enthusiastic answer. "There was this one the time Bill meant to order two copies of an old *Naughty Teacher Nancy* DVD but got two cases instead. You should have seen the cool display I made with a chalkboard and some notebooks. We sold, like, twenty DVDs in one day."

Great. Marketing tips courtesy of the adult bookstore industry. Darla rolled her eyes. But hey, if it had worked for *Naughty Teacher Nancy*, maybe it would work for the flavor-of-the-month politicians, too.

"Go ahead, then," she agreed, "but only use whatever you find lying around the shop for props. I'll be back as soon as I can."

As she hung up the call, Robert's mention of window displays made her think of Hilda Aguilar, whose talent at window dressing had always made her envious. What would happen to Jake's investigation, given that the subject of said investigation was now dead? And more important, what would Tera Aguilar's reaction be to her boyfriend's untimely end? Even if Tera had felt as casual about the relationship as

Curt apparently had, this would still have to come as a huge shock.

A heavy pounding on the open front door was accompanied by a barked demand: "Police. Anyone home?"

"In here," Barry called, promptly rising and offering Darla a hand up.

Her relief at seeing a uniformed officer arriving on the scene was tempered by the fact that she recognized the broad-faced, mustachioed cop. Officer Hallonquist had once caught her parked in Great-Aunt Dee's old Mercedes in a no-parking zone. Despite Darla's honeyed attempt at explanation, Hallonquist had gleefully written her a traffic citation, disproving her previous theory that all middle-aged New York men were suckers for women with southern accents. The fact that Jake's former partner Detective Reese had later managed to get the ticket dismissed hadn't tempered Darla's displeasure over the situation. Would the officer remember her now, with equal annoyance?

He did.

"You again," Hallonquist said with a shake of his head as he trudged through the open door to join them. Giving Barry a curt nod, he turned back to her and went on, "Dispatch says you got something worse than an illegally parked Mercedes this time."

"Hello, Officer Hallonquist. Nice to see you again, too," she said with deliberate politeness, stretching her Texas accent into an even more exaggerated twang for his benefit. "And, unfortunately, yes. There's been a bad . . . accident."

"I'll show you," Barry interrupted and pointed toward the open basement door.

He led the way down the steps, Hallonquist behind him and Darla bringing up the rear. Not that she cared to see Curt's body a second time, but she wanted to be there when Hallonquist took his first look at the scene. With luck, the officer would immediately tag the incident as a likely accident, so that she could stop worrying about scrap thieves and random, bloody violence. But then she remembered something Reese had told her once: that unless a doctor was holding the corpse's hand, any unexpected death was treated as a homicide until proved otherwise. "Stop right here, sir," Hallonquist told Barry when they were a few steps from the bottom. "Homicide will be here in a minute to secure the area, but in the meantime we don't want you wandering around the scene any more than you already have."

He'd drawn his oversized police flashlight, and now he clicked it on, the burst of LED illumination far brighter than the clamp-on lights that Barry had set up earlier. He swept his beam in the direction that Barry indicated, the white light washing over Curt's stiff form. Hallonquist reached for his radio, and Darla heard him speak briefly into it, though she couldn't make out his words or the answering squawk he got in return from his dispatcher. But from the stern expression on his face, she suspected that he had decided there was nothing natural about Curt's death.

"All right, folks," Hallonquist announced as he turned his radio down again, "time to go back upstairs so we can get some statements."

He swung his flashlight beam over the scene again, and that was when Darla noticed something she had not spied earlier. At the sight, her stomach gave a small lurch.

Half a dozen rust-colored paw prints, each successively fainter than the previous, led away from Curt's body.

EIGHT

"HELL, DARLA, IF YOU'D WANTED TO SEE ME AGAIN THAT BAD, you could've just dialed my cell."

Detective Fiorello Reese—known simply as Reese by those who wished to avoid extreme bodily injury—had walked through the open front door just as she, Barry, and Officer Hallonquist exited the basement. She'd almost not recognized him, however, given that he'd exchanged his usual personal uniform of jeans and black leather jacket for navy slacks, striped tie, and brown tweed sport coat.

Tall and blond, with the physique of someone who hung out in the gym a lot, Reese was a year or two younger than Darla and possessed of what she called midwestern corn-fed good looks—this despite the fact he was Italian on his mother's side—though he was saved from being a pretty boy by a strong nose that had been broken and never reset. And he had the reputation to go along with the nose. In fact, Reese had been the one to pull an injured Jake to safety during the gun battle with a homicide suspect that had left her permanently disabled.

Darla's relief that Reese was the homicide detective apparently assigned to the case had been tempered by a flash of annoyance at this bit of levity on his part. Reese didn't seem to notice her consternation. After delivering that offhanded greeting, he switched into detective mode and hustled them all outside again.

"Sir," he addressed Barry, "I need you and the lady to wait out here until I can take your statements. Please don't leave the scene yet."

Not waiting for Barry's assent, Reese turned to confer with Hallonquist for a few moments. Then he headed back inside the brownstone and presumably down into the basement for a look while a dour Hallonquist remained behind to stand guard over her and Barry. As he was jotting down their names and other pertinent information, Darla saw the crime scene van pull up. Two technicians—both blond, female, middle-aged, and wearing dark blue medical scrubs—fastened official yellow "Do Not Cross" tape along the perimeter of the narrow property. Then, reaching into the back of their van to don gloves and what resembled shower caps, each picked up what appeared to be a metal tackle box and marched over to where Officer Hallonquist stood.

"Body?" the shorter of the pair barked, not bothering with a greeting.

Hallonquist thrust a thumb in the direction of the front door, from which Reese was now emerging. "Basement," was his equally succinct reply.

She nodded. "Gimme the Cliff Notes," she commanded in a strong Brooklyn accent overlaid with the characteristic rasp of a two-pack-a-day smoker.

Hallonquist gave the woman a terse recitation of what was obvious from the scene: middle-aged male, dead several hours, apparent cause a blow to the head, possibly from a fall down the steps, but a crowbar had been found near the body.

"Anyone touch anything?" Shorty asked when he'd finished, her pointed look encompassing Darla and Barry. The latter nodded.

"I, er, moved the crowbar off him," he admitted, earning a snort of disgust from the tech.

"Civilians! They'll screw up a scene every time. We'll need his prints, and hers, too," she added with a meaningful glare at Darla before she headed up the steps.

Her partner, meanwhile, shot the rest of them a baleful look. "No one comes back inside until we give the okay."

"All right, folks, statement time," Reese said, all business now as he gestured Barry to join him. "Darla, why don't you hang with Officer Hallonquist for a minute while I talk to your friend?"

The officer appeared just about as thrilled as Darla felt at the prospect. To her relief, however, Hallonquist's definition of "hang" turned out to be "stand around silently and shoot dirty looks at the passersby who were gaping at the police vehicles and yellow tape." Since the strip of trampled grass in front of the brownstone hardly qualified as a lawn, that meant Darla was close enough to Reese and Barry to catch bits of their conversation. She noted that when the latter got to the part about how they had located Curt by means of the dead man's ringing cell phone, Reese quickly confiscated the phone in question still in Barry's pocket. No doubt some official police hacker would be able to get all of Curt's saved messages even without the benefit of the man's password. Knowing Curt, she hoped for his sake that he had deleted any suggestive voice mails from Tera or any of his other conquests.

When it was Darla's turn to talk, Reese went through the timetable of the morning's events with her, up to and including their discovery of Curt. She included how they'd followed the ring of the cell phone, earning an approving nod from the cop at the unconventional tactic. When she mentioned how Curt had warned her about the scrap thieves last time he stopped in at the bookstore, Reese prodded her for everything she could recall about that conversation.

"Curt seemed pretty upset about having that copper tubing stolen," she explained. "I'm sure he thought they were some street punks who'd run off at the first sign of trouble, but he warned me that they were hitting occupied buildings, too, and that I'd better keep a close eye on my place."

"No mention of anyone else he was having trouble with? Creditors, ex-wives?"

"Actually, there is someone," Darla replied, abruptly recalling the recent confrontation in her store. "You heard about my new employee, Robert? Last week, his old boss stopped by the store basically to harass him. Curt happened to come in at the same time, and it turned out the two of them knew each other. They got into a pretty nasty argument before I kicked Bill out, and he said something about unfinished business between them."

"I don't suppose you know Bill's last name, do you?" Reese asked, looking up from his notes to give her a keen look.

Darla shook her head. "I can find out from Robert if you need me to. All I know is that he owns an adult bookstore a few blocks away called Bill's Books and Stuff."

"Short, ugly guy, looks like he escaped from the monkey house?"

At Darla's nod, Reese gave a cold, satisfied smile, though his look for her was one of approval. "That would be Bill Ferguson. Let's just say he's not a stranger to the department. I'll stop by that cesspool he calls a store and have a little chat with him. Anyone else?"

"You might want to ask Jake that," Darla replied. "She's poking around into Curt's background for a new client. She might have something for you."

The suggestion earned her another approving nod, and Darla tried not to feel guilty. It was probably more than she should have said without Jake's permission, but maybe it would offset the one thing she did not intend to mention: the set of bloody paw prints she'd noticed near Curt's body. No way was she going to implicate Hamlet—and, by default, herself—by telling Reese she suspected her store mascot might know something about what happened to Curt. The crime scene tech looked like a pro. She would surely spot the paw prints and draw her own conclusions as to what they meant.

Not that the prints were necessarily Hamlet's, or even feline in origin, Darla reassured herself. For all she knew, they might belong to one of those giant rats she was always hearing about that lived in the New York City sewers. But she couldn't help recalling Curt's assumption that it had been Hamlet he'd seen the previous week slinking out of the brownstone.

What if Hamlet had found his way outside again last night and paid a return visit to Curt and Barry's brownstone in the wee hours of the morning? While Curt was headed up the basement steps with his crowbar, Hamlet might have been lurking down there looking for some entertainment. What if he had decided to play his favorite cat game of rushing up the stairs while dodging a human's legs? If he'd startled Curt and the man had actually tripped over him, could Hamlet be guilty of manslaughter?

Darla had no idea what the ramifications might be, but she suspected it would not bode well for either Hamlet or Pettistone's Fine Books. Animal control for Hamlet, perhaps, definitely a lawsuit for her! She suppressed a shudder.

"Getting chilly?" Reese asked sympathetically as he shut his notebook.

She nodded. "A little."

"I think we're done here. You can go, and we'll see about getting your prints later, if we end up needing them. Mr. Eisen," he called to Barry, "I'm finished with the witness statements. You can wait here until our techs are finished and the body is removed to lock up the place, or you can go and we'll lock up for you. But I can't let you back inside again until probably tomorrow, when we'll release the scene."

Barry left his post by the construction Dumpster and joined them. "Yeah, I'll stick around. It doesn't seem right to leave Curt there with strangers."

"Do you want me to wait with you?" Darla asked, a lump in her throat. Though her emotion was not so much for Curt as it was for Barry. If something like this had happened to one of her friends, she couldn't imagine wanting to stay and watch the blanketed body being carried out on a gurney . . . and yet she knew she'd feel compelled to do so, all the same. Having been friends with Curt since high school, Barry must surely feel as if he'd lost a brother.

He gave her a faint smile and shook his head. "I appreciate the offer, but you need to get back to the store. You don't want to leave that kid running the place by himself all afternoon. I'll be fine here. I'll give you a call or something later, okay?"

"I'll hold you to that," she replied and managed a smile in return.

While Barry took a seat on the partially demolished stoop, Reese walked with her the short distance to the sidewalk. Holding up the crime scene tape so that she could walk under it, he asked, "So, you dating that guy?"

Darla stared at him in surprise. The detective's words had been casual, but something in his deliberately bland expression told her that his interest in the answer was not. Surely Reese wasn't jealous . . . was he?

"We're just friends. At least, at this point," she replied, surprised to find herself complimented by Reese's apparent interest in her love life. Maybe he was regretting not putting forth a little effort back when they'd first met. Maybe now he was gauging the situation to see if he should try moving in on what he considered Barry's territory. The question was, should she give him any encouragement?

What the heck, she decided. *Why not?* True, she couldn't see things between her and Reese going anywhere—for one thing, he had a distinct aversion to the printed word—but the notion that he was interested in her added a cheery note to what had been a distinctly unpleasant day. And so, with a deliberately casual air of her own, she clarified, "We're not exactly dating, but Jake has been encouraging me to go out with him. She thinks he'd be good for me."

"Hey, that's great." Reese gave her a brotherly slap on the back. "I sure hope it works out for you. A broad your age, you can't afford to wait around too much longer for the right guy to show up. Tick, tock, and all that."

Tick, tock?

Darla's previous warm, fuzzy feeling took an abrupt header into cold and prickly territory. Seriously, Reese's whole "hates books" attitude should have been fair warning. Good a friend as he might be to Jake, the man was definitely a Cro-Magnon when it came to more personal relationships.

"If that was a crude reference to my biological clock, then I'll pretend I didn't hear you," she replied in as frosty a tone as she could muster. "In case you didn't get the memo, a woman doesn't need a man to have a fulfilling life. And she sure doesn't need one to have a baby . . . at least, not after that first ten minutes."

"Hey, that first ten minutes is the best part," Reese

countered with a wink that made her blush despite her out-rage. "Don't get your panties in a twist, Red. I was just kidding with you."

"And I've told you before, don't call me Red," Darla gritted out. Her ex had called her that—usually followed by some obnoxious statement that he'd thought was unduly clever—and she had come to loathe the nickname.

He pantomimed an erasing motion with one hand. "Sorry, I forgot about that whole Red thing. Don't send your boyfriend over to kick my ass about it, okay?"

"I can handle my own ass-kicking, thank you very much." She was about to add a few more choice remarks, when she glanced past Reese to see Barry staring curiously at the pair of them. No point in creating a scene, particularly under the circumstances.

Favoring Barry with a sympathetic wave—and Reese with a parting glare—Darla started back in the direction of the bookstore. The weather seemed colder now than when she and Barry had so companionably made their way to the brownstone a couple of hours earlier. Also, reaction to Curt's death had begun to set in, and she felt suddenly drained of energy.

Still, visions of crowbar-wielding thieves kept her moving at a brisk pace down the street, though force of habit made her slow as she passed by Great Scentsations. The Halloween graveyard scene had been modified by the addition of a stuffed figure of a sexy, miniskirted witch chasing a fuzzy black cat through the soap tombstones.

Cute, Darla thought with a flash of a smile, feeling more than a little sympathetic toward Ms. Witch. Her amusement faded just as swiftly, however, as she debated whether or not she should stop in to tell Hilda about what had happened to Curt.

She and Hilda were friendly enough, but their acquaintance was strictly a business one. Breaking this sort of news seemed to require a more personal relationship than they had. And she hadn't thought to ask Barry if he planned to break the news to Tera about her boyfriend. But since Barry was still at the brownstone for the foreseeable future, who knew when he'd have the chance? If she gave Hilda a heads-up now, the woman could tell her daughter right away, rather than having Tera learn about it in some impersonal way. On the other hand, maybe it should be Jake who talked to Hilda. After all, she was the one who'd been hired to—

"Hello, Darla, how are you?" Hilda's cultured voice broke in on her musings, the unexpected greeting making Darla jump.

Guiltily, she tore her gaze from the window display to see Hilda's neatly coiffed head poking out from around the shop doorway. The woman smiled apologetically.

"I'm sorry, I didn't mean to startle you, but you've been standing outside my window for several minutes now looking dazed. Is something wrong?"

There's an opening if ever I saw one. Darla took a deep breath. "Actually, there is," she said aloud. "Why don't I come inside and tell you."

Hilda gave a gracious nod and held open the door. She was wearing a turquoise Chanel skirted suit and matching pumps, and Darla couldn't help but feel dowdy by comparison. Once over the threshold, however, the faint sound track of New Age music that Hilda always played—heavy on flute and chimes—made her feel as if she'd stepped into a yoga studio. Some of her earlier tension dissipated. Unlike those expensive perfumes that lined the department store counters and assaulted the senses, the fragrances that filled Hilda's small shop were subtle and inviting. Each day of the week, Hilda lit a different handmade soy candle, which either soothed or invigorated, depending on its scent. So far, Darla had stopped in on gardenia, sandalwood, rose, and honey-suckle days. This was the first time she'd been there for lav-ender, and she made a mental note to come back later to purchase one of those candles to burn in her own shop.

"So tell me, what's wrong, Darla?" the woman urged in her polite but no-nonsense manner. "You have lines under your eyes . . . very bad. Here, you should try these all-natural compresses."

She lifted a small jar from a nearby shelf, explaining, "They are made with cucumber, twenty to a jar. Gently squeeze out the liquid and put one compress over each eye for fifteen minutes. They work wonders, I promise you."

"Maybe next time," Darla said, hedging as she glanced about the small shop. A smartly dressed young Asian woman with a pigtailed toddler in tow was slathering on hand lotion from one of the sample bottles on the next aisle over, but otherwise the store was empty of customers. "Is Tera here today?"

"Not yet. She has classes in the mornings, so she never comes into the shop until after lunch."

Then Hilda checked at the small gold wristwatch she wore and frowned.

"She should be here by now. That girl, I don't know what to do with her," the woman went on, a hint of Cuban lilt softening those words of maternal rebuke. "She stays out all night long with that so-called boyfriend of hers when she should be at home studying. And then, she's too tired to get up in the morning and skips class. That, or else she goes home again as soon as class is over and sleeps all afternoon instead of helping me here in the store."

Hilda glanced over at her customer, who had dragged her protesting little girl to the children's section to look at organic baby shampoo, and then lowered her voice.

"That Curt Benedetto, he's a bad influence," she confided

with a refined sniff. "Tera was making straight A's in her all classes until she took up with him. What she sees in a man old enough to be her father, I'll never understand. And that shifty look in his eyes . . ."

She paused and clicked her tongue. "I just know he's hiding something. Probably a wife and five children. I hired your friend Jake to check up on him. If Tera won't listen to her own mother, then maybe she'll believe the evidence in black and white."

"That's what I wanted to tell you," Darla broke in when the woman finally paused for breath. "I have some bad news about Curt."

"Humph. The only news I want to hear about him is that he left town."

"Well, it's close to that." Darla hesitated, and then forged on. "I went with Barry this morning to see the brownstone that he and Curt are remodeling. We found Curt dead in the basement."

"Dead?" He artfully made-up eyes widening, Hilda took a step back and traced a quick sign of the cross. "*Dios mío*, who killed him?"

The woman's porcelain skin had turned appreciably paler, while her gasped exclamation was loud enough to draw her customer's attention. The young mother shot them both a look of alarm and promptly dragged her child toward the door, ignoring the little girl's outstretched hands and plaintive cry of, "Mama, want!"

Hilda didn't seem to notice that she'd lost a customer. As for Darla, she hesitated. Why had Hilda immediately assumed that Curt had been murdered? The more obvious possibility was that he'd succumbed to a fatal heart attack or else had an accident. It sent alarm bells jangling in Darla's head. Could Hilda possess some knowledge of what had actually happened to the man?

Carefully skirting a direct answer, Darla replied, "The police made us leave the building, so I really don't know any more. But I didn't want Tera to hear this kind of news on the radio or read it online."

"That's good of you, Darla." Sounding distracted now, Hilda reached into her jacket and pulled out a slim white cell phone. "I'd better call Tera right now and tell her. You know how young people are . . . they take things so personally. She shouldn't find this out from anyone but her mother."

Realizing she had been dismissed, Darla took the hint. "Sorry to be the bearer of bad news," she said as she headed toward the door. "And I'll think about those compresses."

Hilda nodded, but her attention was on her phone as she dialed. Before she stepped outside, Darla heard Hilda genteelly shout her daughter's name—"Maria Teresa Aguilar!"—followed by a flurry of Spanish that Darla roughly translated with her minimal knowledge of the language to mean, "It's your mother. Get your lazy butt out of bed and pick up the phone!"

Darla let the door close behind her on that little drama, her concern more over Hilda's earlier reaction than what Tera might say or do. While Reese hadn't specifically told her not to speak to Hilda, she suspected that he might consider it interference in police business. But as she started down the street toward her own store, another concern was on her mind: Hamlet. Some wily animal had been in the brownstone's basement during the early morning hours. For her own peace of mind, she needed to know if Hamlet was the creature in question. She had an idea how to prove that that he'd been present—or else how to eliminate him as a four-legged suspect—but it would take Jake's help.

She pulled out her cell phone and pressed the speed dial for Jake. The ex-cop picked up on the first ring, as if she'd been waiting for Darla's call. "Hey, kid, I heard via the blue grapevine that there was some trouble over at your friend Barry's place."

"You can say that again. Curt's dead—probably murdered, according to Reese—and Barry and I were unlucky enough to find him."

"Yeah, that's what I heard. A shame," Jake replied, sounding like she meant it. "Are you back at the store yet?"

"I'm a block away. Can I meet you at your place in about fifteen minutes, once I make sure everything is okay in the store? I need your help with something related to this whole awful business."

"Sure, what's the problem?" Jake wanted to know.

Darla took a deep breath. "If you talk to Reese before I see you, tell him he'd better take a crash course in Meow 101. You see, I think I have a witness to Curt's murder."

NINE

"MR. BENEDETTO IS DEAD?" JAMES ECHOED IN WELL-BRED disbelief once Darla had broken the news back in the shop. "Are you quite certain?"

"Yeah, it was pretty obvious from that whole stiff-as-a-board-not-breathing thing he had going on."

James shot her a long-suffering look. "I am not questioning your diagnosis of death, Darla, only your identification of the decedent."

She gave a weary sigh. "Sorry. Yes, we're absolutely certain it was Curt. He was still, um, identifiable."

"And how fortunate that Officer Reese is the one handling the case," her manager went on. "Do we know the official cause of death?"

"For the moment, the police are treating Curt's death as a homicide until the medical examiner says otherwise. But I'm pretty sure Reese thinks he was murdered. Barry thought at first that he'd fallen, but there was a crowbar lying on top of Curt, and he had a crowbar-shaped dent in his head. So it's a logical leap that someone whacked him with it."

"I would assume so," her manager agreed. "Even if the man had been holding the crowbar when he fell down the steps, what are the chances that he could hit himself in the head with it *and* manage to fall so that it landed on top of him?"

"I knew someone who, you know, did that," Robert interjected, setting down the carton of paperbacks he was unloading and walking over to join them at the register.

When she and James both turned to stare at him, he shrugged, or rather, tried to. With Hamlet slung around his neck like an inky fur stole, the cat's forepaws and back paws draping over either shoulder, it was not an easy gesture to make.

Darla shook her head. She wasn't sure who had come up with this sartorial idea, Robert or Hamlet, but the latter was staring at her with gleaming green eyes that seemed to say, *No way would I let you get away with carting me around like this.* She shot him a sour look in return. She'd deal with Mr. Furry Witness for the Prosecution later.

"It wasn't a crowbar, though," Robert clarified. "The dude, he was on a skateboard and tried to, like, skate down the handrail. He fell off, and the skateboard hit him in the head in midair. And then when he landed, it was, you know, on top of him. I can show you on YouTube if you want to see it."

"Thanks, I'll pass," Darla said. "But until we know what really happened to Curt, the new rule is that no one works alone in the evenings, and the doors all stay locked and the alarm stays set before and after business hours, no exceptions."

"I concur with your plan," James said. "Better to be overly cautious than overly confident in this sort of situation. Between the Russian gangs and the scrap thieves, we could be dealing with some very dangerous customers, indeed. Perhaps we should review the schedule to make certain that our shifts will overlap accordingly?"

"Yeah, and I can look at the security videos in the mornings for you if, you know, you want me to," Robert added. "See if anyone is prowling around outside."

Darla nodded as she pulled up the weekly schedule on the computer. "Good idea, Robert. That can be your job every morning from now on. I'll show you how to play back the recordings. James, see what you think if I switch around your hours a bit on these days."

She made some quick adjustments to the schedule and got James's blessing, then printed off a few copies. "Robert," she said, "can you stay on the clock a little longer? I need to run down to Jake's place for a bit. I'll show you the security system routine as soon as I get back."

"Okay. Hey, are you gonna look at the window display I made?"

He sounded so eager that she smiled. She'd forgotten that she had given him free rein to do something with the two political autobiographies that had been gathering dust for a week. So distracted had she been by thoughts of Curt that she'd walked right past the window without even looking at it. She glanced over at James, who merely nodded. She wasn't sure if the gesture indicated a positive review of the teen's artistic abilities or not. But if his skills were good enough for Bill's Books and Stuff . . .

"You should look at it from the outside," he added. "I'll go with you, if you want."

"Sure," she agreed, "but leave Hamlet in the store. He's not allowed out of the building."

The feline in question gave her a peeved look as Robert obediently dislodged him onto the register counter. "Sorry, bro," he explained as Hamlet stalked to the counter's far edge and sat with his back deliberately to them, "but Ms. Pettistone is, like, the boss."

Darla could almost hear the she's-not-the-boss-of-me

vibes emanating from the disgruntled cat. But whether or not Hamlet liked it, she was on a campaign to keep him safely indoors, particularly in light of recent incidents.

With Robert trailing her, she left James to deal with Hamlet's mood and headed outside. Unlike Hilda's shop, which was at ground level, the windows of Darla's bookstore were almost head high—one reason she'd been lax in doing much more than putting out the occasional "Big Sale" sign behind the glass. Almost any halfway competent display would thus be an improvement. She only hoped that Robert's efforts were not so amateurish that she'd have to find some excuse to redo his work that wouldn't hurt his feelings.

"So, uh, what do you think?" he asked as she dismounted the final step and turned for a look at what he'd done.

Darla stared in surprise. The end result was as professional as any window display that Hilda had ever created. She recognized the two table runners—one blue, one red—that had been tucked on a shelf in the storeroom ever since she'd taken over the shop. Robert had arranged the fabric on the broad inner sill so that the two pieces met in the middle of the display, each half of the display space lined now in its own color. The two authors were of different political persuasions, and she saw that he had put their respective books on the appropriate color for their particular affiliation. Even better, both covers featured three-quarter photos of their authors, so the two politicians appeared to be facing each other in point-counterpoint style. In between the figuratively dueling politicos, Robert had built a pedestal combining both of the books, which he'd topped with a Statue of Liberty figure he must've found somewhere.

As a final touch, he had strung a length of red, white, and blue twinkle lights left over from a July Fourth display like bunting from the window's top edge. Red letters spelling out "Hot Seller" ran along the bottom edge.

"If you don't, you know, like it, I can change it," Robert said in a diffident tone when a few moments had passed and Darla still had made no comment.

Smiling, she turned toward him. "You did a wonderful job, Robert. I was simply admiring your work. But wherever did you find Lady Liberty?"

"I remembered seeing it in Mr. Plinski's store, and Ms. Plinski said I could borrow it."

"Very clever. I think I'll make you our official window dresser from here on out. That is, if you don't mind taking on an extra duty."

"Yeah, I could do that. And maybe some stuff inside, too. No offense, but the Halloween decorations inside are kinda lame."

Once again, the tone was offhanded, though she could see the pleased color in his cheeks. Darla's smile broadened. Really, Robert was a good kid despite a few annoying quirks. She'd have to ask James if he'd noted the vest homage thing.

Then, recalling her errand, Darla's smile faded. "Finish up the stocking with James, and I'll be back in a few minutes. Oh, and see if you can keep Hamlet somewhere readily accessible. I might need him."

"You've got it, boss."

He took the stairs in two oversized hops and went back inside while she made her way more conventionally down the few steps to Jake's place. With luck, her friend wouldn't think what she was about to suggest crossed some sort of crazy-woman line.

"Hey, kid," Jake greeted her as Darla gave a perfunctory knock and stepped inside. Gesturing Darla to join her at the kitchen table turned desk, she asked, "How are you holding up?"

"It's still a bit of a shock," Darla admitted as she sank onto one of the chrome chairs. "I mean, Curt was a royal pain in the butt, and I didn't much like him, but no way did I want to see him dead, especially like that."

"Don't worry, you're allowed to be upset. In fact, I'd be concerned if you weren't. I was a cop for twenty years, and I still wanted to puke every time I had to call in another stiff." She paused and gave a dismissive wave. "Oh, they claim you get used to it after a while, but if you're halfway human, you never really do. The kids, they're the hardest . . ."

She trailed off, and Darla saw a fleeting expression of remembered pain in the older woman's eyes before she focused back on Darla again.

"But what was all that you said on the phone about meows and witnesses?" Then, as Darla opened her mouth to reply, Jake shook her curly mane and put out a restraining hand. "Wait. If this involves a certain black cat, you'd better start from the very beginning and tell me what happened from the time you arrived at the brownstone until the police showed up."

Darla complied, starting with Barry's concern that the door had not been properly locked and ending when she had left Reese and Barry at the scene—omitting, of course, the whole "tick, tock" conversation. Jake listened intently and then flatly stated, "Okay, so you saw cat paw prints near Curt's body. Why would you think they belong to Hamlet? There's got to be two dozen feral cats in the neighborhood."

"Yes, but remember I told you last week how I found what looked like grease on his fur, and that I thought he was getting out of the apartment somehow? Well, the same day that Porn Shop Bill came by to harass Robert, Curt told me that he'd seen a cat he was sure was Hamlet running out of his building that very morning. And the prints I saw next to Curt's body today were pretty darned big. The feral cats I've seen around the neighborhood are all scrawny things."

Jake sighed. "All right, so maybe it *was* the little hell-raiser who was down in the dead guy's basement. But it's not like

Reese can drag his furry butt down to the precinct and question him about what he saw. So why does it matter?"

"Curt's death might still have been accidental," Darla explained. "If it was, I-I need to know if it was Hamlet's fault that it happened. You've seen that game he plays, running between people's legs on the stairs. If that had something to do with Curt falling, then I'd rather live with knowing my cat is guilty of—"

"Involuntary cat-slaughter?" Jake interjected with a hint of a smile.

Darla shot her a sour look but let that last good-natured jibe go unchallenged, knowing there was more to come. "—of causing a fatal accident, than always wondering about it. If you know what I mean."

Darla took a deep breath before continuing. What she was about to say would doubtless make her sound like a crazy cat lady despite the fact that (a) she wasn't crazy and (b) she wasn't that much of a cat lover. Wincing a little, she forged on. "If Curt *was* murdered, and we can prove that Hamlet was a witness, maybe he can help identify the killer."

Jake's lips twisted in what was an obvious effort to hold back a laugh, but to her credit she merely said, "Okay, okay. What do you want me to do here?"

"Thanks, Jake," Darla replied with genuine gratitude. "I figured maybe you could do one of those CSI things like you see on television and test Hamlet's paws for blood."

"Jeeze, they ought to outlaw those shows," Jake said with a shake of her head. "You civilians watch that stuff and come away thinking every crime can be solved in under sixty minutes, counting commercials, just so long as you have a full lab at your disposal. Well, that ain't the way it works, kid."

"I know that, but isn't there some sort of home test you can do?"

"Like a home pregnancy test?" Jake asked with a grin. "Yeah, actually, there is. Let me see what I have in my bag of tricks. Wait right here."

She headed off in the direction of her bedroom while Darla waited at the table, virtuously resisting the temptation to do a little upside-down reading of the open file on the table. She could see the preprinted tab on the folder with its big "A" and assumed this was Hilda's file. So much for Jake's first official case.

"Here you go," Jake said, returning to the room with a smaller version of the tackle box the crime scene investigators had carried. "Ye olde evidence-collecting kit," she explained, "aka my bag of tricks."

Popping it open, she pulled out a screw-top cylinder that resembled a skinny plastic vitamin bottle. "We can swab Hamlet's paws with these test strips and see if they detect any blood residue," she went on. "They won't distinguish between animal or human blood, but for some quick and dirty results, they'll do the job."

Then she frowned. "Wait. We're talking maybe eight, ten hours since he would have stepped in the blood. And then he walked a couple of blocks through God knows what kind of crud on the streets to get back home again? If there was any blood left behind after all that, he probably licked it off."

Darla felt her stomach roil at the mental image that statement conjured and was abruptly glad she'd missed lunch. Even considering everything else that had happened today, the idea of Hamlet casually licking Curt's blood from his paws somehow seemed more ghastly than the rest. "Ew, Jake!" she exclaimed.

Jake snorted. "Darla, he's a cat. What did you expect him to do, grab himself a pawful of hand sanitizer and tidy up? He probably ate a few nasty little mice while he was out, too."

"Stop!"

Now it was Darla's turn to raise a warning hand, even as a giggle bubbled up in her throat. Despite her best efforts, the giggle ballooned into a laugh. The mental picture of Hamlet pumping a few squirts from the industrial-sized container she kept by the store register was ludicrous enough to counteract the unpleasant images of Curt that had been drifting in her mind since that morning.

Finally regaining her composure, she conceded, "You're right, I didn't even think of that—I mean, the part about it being so many hours and him walking around. Bad idea, I guess."

"Not necessarily. The pad on a cat's paw has creases just like your skin does, so there is a chance some blood residue might be left. If you want to bring him down, we can give it a try."

"Actually, I was hoping you could come up to the store. The only way to get him down here is in his cat carrier, which means any blood you'd find on him would probably be mine."

Darla had endured a similar scenario when she'd had to take Hamlet to the vet for his annual exam a few months earlier. Her first attempt to load him into the plastic crate had dissolved into a contest of strength, with Hamlet gripping the carrier's opening with all four paws and stubbornly refusing to be pushed inside. A second try had ended much like the first, save that Hamlet had cut short that round with a swipe of claws that nicked one of Darla's fingers and left her muttering bad words as she sucked on that bloody digit.

She'd finally resorted to donning elbow-length oven gloves as protective gear. Then, sneaking up on him from behind, she managed to grab Hamlet and stuff him into the carrier before he had time to react. She doubted he could be fooled with that tactic a second time.

Jake grinned, apparently familiar with Hamlet's aversion

to being transported via crate. "Let me grab my keys and phone, and I'll go up with you," she said and then packed the vial back into her evidence-collecting case.

Not surprisingly, Jake's trip upstairs took a couple of minutes longer than Darla's, since she paused outside for a few clandestine puffs on a cigarette before heading into the store. By the time she walked in, Darla had already taken stock of her employees. James was in the reference section assisting two college boys—in what Darla could only assume was an homage to ghosts of students past, they wielded briefcases rather than the requisite backpacks—while Robert was busy rearranging the new arrivals table. As for Hamlet, he was still in classic p.o.'d mode, sitting on the register counter, tail tucked around him, ears flat. But Darla took the fact that he hadn't stalked back up to the apartment as a positive sign.

"Robert," she called out, "Jake and I need your help for a minute."

"Sure." Carefully squaring off one of the stacks, Robert sauntered over, fists crammed into the pockets of his black vest. "Hi, Ms. Jake. How's the PI biz?"

"Not bad, kid. Say, do you think you could hold Hamlet still for a minute while I rub a little something on his paws?"

Robert looked alarmed. "What, like, medicine?"

"Nothing bad," Darla hurried to assure him. The last thing she wanted to tell the teen was that they were swabbing her cat for a dead man's blood. Though, knowing Robert, he would probably find that pretty cool. "We're afraid he got out last night and stepped in, er, something he shouldn't have. We need to clean him up."

"Oh, okay, then."

He scooped up the cat and cradled him so that all four paws were sticking out. "Hey, little bro," he comforted Ham-

let, who was giving Darla a suspicious look, "don't get all
bent. They just want to wash your feet."

"This will only take a minute and a little bit of water,"
Jake added as she dug into her metal box. She pulled out four
test sticks and an ampoule of clear liquid. While Darla
watched in interest, Jake applied a drop of water to the pad
on the first test stick and then rubbed the dampened strip
against Hamlet's right-front paw pad. The "little bro"
squirmed, but to Darla's relief he let Jake repeat the process
on his other three feet, using a fresh stick each time.

"All finished," Jake cheerfully said as she set the final
strip on the counter. "You can let the witness, er, cat, go now."

"Good job," Robert praised him and set him down on the
floor.

Hamlet hissed and shot the youth a narrow green look
that said, *Yeah,* bro, *and this better not happen again.* Darla
suppressed a smile, feeling vindicated. Apparently, even
Robert was subject to dropping a notch down Hamlet's ever-
sliding scale of acceptable human behavior.

Jake, meanwhile, was comparing each strip against a little chart on the side of the bottle that reminded Darla of a
swimming pool chlorine test.

"Anything there?" she anxiously asked her friend. Then,
recalling that Robert was still standing there and listening
in while pretending ennui, she reached under the counter.
She dragged out a three-ring binder the size of a New York
City phone book—assuming such a thing was even printed
anymore.

"Here you go," she said and thrust the manual in his
direction. "These are the instructions to the security system.
Why don't you thumb through it for a few minutes while I
finish up with Jake, and then we'll do a test run on how to do
a replay?"

"Sure, boss," he obligingly agreed and headed over to the children's section, landing with an alarmingly loud *plop* in the beanbag chair. At another time, Darla would have lectured him on the proper care and handling of beanbags, but now her attention was on Jake and her test sticks.

"We have a winner," the older woman said, holding up one strip that now sported a faint bit of green on the formerly white pad surface. "Definitely blood, but like I told you, there's no way to tell if it's human or not."

Darla stared uncertainly at the strip. Finding the blood traces could mean that Hamlet had indeed been at the crime scene and been the one to leave the paw prints. On the other hand, the blood could be his own, or else have been the aftermath of Jake's suggested nasty little mouse massacre. Bottom line, they still had no proof one way or the other that Hamlet had witnessed the crime.

Jake, meanwhile, had pulled out her phone. She snapped a quick picture of the strip next to the container's color chart, then slipped the strip into a small paper bag and wrote *Hamlet, left-rear paw* and the date before initialing and sealing it. The remaining used strips she stuck into a mini biohaz bag.

"Normally, we'd need the original item as evidence," she explained as she stowed everything back into her kit, "but I don't think Hamlet will let me lop off his back paw."

"And why would you want to perform an amputation on our store mascot's extremity?" James asked—rhetorically, Darla assumed—as he slid past them to reach the register. With swift efficiency, he rang up his customers' purchases (Latin grammar; Darla saw him nod in approval) while she and Jake prudently hung back and did their best to be invisible.

"Wonder what's in those briefcases," Jake whispered in her ear.

Darla gave the customers a professional smile as she murmured back, "Either dirty laundry or bomb-making materials."

James finished the transaction but waited until the two young men had left the store before he coolly replied, "I believe it was the former, as I detected a distinct whiff of gym socks emanating from one of the gentlemen. And now, would you care to share what sort of experiments you were performing on Hamlet?"

"Just testing a theory of Darla's," Jake airily dismissed the question as she collected her kit. "Gotta go. I've got some reports to write up and a couple of errands to run." To Darla, she added, "I keep forgetting, the man has bionic hearing. I swear he could hear a mouse farting in the next room."

Not waiting for a reply, she headed for the door. James fixed Darla with a quizzical look, one gray brow quirked in question. Darla debated fobbing him off the same way that Jake had, but she couldn't just leave, as the store didn't close for a few more hours yet. Finally, she said softly, "I'll tell you more, but wait until after our part-timer goes home for the day."

"Yo, I can hear mice farting, too," Robert called from the beanbag. "It's not nice, keeping secrets from the hired help."

"Actually, keeping employees in the dark is a time-honored tradition," James countered before Darla could respond. "I presume you are familiar with the concept of information being dispersed on a need-to-know basis?" At Robert's nod, he clarified, "Let us just say that you do not need to know."

Darla heard a bit of grumbling from the beanbag, but Robert obediently subsided back into his study of the manual. Hamlet, meanwhile, had slipped out from behind the main shelf in the kids' section. He planted himself beside the beanbag in what appeared to be a gesture of solidarity with the teen, despite Robert's earlier bit of betrayal.

Shaking her head, Darla said, "Robert, let's do this training now, so I can throw you out of here before James dies of curiosity."

"Believe me, there is no danger of that," James countered with a hint of a smile. Tugging his vest into place, he headed toward the stairs leading up to the storeroom.

Robert slapped shut the manual and flung himself out of the beanbag with much the same gusto as he'd dropped into it. Darla waited until he'd joined her at the counter and then opened the security program on the computer.

"That's the icon," she said, pointing at the screen, "and here's how you get in."

Taking the manual back from him, she flipped it open to page 99 and showed him where she'd written the password information. She typed that in, and a welcome screen appeared. She used the mouse to click on the button marked "Menu."

"You've seen the cameras inside the store. There are six total: the four inside, and one each at the front and back doors."

"You mean there's, like, one in the courtyard?"

"It's pointed at the door," she explained, pulling up a screen that showed all six views at once. "You don't need to be paranoid; no one is spying on you if you sit out there to eat your lunch. Though pretty soon, it's going to be too cold to be out there without a parka."

"Yeah, I heard there might even be snow for Halloween. I think about how that would suck, you know, being homeless in the snow."

"Don't worry, there are plenty of shelters and volunteers to help folks in need when the weather gets bad," she absently assured him, concentrating on the screen. "Here, the program's set to run automatically. This is how you can tell it's in real time, and here's how to play back what you've previously recorded."

She spent the next twenty minutes going over the features and letting Robert try it himself, until she was sure he had it down pat. "You can go through the review first thing tomorrow when you get here. You won't have to watch every minute, just fast-forward through until you make it back to real time. Or you can stop it sooner if you see something that needs a closer look . . . like Hamlet sneaking out of the building. We've got to put a stop to that before he gets hurt."

Or before he stumbles over another dead body.

"Don't worry, boss, I'll keep a sharp eye out," the teen said with another of his snappy salutes. "And I'll try to, you know, think like a cat so I can figure out where he's getting out."

"I'd appreciate that." She glanced at her watch and added, "You can sign out now, but why don't you plan on getting here about thirty minutes early tomorrow morning so you can look at the video."

"Got it." He initialed the printed schedule on the clipboard she kept beneath the register, and then reached for the backpack he kept stashed beneath the counter. As he did so, a couple of candy bars tumbled out of the unzipped side. While he stuffed the snacks back in and zipped up the pack again, Darla noticed that today he had a thin sleeping bag cinched to the bottom.

"Going camping tonight?" she asked with a smile.

He shrugged and then pulled the straps over his narrow shoulders. "Sometimes some of us go to the park at night to hang out. The girls, they always complain that it's, like, too cold. But if I bring along a sleeping bag, we can crawl inside, and they don't have an excuse to, you know, leave early."

"Got the picture," Darla said, hurriedly cutting him short.

She didn't want to think about what else might go on in that sleeping bag. "See you tomorrow, then."

Robert headed for the door, sending a long-distance fist bump in the direction of Hamlet, who had taken over his spot on the beanbag chair. Darla frowned a little as she watched him leave. She'd hung out in parks at night as a teen a time or two herself. Still, that had been close to twenty years ago and in Dallas, which—contrary to its natives' protests—had still clung to a small-town mentality despite its sprawling geographic bounds. But what was it like in Brooklyn, in this day and age? Besides, there could be a killer on the loose!

"You're acting like someone's mom," she told herself with a wry smile. Robert was over eighteen and presumably had a mother of his own. If he wanted to go out at night, that was his call. But as for another of her employees—

She glanced again at Hamlet, who was busy kneading the beanbag chair into a more comfortable shape to accommodate his furry self. He'd been darned lucky so far to have returned home unscathed from his unauthorized forays outside the building. With luck, Robert would eventually discover the crafty feline's escape route, but until then, she intended to keep a keen eye on Hamlet, as well as on her shop's exterior fixtures . . . at least, until the roaming scrap thieves were caught and jailed.

Though heaven help any scrap thief—or murderer—unfortunate enough to cross paths with the official mascot of Pettistone's Fine Books.

TEN

BY EIGHT P.M., DARLA WAS LOUNGING ON HER LIVING ROOM couch—a prickly, old-fashioned horsehair sofa inherited from Great-Aunt Dee—clad in gray sweats and a matching hoodie. Unfortunately, the fleece fabric wasn't thick enough to protect against the sofa's prickly hide. Grabbing a well-worn quilt, she spread the blanket over the offending cushions and then flopped again, this time with a sigh. She'd twisted her auburn hair into a knot held in place with a couple of her late great-aunt's lacquered chopsticks, and her bare feet were planted on the coffee table as she watched a video of one of her favorite vintage British comedies. The show was her visual equivalent of comfort food after a particularly stressful day. And this day had definitely counted as stressful. She wasn't sure how she was going to sleep tonight, since images of a waxen-faced Curt had continued to pop into her head all day.

But with any luck, she told herself, an evening's marathon

of *To the Manor Born* would be enough to relax her. Otherwise, she'd have to take more drastic measures and dig out the grainy VHS copy she had of *The Joy of Painting* and watch that a few times. If the soothing tones of Bob Ross talking about happy trees and clouds couldn't improve her day, then nothing could.

She was halfway through both the second episode and her supper of leftover Thai takeout when the sound of a beehive on steroids nearly made her dump the carton into her lap.

She yelped in surprise, startling Hamlet, who was lounging behind her on the back of the horsehair sofa. A heartbeat later, she realized that the source of the sound was, of course, the buzzer linked to the glass entry door in the downstairs hall.

"Sorry, Hammy," she told him as she set down the carton and shut off the video, and then padded over to the door.

The security system, similar to the kind one would find in a typical walk-up, had been nonfunctional when she'd first moved in. She'd only gotten it repaired when Jake had bluntly informed her that she was resigning as unofficial lookout for Darla's evening visitors who didn't realize their knocks couldn't be heard two stories up. The intercom had only buzzed a couple of times since it had been restored to working order. Each time, the noise had startled the heck out of her, to the point she was considering bringing the repair guy back to upgrade it with a nice, soothing *ding-dong* chime.

She pressed the talk button and cautiously asked, "Hi, who is it?"

Except for a couple of food-delivery guys, her only visitors had been after-hours customers rightly guessing she lived over the store and hoping she'd pop down to open up just for them. She had politely declined both opportunities, leaving said would-be customers to go away disappointed. This time, however, she had an uneasy feeling that she knew who was standing down there at her door.

"Yeah, it's Reese," came the familiar Brooklyn-accented voice, made tinny by the intercom. "We need to talk, pronto."

Darla winced. *Time to face the music.* She could probably think of a few other appropriate clichés, but what it all boiled down to was that she likely was about to get a lecture royal from the detective for breaking the news of Curt's death to Hilda.

"All right, come on up," she replied and buzzed him in. This, at least, was a major improvement, saving her from having to trot down two flights of stairs to manually open the door.

Reese must have taken the steps at a run, for a firm knock sounded on her door sooner than she expected. Deciding she'd better find out before she let him in if he was simply mildly ticked or if he was super torqued off, she fastened the security chain and popped the door open the couple of inches it allowed.

"Just making sure it's really you," she explained in as casual a tone as she could muster. "You know, safety first and all that."

"Yeah, better safe than sorry," was his wry response. "I think they teach something like that at the police academy. So, you gonna let me in?"

Darla hesitated, trying to judge the extent of Reese's disapproval from her glimpse of chiseled cheekbone, crooked nose, and stern blue eye. Since he was doing a pretty sphinx-like job of hiding his emotions, however, she sighed and quickly unlatched the door.

Reese strode on in. He had on one of those ubiquitous beige trench coats, the official Columbo model, with the addition of a jaunty plaid lining but minus the wrinkles. Its belt was buckled behind his back so that the garment swung open, revealing the same navy slacks and brown tweed sport coat from earlier that day. Definitely not the black-leather-clad Reese she was used to seeing.

"Where's the motorcycle jacket?" she asked, recalling how it had always made him look like a blond Mad Max. Not that she disapproved of that particular image.

Reese shrugged. "It's in the closet. Peer pressure and all that."

When Darla gave him a quizzical look, he went on, "It was brought to my attention by the powers that be that I'd better start toeing the line as far as departmental dress code if I want to see a promotion in my future. The old dress-for-success thing, know what I mean? Hell, I think I'd rather be wearing a uniform than be stuffed into a tie and jacket."

"Too bad," she said somewhat sympathetically as he peeled off the trench coat, loosened said tie, and gave a tug on his shirt collar. Feeling distinctly underdressed in her sweats, Darla shut the door and gestured toward the horse-hair couch. "Go ahead, have a seat. I'd offer you some of my supper, but it's only leftovers and there's not much."

"I won't be staying that long."

He eyed Hamlet, who gave him a wary green look from where he was stretched out along the sofa back. Apparently deciding not to test their previous unspoken détente—the two had clashed more than once, with Reese on the losing side of those battles—the cop bypassed the sofa and instead settled on one of the ladder-back chairs Darla kept for extra seating.

Darla resumed her own seat on the couch and picked up her Thai food, casually scooping up a forkful of noodles. Between chews, she asked, "So, any updates on the Curt situation?"

"Nothing yet on cause of death. If we're lucky and the

ME's office isn't too backed up, we might have a ruling by tomorrow afternoon. Depending on what she says, we'll probably release your boyfriend's building back to him tomorrow, too."

"Barry's not—"

She was going to say, *Barry's not my boyfriend*, but Jake would probably tell her that smacked a little too much of junior high. Instead, she finished, "—not worried about that. His concern is for finding out what happened to Curt."

"So's mine."

Reese leaned back in the chair, which creaked ominously. "Let's say that your friend Mr. Benedetto wasn't clumsy enough to fall down the stairs on his own and hit his head on that crowbar. Statistically, about half of all murder victims know their killers. So one of those police things we sometimes do is spring bad news on people we want to question. That way, we can see how they react. You know . . . mad, glad, scared. And a lot of times, the way they react lets us know if they're telling the truth when we start asking them questions."

He let the chair tip back down, so that it rested on all four legs again, and finished, "So a couple of hours after you leave the scene, I go to track down Hilda Aguilar, mother of the dead guy's girlfriend. I want to ask her a few questions about the deceased and find out how to get in touch with her daughter, maybe even get a reaction. And then she tells me you already spilled the works to her, which means, no more surprise."

Darla swallowed her noodles along with a bit of lingering guilt and tried not to sound defensive as she countered, "You didn't tell me *not* to talk to Hilda . . . or anyone else, for that matter. And it wasn't like I tracked her down. She saw me outside her shop and asked what was wrong. I wouldn't have said anything, except that I really didn't want Tera hearing about her boyfriend's death on the street. I thought it would be better if her mother told her."

"I'd probably have done the same thing in your shoes," he agreed, lobbing her argument right back at her, untouched. As she stared at him in surprise, he went on, "That'd be pretty harsh, Tera getting a text from someone with the news, or something. And you're right; I didn't ask you not to talk to anyone. Technically, there's no way I could keep you from blabbing the news all over town, if you felt like it."

"Don't worry, Hilda is the only one I blabbed to . . . well, besides Jake. Oh, and James."

Reese rolled his eyes and then plucked a notebook and pen from his sport coat pocket. "All right, so how about you do a little blabbing to me. Tell me what Mrs. Aguilar said and did when you told her about Mr. Benedetto."

Feeling relieved that the expected lecture apparently wasn't forthcoming, Darla nodded. "I told her how we found Curt lying in the basement—pretty much everything I told you—and she definitely was shocked. She actually turned pale." Then, recalling the reaction that, to her, had been the most odd, she added, "But the thing was, she didn't ask me how he died. She wanted to know who killed him."

"She asked who killed him?" Reese's neutral tone sharpened, and he looked up from his notes. "That's what she said . . . in those words?"

"In those words," Darla confirmed with another nod. "She didn't ask if Curt had been in a car accident or keeled over from a heart attack. She just assumed he had been murdered."

"Keeping in mind we don't officially know that for a fact," Reese reminded her. "So what about Tera? Mrs. Aguilar told me she had been trying to get hold of her daughter since she talked to you, but no dice."

Darla explained what she knew about Tera's schedule and Hilda's opinion of her daughter's relationship with Curt.

"But surely Hilda has heard from her by now," she added with a frown, though a very bad feeling abruptly made her put down her fork, her appetite gone. "Reese, you don't think the reason no one has heard from Tera is because she had something to do with Curt's death, do you?"

The detective shrugged. "That's one possible scenario. I could give you five or six more off the top of my head. For all we know, your hellcat over there"—he pointed his pen at the hellcat in question, who responded with a lazy yawn—"took a little stroll down the street that night and ended up at Mr. Benedetto's place. Maybe he decided to explore a strange basement, chase a few rats. And then, when the poor schlub went downstairs to figure out what was causing the racket, he ended up tripping over the cat as he was going down the steps."

"Yes, well, about that . . ."

She hesitated, wondering how best to explain that she'd been worried about that identical scenario, and that Jake already had proved quite scientifically that Hamlet had been stomping about in someone's blood. Her confusion must have been reflected on her face, she realized, for Reese abruptly leaned forward in his chair.

His eyes narrowed as he glanced from her to Hamlet and back again. Then he shook his head. "Okay, spit it out, Red. What have you and that cat of yours been up to?"

For once, she didn't bother to chastise him about the "Red" nickname. "Didn't your CSI person mention it to you?"

"I haven't seen the report yet. Mention what?"

"The bloody paw prints near Curt's body."

"Bloody paw prints." Reese sighed and scrubbed a hand

over his face. "I saw what looked like a few drops of blood spatter near the body. You're saying you think they were actually paw prints? All right, let's hear this story from the top."

Darla obliged for the third time that day, having already given James as well as Jake a recap of events. Surprisingly, James had been more inclined than Jake to believe Hamlet might have been the feline culprit in Curt's basement.

Yes, Hamlet has managed a few midnight forays over the years, he'd told her when she had finished . . . much to her dismay. Why in the heck hadn't James mentioned that fact a long time ago? *Unfortunately, we still have not figured out how he makes good his escape.*

For his part, Reese listened intently, scribbling a note or two in his book as she spoke.

"Jake has the strip all officially bagged and photographed if you need to see it," she finished, and then hurried to add, "But I'm sure that Hamlet wouldn't have deliberately tripped Curt."

"Don't worry, Darla, I'm not going to arrest your cat. I'm not even going to bring him in for questioning. But I wonder if—"

The intercom abruptly buzzed again, cutting off Reese in midword and making Darla jump.

"Sorry, didn't know you were expecting someone," Reese said as, apparently deciding to leave his last observation unsaid, he flipped his notebook shut and rose.

Darla scrambled to her feet as well and hurried to the door. "I'm not. It's probably a customer who doesn't get it that *closed* means closed." Pushing the intercom button, she called, "Hello, who's there?"

"Um, Darla?"

Darla frowned. The tinny male voice sounded vaguely familiar, but she didn't recognize the speaker until he went on, "It's Barry . . . Barry Eisen. I know I should have tried calling you first, but I was in the neighborhood. You're not busy or anything, are you?"

"Hi, Barry. Actually, I—"

Before Darla could finish, Reese was at her side gesturing "no" and doing the old slice-across-his-throat routine. She quickly released the button and hissed at him, "What, am I not supposed to tell him you're here?"

"Keep me out of it. Tell him you're eating your dinner and see if he wants to come up."

She gave him a fair version of Hamlet's *what the heck?* look but gamely pressed the "Talk" button again and went on, "Actually, I was just finishing my supper. Did you want to come up for a cup of coffee or something?"

"Sure, that would be great," came his reply, the slight eagerness she heard now in his voice making her wonder abruptly if he thought that something meant, well, *something*.

Frowning a bit, she buzzed him in and then swung back around to Reese to demand, "Why am I pretending you're not here?"

"The same reason you're pretending he's not your boyfriend," the detective replied. Before she could decide if he was joking or not, he went on, "Remember that whole element-of-surprise thing we talked about? I just want to check this guy out, see if he's on the level. Get him talking about finding the body and anything else you can think of that has to do with what happened. Now that he's had some time to think about things, he might mention a few details he forgot to tell me—like maybe a motive."

"Surely you don't think Barry killed Curt?" she gasped. "Why, they've been friends since high school. And he and I were together when we found the body."

"Remember what I told you? Until we know it's an accident, we assume it's a murder, and everyone's a suspect."

"Fine. And what are you going to do while I'm quizzing Barry, hide behind the curtains?"

"Nope, I'm going to hang out in the john. Remember, keep him talking," he said, taking his coat from the chair and heading for the half bath next to the kitchen. Hamlet, following suit, leaped off the sofa and stalked toward the bedroom, apparently tired of having his evening nap interrupted. Darla barely had time to pick her remaining takeout off the coffee table and stash it in the kitchen before Barry's polite knock sounded at her door.

"Hi, come on in," she told him, gesturing him into the few square feet of exposed oak flooring that served as her foyer and closing the door behind him. "Here, let me take your coat."

"I hope you don't mind me dropping by like this," he apologized, unzipping a drab green jacket that looked like it had come from the army surplus store and handing it to her. "I needed to talk to someone, and since you were there today with me . . ."

He trailed off, and she nodded sympathetically. "I understand completely. It's kind of like the way you can't really talk about surviving a disaster—a flood or a hurricane, or something—except with someone else who survived the same thing. So, how are you holding up?"

"Not too bad, I guess."

His lips quirked a little, as if he were trying for a smile; then, giving up the attempt, he instead ran a hand through his thinning hair and shook his head. "It's all still such a shock. Curt's always been a phone call away ever since high school. I keep reaching for my cell to dial him, and then I remember."

Then he paused and gave her a quizzical look. "You, um, have something there," he added, touching his forefinger to a spot below his lower lip.

He tactfully looked away as she hurriedly used the back of her free hand to scrub away a few drops of peanut sauce that had dripped unnoticed onto her chin. *Thanks a lot, Reese*, she thought with an irritated frown. The least he could have done was tell her that she was wearing her supper. She only hoped she didn't have broccoli stuck in her teeth, to boot.

"Why don't I make you that cup of coffee, and we can talk," Darla suggested. Which would leave Reese stuck in his bathroom hiding place for a while, she thought in evil satisfaction. "Go ahead and make yourself at home on the couch."

While Barry settled on the sofa, she hung his jacket on the hook near the door and then headed for her small kitchen, where she stopped for a surreptitious look in the shiny surface of her chrome toaster. Relieved to find no more stray remains of her meal reflecting back at her, she filled the coffeepot with filtered water and measured out enough Kona blend for a few cups.

"Ready in a couple of minutes," she announced as she returned to the living room.

Barry had been studying the cover of the DVD case she'd left on the coffee table. Now, as she took the wingback chair, he gave a nod of approval. "I'm a British comedy fan, too. If you ever want to borrow some of my collection, I'll be glad to drop them off to you."

"Sure, thanks," she told him, favorably impressed. Had Reese made a similar offer, it likely would have been for the collected works of Stallone, Schwarzenegger, and Willis.

They sat in awkward silence for a moment while she waited for him to steer the conversation to what had happened that morning. But when he merely fiddled with the jewel case, she took the initiative.

"What about Curt's family?" she asked in a sympathetic tone. "I didn't know him well enough to know if he had any relatives living in the area."

"His dad passed away a few years ago. He has a mother and a married sister—Peggy is her name—who are in Connecticut. I called Peggy this afternoon and broke the news to her. I figured it would be better if she was the one who told her mother. I told her to let me know if she needed help with the funeral arrangements or anything."

Darla nodded; then, mindful of Reese hiding out in her powder room, she dutifully added, "I really thought when we first found him that he'd fallen down the stairs and hit his head, but now I'm not so sure. What do you think happened? Was it an accident?"

"I think someone hit him with that crowbar and killed him, Darla."

The stark words made her shiver. Barry's blunt assessment somehow made the likelihood of murder a given. Worse, a sudden image of an impeccably groomed Hilda Aguilar in her turquoise suit smashing a wrecking bar against Curt's skull flashed through her mind.

No, not right.

Then, since Reese had mentioned it, she replayed the scenario in her mind but with Barry wielding the crowbar. And again, she gave a mental shake of her head.

No, he doesn't fit the picture as a killer, either.

Aloud, she asked, "Do you think it was the scrap thieves who did it?"

He shrugged. "It could be. I hear they're some pretty rough characters, maybe even tied in to one of those Russian gangs. Or it could have been a druggie, or someone mad about the fact we got that building for a song. Not that we did anything illegal," he hurried to clarify, "but sometimes there's a lot of behind-the-scenes politicking in the renovation business. You know, a little you-scratch-my-back-and-I'll-scratch-yours kind of thing."

Darla stored that last comment for further thought,

hoping that Reese could hear everything clearly from his bathroom vantage point. Raising her voice for the detective's benefit, she asked, "Do you know if Curt had any enemies?

Now, Barry smiled a little.

"Are you asking me if a sweet, mild-mannered guy like my buddy Curt had ever pissed someone off enough that they'd contemplate murder? Let me put it this way: I've been tempted to throttle him a time or two myself, over the years. But under that obnoxious exterior he was a pretty good guy. Not a Mother Teresa or anything, but his heart was in the right place."

"He did have a way about him," Darla agreed with a fleeting smile of her own. "But I did hear somewhere that about half the time a murder victim knows his or her killer. So if it turns out not to be an accident, the police will probably be taking a pretty close look at all of us."

"Yeah." Barry dropped his gaze to the DVD case, where he appeared to be studying the product information with great interest. "I don't mean to make this all about me, but I'm a bit worried about how that's going to work out. I picked up that crowbar, remember? That means my fingerprints are all over it."

"Maybe . . . but if you'd both been using it during the remodel, then your fingerprints would have been on it anyhow," she pointed out in a reasonable tone.

He looked up again and sighed in audible relief. "You're right. I guess I wasn't thinking straight. It's just that I have a really bad feeling about the whole situation."

"It's awful enough that Curt is dead," she said, "but if it turns out that it wasn't an accident, then that could mean no one in the neighborhood is safe."

"Well, that's one thing I wanted to talk to you about. You see, there was something I didn't tell the police this morning."

Darla could almost feel her ears flick forward in sudden

interest, just as Hamlet's did when he heard the sound of kibble pouring into his bowl. No doubt Reese's ears were doing the same trick. Trying not to appear too anxious, she said, "If it's important, you should say something. Can you at least tell me?"

"It's about Tera."

Barry hesitated, shifting the DVD case from hand to hand as he seemed to consider whether or not, in Reese's words, to blab.

"It probably doesn't mean anything, but yesterday while we were doing some work at the brownstone, I overheard Curt on the phone with her. I don't want to repeat some of the things he said, but they weren't exactly nice. I've met that girl before, and I know she has a temper. She might have tracked him down there last night to finish the fight . . . and, you know, ended up finishing it for good."

Before Darla could respond to this unsettling revelation, the sound of a flushing toilet interrupted them. The powder room door swung open, and Reese came strolling out, coat over his arm.

"Thanks for letting me borrow the facilities, Darla," he told her. "It's a long way back to the precinct." Then, to Barry, he added, "I thought I heard voices. How ya doing, Mr. Eisen? Darla didn't tell me you were stopping by."

"She didn't tell me you were here, either," the other man said with a sidelong look at her.

Darla managed an innocent smile. "Oh, I thought I mentioned it when you came in. But Detective Reese was just leaving, weren't you?" she added with a pointed look at the cop.

Reese, however, was giving an exaggerated sniff. "Hey, Darla, is that coffee I smell? I might stick around for a cup, if you don't mind. The stuff you brew is a hell of a lot better than what I can get downtown. How about you, Mr. Eisen? You going to join us?"

"Actually, I need to head back home." He set down the DVD case and rose. "Darla, I apologize for not calling beforehand. I promise I will next time."

He headed for the door, pausing to grab his jacket off the hook. "Detective, you'll let me know as soon as I can go back into the brownstone, won't you?"

"Should be tomorrow, probably when we know the cause of Mr. Benedetto's death."

"I trust you'll let me know on that, too. Curt was . . . a good friend."

So saying, he gave Darla a small wave and slipped out the door. She could hear the faint sounds of footsteps going down the stairs, and she went to the window to watch as he exited the front entry and started down the street.

Darla let the curtain drop again and turned back to glare at Reese, who had his notebook out and was scribbling again. "Thanks for making me look like an idiot a couple of times over. I'll be lucky if Barry ever talks to me again."

"You did fine," he said in an absent voice as he flipped the page. "Oh, and I wasn't kidding about the coffee. I could go for a cup . . . no sugar, just cream."

Darla ran through a mental list of several rude retorts but in the end gritted her teeth and went to pour him his drink. "Why didn't you let Barry keep talking?" she called from the kitchen as she pulled down a *Twilight* mug that she'd bought as a joke from a street vendor and poured Reese's coffee into it. "I thought you wanted to see if he was on the level."

"Yeah, well, I was getting bored. All you had in there to read were a bunch of decorating and reorganizing magazines."

"Sorry, next time I'll throw in a couple of *Sports Illustrated* copies just for you." Still rolling her eyes, she returned to the living room to find Reese staring intently at his phone.

"Anything interesting?" she asked as she handed over his cup.

She was disappointed not to get a reaction to the sparkly rendition of a brooding teen vampire on the mug she'd deliberately chosen to goad him. All he did was take an absent sip and nod.

"Yeah, I just got a text from my friend at the ME's office. Apparently they had a slow day for a change and got to Mr. Benedetto already."

Something in Reese's expression made her certain she already knew the answer, even before she cautiously asked, "Did they decide on a cause of death?"

He glanced up from the phone and thrust it toward her. "Turns out Hamlet is in the clear. Here, read for yourself."

Squinting, she made out the phrases, *Estimated TOD between 3 a.m. and 6 a.m. . . . Blunt force trauma to head . . . DNA material found on possible weapon collected . . . Being sent to outside lab to confirm tissue match.* Handing back the phone, she asked in as small voice, "I guess this means . . ."

He nodded. "Your boyfriend had it pegged right. To put it in layman's terms, someone bashed Curt Benedetto over the head with that crowbar."

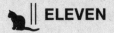 **ELEVEN**

"NOTHING TO REPORT FROM LAST NIGHT," ROBERT ASSURED Darla come Friday morning as he switched the computer screen of the security software from review mode to the multipicture live view. "Not unless, you know, you count all those guys I saw going up to your place."

"Guys? There weren't any . . . oh, wait."

Snatching the mouse from him, Darla pulled up a full-screen view courtesy of the front exterior camera. Sure enough, not only did that camera capture the store's front door, but now her private stoop as well as the Plinskis' stoop next door was also visible.

Darla gave the teen a stern look. "Last I saw, the camera covered just the store's front door and window. Any idea who changed the angle?"

"Sorry," he replied, ducking his head. "It's just that the owner of the barbershop down the street came by a couple of days ago when you were at lunch. He said the scrap thieves hit his shop and stole his fancy mailbox. And Professor James was like, all worried about you, so he had me get out the step ladder and move the camera so it recorded your door, too."

"And no one was going to tell me about this?"

"I guess we figured you'd notice sooner or later." He pointed to the screen. "I mean, it's pretty obvious. And with what happened to Mr. Eisen's friend—"

Robert broke off dramatically with a gesture of hitting his head with an invisible crowbar, and Darla suppressed a sigh.

"Oh, and boss, about the guys . . . that's all good," he added, giving her a grin and an exaggerated thumbs-up.

Darla felt herself blush as bright a pink as the sweater set she was wearing over her brown woolen slacks, even as she firmly informed him, "Sorry to break it to you, Robert, but the guys you saw were Detective Reese and Mr. Eisen. We were all just talking about what happened to Mr. Benedetto."

Reese had left soon after Barry, staying only long enough to gulp down his coffee before heading back out into the night. His parting comments had been to warn her that Curt's death was now a full-fledged murder investigation.

"I particularly want to talk to Tera Aguilar," Reese had told her, "so do me a favor and don't give her any early warnings if you see her before I do. That little hint your boyfriend dropped about a fight between her and Benedetto might turn into a motive."

"Maybe Jake can help you track her down," Darla had suggested, nobly eschewing offense that he'd assume she'd make the same mistake twice. "Hilda might be more open to talking about Tera to her than to you."

"You're reading my mind, Red. That's where I'm headed next."

Continuing her virtuous streak, Darla had bit back another reflexive *Don't call me Red*, and also resisted the temptation to keep a surreptitious watch out the window until

Reese left Jake's place so that she could run down and pump her friend for details. Not that she wouldn't see if she could pry a little bit of gossip out of Jake today, though she suspected that the ex-cop would likely be as closemouthed as Reese on the subject.

For the moment, though, there was an even more important issue that needed to be addressed.

"What about Hamlet? Did you catch him on surveillance?" she asked.

Hamlet looked up from where he was sunbathing on the faded Oriental throw rug in front of the main door and returned Darla's annoyed look with an innocent green blink. Not that she was taken in by his whole I'd-never-dream-of-sneaking-out act. She knew better.

Darla was pretty sure that he'd gotten out again last night. She had walked through her whole apartment after Reese had left, looking again for possible Hamlet escape tunnels. She hadn't discovered any likely exits, and Hamlet was once more snoozing atop the horsehair sofa. Feeling confident that the ornery cat was safely contained for the night, she had finished watching her video and then reluctantly tuned in to the local news channel. To her relief, Curt's murder wasn't mentioned, and so she'd headed off to bed.

But she woke a few hours later from a ghastly dream of stumbling over Barry dead in his basement to discover Hamlet nowhere to be found in the apartment. Anger had battled with worry. The overnight forecast was for temperatures in the high thirties—not low enough to freeze an AWOL cat, but cold enough that he'd be pretty frosty despite his warm black fur coat.

"You'll be sorry," she'd declared as she headed back to her own warm bed. Hamlet was a grown-up cat, she had reassured herself as she pulled up the covers. If he wanted to freeze his fuzzy butt off partying on the streets overnight, then let him. But despite repeating that mantra several times, worry had clung to her even as she drifted off to sleep again.

When she'd awakened again at the usual time, she had made a beeline for the kitchen, where she'd been relieved to find Hamlet waiting for his breakfast. Rather than haranguing her with his usual demanding *meow*, however, he had sat patiently next to his dish, head tilted and green eyes wide as if to say, *Look at the good kitty . . . I've been inside the whole time.*

"Yeah, like I believe that," she had groused. Not only was his fur still cold to the touch, but a few spots of dirt clung to him. The sly little beast had definitely been out on the town.

Now, Robert shook his head. "If he snuck out, it wasn't any place that the cameras could see. But if you want, I can poke around outside later and see if I find any Hamlet-sized escape holes."

"That would be great. Bad enough the neighborhood is being taken over by murderers and thieves. We don't need Hamlet on the loose to boot!" Then, glancing at the clock, she added, "Oops, opening time. Robert, go ahead and unlock the front door."

While the teen complied, Darla powered up the register and wondered again if Reese had learned anything from Jake about Tera Aguilar. Maybe she should see if Jake could join her for lunch today. Even if her friend claimed client confidentiality, they'd be walking past Great Scentsations on their way to the deli. She could peek in and see if Tera was working, and at least satisfy herself that the girl hadn't turned fugitive. As far as Barry . . .

She shook her head. No doubt Reese's little stunt last night hadn't earned her any points with the man, though she suspected he was too polite to admit any aggravation. And since she still hadn't gotten around to getting his phone number—the whole finding-Curt's-lifeless-body thing had caused that detail to slip her mind—she would have to wait for him to call or stop by again before she could learn where she stood. The realization left her feeling oddly regretful. Though he wasn't her boyfriend—despite what Reese said—and they hadn't even technically gone out on a date yet, Darla could see developing a more personal friendship with him. Besides, under the circumstances, she suspected he could use a friendly shoulder to lean on.

"Hey, Ms. Pettistone, look who's here!"

Robert's enthusiastic tone and the sound of the front door chiming roused her from her reverie. She looked up to see a smiling Mary Ann making her way around Hamlet, who as usual was refusing to relinquish his official sunning spot to any incoming customers. Mary Ann's long, navy blue corduroy shirtdress brushed him, and he put out a sheathed paw in an obligatory "back off" gesture, but Darla knew he wasn't serious. The old woman was on his permanent BFF list.

"Hello, Darla . . . and Hamlet. And good morning, Robert," Mary Ann greeted the teen, who surprised Darla by giving the septuagenarian a gentle if enthusiastic hug. "I must say, I do like this new look of yours, all dressed up like a successful businessman."

Darla suppressed a smile. Robert wasn't exactly Brooks Brothers material, wearing his usual black shirt and jeans topped with another James-inspired vest—this one, in shades of red, blue, and yellow in a distinctly southwestern pattern—but he looked neat and professional.

"Thanks again for, you know, lending me the statue, Ms. Plinski," he told her. "Ms. Pettistone really liked my window display."

"I just saw it, and I think you did a marvelous job! It's—how do you young people call it?—really rad. In fact, I may come back later to buy both books."

"We sold half a dozen copies yesterday afternoon alone,"

Darla told her, noting in amusement Robert's expression of teenaged horror over an adult using sadly dated slang. "That's as many as we sold in two weeks, and all thanks to Robert's creative work. Why, I wouldn't be surprised if we sell most of the remaining stock this weekend."

"I'm so glad. And, I must confess, Robert is the reason I'm stopping by," she explained, joining Darla at the register. "You see, Brother hurt his arm yesterday. Oh, he'll be all right," she added as Darla made a sound of concern, "but we received a delivery this morning, and I can't carry the boxes by myself. I was hoping to borrow Robert for a few minutes."

"Sure, no problem," the teen exclaimed, and then gave Darla an apologetic look. "Uh, that is, if it's okay with Ms. Pettistone."

"Certainly," Darla agreed. "Now's the perfect time, before the customers start coming in."

"I knew I could count on you both," Mary Ann said cheerily. "And I made some lovely pumpkin and cranberry bread last night. Why don't I send him back with a few slices for you and him and James?"

"Yum," Robert replied.

"It's a deal," Darla agreed with a smile that promptly faded as she recalled that the old woman probably had not heard about Curt Benedetto's murder yet. "Mary Ann, before you go, there's something I'd better tell you so you can let Mr. Plinski know, too."

Darla filled her in, and when she had finished, the old woman clasped her age-blotched hands together and gave a despairing look. "Oh my gracious, Darla, what is this world coming to? Brother will be *so* distressed when I tell him. Do the police have any idea who killed the poor man?"

"Not yet. Detective Reese is the one handling the case, though, and I know he's busy questioning people."

"Oh, yes, Detective Reese. Such a nice man," she added

in a confidential aside to Robert, "even though he did almost arrest me that one time for breaking and entering."

While the teen stared at her in surprise at that comment, she returned her attention to Darla. "Well, we'll just have to trust him to solve the case. But I do wish there was something we could do to take back our neighborhood from these miscreants."

"I'm with you on that, Mary Ann. Maybe we should talk to Reese about setting up a neighborhood watch."

"You mean, one of those things where they, you know, wear red beanies and patrol with walkie-talkies and baseball bats?" Robert interjected in an eager voice. "That would be, like, totally cool. I'm in."

"Oh, my gracious," Mary Ann replied with a small smile. "Though, come to think of it, I do have a baseball bat that I keep by my bed. If Brother didn't object, perhaps Robert and I could patrol together. Do you suppose I could wear a red ski cap instead of a beanie?"

"Sure, ski caps are way better," he agreed. "And you know how Ms. Pettistone sometimes wears those fancy chopstick things in her hair? Those would make, like, really sick weapons, just like in the movies. Hi-yaah!" he finished, mimicking whipping out a pair of hair sticks from an updo and wielding them like twin foils.

"Wait!" Darla gave the pair of would-be crime fighters a look of mild alarm. She'd been thinking more along the lines of handing out fliers to the local homes and businesses, maybe coordinating a lookout post on each block. These two, on the other hand, were prepared to launch their own mini D-Day assault.

"Robert, I appreciate your enthusiasm, but if you want to organize a group like that, your job would be to call the police if there's trouble and then get the heck out of there. No vigilante heroics where someone—maybe the wrong person—winds up getting hurt. It's happened before, and I don't want to be bailing you out on a murder charge one day."

"Don't worry, boss, I get it. I read the news online," he soberly agreed, dropping the imaginary weapons and sticking his hands back in his vest pockets. Mary Ann, meanwhile, shook her head in agreement. "Darla is right. Patrolling a neighborhood is a serious responsibility. Maybe that nice Detective Reese can give us some pointers. But we really should get the lead out and organize this before anyone else in the neighborhood is murdered."

"Don't worry, I'll ask Reese to talk to you two about it as soon as I see him again. Now, why don't you take Robert and get those boxes moved?"

The two of them headed out, sidestepping a snoozing Hamlet, who appeared to have no interest in joining any sort of citizens' brigade. His green eyes remained tightly shut, even when two customers almost tripped over him a few minutes later. He still hadn't stirred even after Robert, bearing the promised cranberry and pumpkin bread, returned from helping Mary Ann.

"Mary Ann's a better crime fighter than you," Darla commented in the cat's direction while heading for the foreign language section to answer a phone customer's question.

That accomplished, she tried ringing Jake's cell, but her call went straight to voice mail. She left a quick message— *Hey, how about lunch at the deli later?*—and then got to work paying invoices and going through the latest publishers' catalogues in between assisting customers. Robert kept equally busy stocking shelves and jumping in to help ring up sales. Every time the bells on the front door jangled, Darla looked up to see if perhaps Barry had decided to stop by, only to be vaguely disappointed each time that it was not him.

It was almost noon when Jake called back on the store phone.

"Hey, kid, I got your message. Sorry, I can't break for lunch. Things are popping."

"That's okay, I understand," Darla told her. "I don't suppose what's popping has anything to do with Tera or Hilda Aguilar, does it?"

She heard a small sigh from the other end before Jake responded, "Remember what I said about client confidentiality? Oops, someone else is trying to ring through. Let me get that, and I'll stop by the store later, all right?"

Jake hung up before Darla could even reply. Frowning, Darla hung up the receiver.

She considered calling Reese to find out if he'd located Tera, but then thought better of it. He'd just tell her it wasn't any of her business. She decided to send him a text instead, asking about the neighborhood watch, and let him reply at his convenience. And maybe at the same time he'd give her an update on the Curt situation.

She waited until Robert finished ringing up the soccer mom he'd been helping. She was pleased to see that the woman had bought one of the books featured in Robert's window display in addition to a DIY book on plumbing and, strangely, a copy of *Robinson Crusoe*. But then, she'd gotten used to customers' eclectic tastes in reading matter.

"Hey, it's lunchtime," she reminded the teen. "I feel like a turkey Reuben special from the deli. How about I buy, you fly?"

"Yeah, sure." He gave her an enthusiastic grin. "Is it okay if I get, you know, one of those big chocolate chip cookies, too?"

"Sure. Consider it a bonus for your good work on the window display. Tell them to put it all on my account."

"Yes!" He gave a little fist pump and reached under the counter for his jacket. "Back in a minute."

She smiled as he tore out of the store like Hamlet on catnip. All in all, Robert was working out quite well, she decided. Once he'd had a little more time and training, she might even manage an extra day off on occasion, with him to take up the slack.

Since this was their usual prelunch lull, Darla headed upstairs to the storeroom. She returned downstairs with a lamb's-wool duster in one hand and an ostrich-feather duster in the other. Picking up where she'd left off a couple of days earlier, she got to work cleaning the inventory, allowing herself the occasional unavoidable sneeze in the process.

She'd been amazed when she'd first taken over the shop to learn how quickly dust accumulated on books. While the regular stock was treated to the standard duster routine, James had a special HEPA vacuum he used on the collectibles and first editions. He'd also explained how, to avoid damage, it was better to clean on a regular basis, rather than making it an hours-long project on occasion. And so Darla tried to tackle the place with her collection of cloths and dusters whenever she had a slow period during the week.

She had barely gotten started on the first shelf, however, when she heard the distinctive *thud* of a book hitting the wood floor.

"Hamlet?"

Darla peered around the corner of the shelf to see the cat still stretched out on his rug near the door. Hearing his name, he yawned, showing sharp white teeth and a bubblegum pink tongue, and then settled his chin back on his paws to sleep.

Frowning, she set down her dusters and headed in the direction from where the sound had come. Sure enough, in the classics section she found a single paperback book lying on the floor. Her frown deepened. The last time that Hamlet had pulled books off the store's shelves, he'd been trying to communicate a murderer's identity. Maybe he was at it again. But could the touchy feline have rushed over, snagged the book, and flown back to his sleeping spot that quickly?

Curious, she picked up the volume and flipped it over. *"The Man in the Iron Mask,"* she read aloud, followed by a thoughtful, "Hmmm."

Of course, Hamlet might have had nothing to do with the book at all. Maybe the customer who'd picked up the copy of Defoe's classic *Robinson Crusoe* had accidentally dislodged this Alexandre Dumas book from its spot on the *D* shelf, with gravity eventually doing the rest of the work. But how often did she have to pick up fallen books after a customer left the store?

Not too often. Darla pursed her lips and nodded. For the moment, she would assume that it *had* been Hamlet who had pulled down the book as a clue—no matter that he was being even vaguer than previously in his hints.

"How about sometime you give me a book title that's an actual name?" she told Hamlet as she carried the book to the counter. "You know, like *Anna Karenina* or *David Copperfield* or *Jonathan Livingston Seagull*. That would really help narrow down the suspect list, you know?"

Hamlet did not deign to reply.

"Fine, so I'll play twenty questions by my lonesome," she told him. "You speak up if I get it right."

Dragging out a pen and sheet of paper, she scribbled *Man in Iron Mask* at the top of the page. Then she halted, momentarily stumped. She hadn't read the book since high school, and even then she'd skimmed it. For better or worse, she'd seen the movie version—which likely bore only a nominal resemblance to the original novel—but that had been quite a while ago. Her memory of the characters' names and the plot was hazy.

"Let's take it a face value and assume that the killer is male . . . as in, *Man*," she said and underlined that word on her page. "Help me out, Hamlet. How about D'Artagnan or Aramis or Porthos or Athos? Any of those ring a bell?"

Once more, the feline remained provokingly silent. "Okay, maybe I need to back up. Since the author is Alexandre Dumas, let's try Alexander for the killer."

Darla wrote down that name, followed by a large question mark. It didn't matter that she didn't know any Alexanders, but maybe Curt had. Or maybe he knew an Al or Alec or an—

"Alex," she exclaimed with a triumphant smile, writing that name in large letters and circling it. "Robert's buddy Alex Putin, the Russian mafia guy. He's in construction, and he's probably killed a bunch of people before."

Not that she had firsthand knowledge of this—either the Russian mafia connections or any actual killings—but his name was as good a place as any to start.

She added *Alex Putin* to her budding list as a second possibility; then, with a snort, she crossed out that name and glanced toward the cat.

"Too easy. If the killer was Alex Putin, you'd have snagged something from Aleksandr Solzhenitsyn or else a Vladimir Putin bio, wouldn't you? Besides, there's no reason to believe that Curt has ever even met the man, just because they're both in construction."

Then she frowned. The more obvious candidate was Porn Shop Bill, though how he could possibly be tied to Dumas's work, she couldn't guess. Maybe there was a "William" somewhere in the story? She turned to her keyboard and did a quick online search.

"Well, close," she decided a moment later as, scrolling through a popular movie database, she saw that the director of an older film version of *The Man in the Iron Mask* had the first name of William. *A bit too much of a reach?* She shook her head even as she wrote down *Bill*. What she needed was a list of characters from the novel. Unfortunately, the publisher had neglected to supply that little convenience in the copy that she held. But she did find a story summary as part of a preface. Swiftly, she began to read bits of it aloud.

"Story opens in the Bastille . . . Aramis was a Musketeer, is now a priest . . . listening to a prisoner's confession . . . he claims he's the twin brother of King Louis XIV."

She paused long enough to scribble down the words *Louis* and *king*, and then went on, "Blah, blah, Aramis decides to free this prisoner . . . will swap him for his brother. Meanwhile, things aren't going well at court. King Louis sulking, blah, blah . . . can't decide between his mistress and his wife, Maria Theresa—"

She broke off abruptly and stared at Hamlet. "Maria Theresa," she slowly repeated as she recalled the overheard phone conversation at Hilda's shop the day before. "Maria Teresa is Tera's full name. But surely she couldn't . . ."

Darla trailed off as her previous mental image of Hilda wielding a crowbar was replaced by the mental picture she'd been trying to hold at bay ever since she'd first heard that Tera was missing: that of the petite girl doing her version of "batter's up" on Curt's skull. After all, hadn't Barry said he'd overheard the pair fighting the day before they found Curt's body? But surely a run-of-the-mill lovers' quarrel couldn't be enough to drive the hot-tempered Tera to murder. Or could it?

Reluctantly, she added *Tera* to her list; then, for good measure, she added Hilda's name, too. Better that she not decide this early in the game that Curt's killer was male, despite Hamlet's choice of book titles. After all, a crowbar was as deadly a weapon in a female's hand as it was in a man's.

Even as she mulled over that unsettling possibility, the bells on the shop door jangled, and in rushed a woman whom she didn't recognize.

At least, not at first.

 **TWELVE**

"HILDA?"

Had Darla passed this version of the Great Scentsations owner on the street, she likely would have slipped the woman a dollar and kept on walking. Never had she suspected that the coolly elegant Hilda Aguilar could look so downright . . . well, frumpy.

Today, the woman's frosted blond hair was pulled back in a stubby, lopsided ponytail rather than styled into the usual sleek French twist or smooth bob Darla was used to seeing. As for the usual professional makeup job—the one that looked airbrushed on—this morning it consisted of simply a slash of red lipstick that had already been partially chewed off. But, the designer handbag over her shoulder notwithstanding, the most surprising aspect of the woman's appearance was the fact she was wearing a tracksuit of the kind septuagenarian Mary Ann Plinski favored when not dressed for work.

Hilda, however, seemed either unaware or unconcerned that her appearance had shocked Darla into momentary speechlessness. Barely missing stepping on Hamlet, who scrambled out of the way just in time, she hurried to the counter where Darla was standing.

"Darla, thank God you are here! I came to see Jake, but she won't be back for a while. I talked to her on the phone, and she said I could wait for her up here, if you don't mind."

Darla shook her head, her concern growing. "No, I don't mind. Why don't you sit upstairs in the lounge area? There's coffee up there, and hot water if you want tea."

Though the woman could probably use a cup of something stronger, Darla decided. Hilda's eyes were ringed with dark circles that were likely owed in equal parts to a sleepless night and yesterday's makeup.

Hilda, however, shook her head, refusing the offer. "I-I'd rather stay down here, if you don't mind. I'm afraid I'll go crazy if I stay alone."

Darla stepped around the counter and impulsively took the woman's hand. "Tell me what's wrong," she urged. "Is it Tera?"

The other woman nodded.

"Darla, she-she never came home last night."

A tear spilled down one unpowdered cheek and left a faint eyeliner trail behind. "I spent all yesterday afternoon calling her, and she never answered her phone. I finally closed the shop early because I thought maybe she was home sick in bed, but she wasn't there, either.

The woman paused and took a shuddering breath. "I didn't know what else to do, so I phoned a few of her friends. No one saw her at school yesterday morning. And then that detective—I don't remember his name—came by my house looking for her last night. He said that when she showed up again, he needed to talk to her right away."

"I'm sure it's just routine," Darla assured her, but Hilda shook her head.

"You don't understand. The questions he asked me about her, I could not believe. Does she have a passport . . . does she have any friends with criminal records? Finally, I got angry and told him to leave."

Probably not the best move, going Mama Grizzly on a cop, Darla thought wryly, though she could understand a parent wanting to protect her child. Aloud, she asked, "So is that why you're looking for Jake, to see if she can find Tera before the police do?"

"That's all I could think to do. Tera has no one in this city besides me. The rest of the family, they're back in Miami or in Cuba. I've always taken care of her. She knows nothing of life, of what it takes to survive on her own."

Hilda paused and gave a swipe at her eyes, which were damp again.

"Me, I was only seventeen when I escaped from Cuba with my husband and his entire family on a little fishing boat meant for just six people. It was the hurricane season, but we didn't know a storm was forming in the Atlantic when we set out. With the wind and the waves, it was a miracle that we stayed afloat long enough to reach Miami."

"Hilda, I didn't know. That must have been a terrifying journey."

"I suppose it was, but I had grown up being frightened and hungry. To me, it was just one more thing to endure. But after that, I was never frightened of anything else again . . . not until now." She paused, and her regal features abruptly crumpled. "*Dios mío*, I am so afraid! I'm afraid that the police think my daughter killed Curt Benedetto!"

"Who wants lunch? Get it while it's hot!"

Darla had been so caught up in Hilda's account that she hadn't heard the bells on the shop door jingle. Robert had returned from the deli and was making his way toward the counter triumphantly waving a large and slightly greasy paper bag. Darla released Hilda's hand and hurried to intercept him.

"Why don't you put mine in the fridge upstairs in the lounge?" she suggested, giving her head a meaningful shake as he peered curiously past her. "I've got a customer I'm helping right now."

Hilda began to sob, and the teen's inquisitive expression promptly morphed into the distressed look common to males who can't bear to see the opposite gender cry.

"Yeah, sure," he verbally backpedaled. "Do you want me to, uh, take my break now, or wait?"

"Go ahead. I've got things under control here."

Which wasn't exactly the truth. For the moment, she had no idea what to say to a mother whose only child had just become a suspect in a murder investigation. And she couldn't just leave the woman there crying, especially since her usual lunchtime customers would be popping in any minute now.

Darla hurried back around the counter, grabbed the box of tissues from the shelf below, and then thrust it into Hilda's arms.

"Let's find you a quiet spot," she said, deftly steering the woman toward the shop's rear room. As in the main part of the store, a few small tufted chairs were tucked in strategic corners so customers could sit and peruse potential purchases. Darla settled the woman alongside the New Age shelves. Maybe she'd gain a bit of serenity by osmosis.

"Here you go," she said and plumped a tapestry pillow, which she then slipped behind Hilda's back. "You can wait right there until Jake comes back. Are you sure you wouldn't like me to bring you something?"

Hilda sniffled a moment into her tissue and then shook her head. "I'm so sorry, causing such a scene in your nice store. But I know my daughter. She's not capable of doing such a horrible thing. How could that detective suspect her of murder?"

"Reese has to check her out, just like he's doing with everyone else who knew Curt. He's only doing his job," Darla gently reassured her. "Remember, she didn't come home the night that Curt was murdered, and you yourself said that she usually spent her evenings with him. It does seem a bit suspicious."

"I know, I know," the woman agreed, breaking into fresh sobs. "But no matter what happened, I can't believe Tera would leave home without telling me."

Darla handed her another tissue and desperately wished that Jake would hurry up. While she was inclined to agree with Hilda that Tera didn't seem to fit the type, she'd heard Reese and Jake recount enough tales about unlikely killers to know that one could never say never when it came to murder. On the other hand—

"Hilda, maybe Tera *did* have something to do with Curt's death," she ventured, "but that doesn't mean it was deliberate. Maybe they had a fight, and he tried to hurt her, and she was defending herself. Or maybe he brought her down to the basement and tried to force himself on her, and she had to hit him with the crowbar to get away. I think on the cop shows they call it justifiable homicide or something."

"You mean, self-defense?"

"Right. And maybe she's afraid to come home because she knows the police will be looking for her. And she won't call you because no one can accuse you of helping her if you don't know where she is."

"Oh, Darla, that does make sense." Hilda looked up from her pile of sodden tissues, her swollen eyes suddenly filling with hope. "I know she could never hurt anyone on purpose . . . but maybe if he had tried to hurt her . . ."

She straightened and reached into her handbag, pulling out a compact. "I look a fright," she exclaimed with a glance in the small mirror. Shoving the mirror back into her purse, she got to her feet again. "Please, I must make myself halfway presentable before Jake gets here."

Darla obligingly pointed her in the direction of the ladies' room and then went to wait on the middle-aged executive who'd just walked in. By the time she'd sent him off with a best-selling business biography and then rang up another customer who'd come in for her weekly fix of the latest romance novels, Hilda had emerged from the restroom looking almost like her usual self.

Darla took in the woman's deftly recoiffed hair and fresh makeup with amazement. *She must have a personal stylist stashed in that purse*, she thought with a wry shake of her head. Even the tracksuit looked suddenly trendier, thanks to a scarf Hilda must have found somewhere in the handbag and which now was wrapped jauntily around her throat.

"Darla, I am so sorry for dropping in on you like this with my problems," Hilda exclaimed, the earlier quaver in her voice all but gone. "I must have faith that Jake will find Tera before the police do and bring her home so we can work this out together."

"I'm sure she will. And even if Detective Reese finds her first, I promise you he'll treat her fairly."

"Perhaps." That last was said with a shrug that seemed to speak of more than a little distrust of authority. Though, now knowing the woman's history, Darla couldn't quite blame her.

Bells jingled again. This time, to Darla's great relief, it was Jake walking through the front door. She was dressed for serious investigating, her unbelted black leather duster swirling around her jean-encased calves with every stride, her stacked-heel boots effectively camouflaging her limp.

A pair of mirrored sunglasses hid her eyes, and her curly black hair sprang from her head like a lion's mane, everything combining to give Jake the look of a kick-butt anime heroine come to life.

Just what Hilda and Tera needed right about now, Darla thought with a grateful sigh.

"Hey, kid, thanks for filling in." Jake gave Darla an approving nod before turning to Hilda. "Sorry you had to wait. I was making a few inquiries about Tera."

"Did you have any luck?" Hilda greeted her, the crispness of her tone belied by the anxious way she was twisting her hands. "Has anyone seen my daughter?"

"So far, none of her friends have seen her since her Wednesday morning class. And I can't find anyone who saw her after you said she left the house again Wednesday evening. Late Thursday morning is when Darla and Barry found Curt's body, so we've got about twelve hours we have to account for to get her off the hook. Do you have that picture I asked you to bring?"

"Of course." Hilda reached into her magical handbag and pulled out a small framed photo, the size one would keep propped on a bedside table. "That detective—"

"Detective Reese," Darla helpfully supplied.

"—Yes, that Detective Reese, he wanted a picture, too, but I lied and told him I didn't have one," Hilda replied, a faint look of defiance adding color to her pale cheeks. Darla caught a glimpse of the photo as the woman clutched the frame to her with a possessive air.

The image appeared recent and professionally shot, although the setting was casual and outdoors. The photo captured the girl from the waist up, turned so that she peered back over one shoulder toward the camera. For once, it looked like Tera had abandoned the exaggerated makeup she usually favored, wearing just enough color on her wide brown eyes and full lips to accentuate those features. Her shoulder-length, dark blond hair was loose and windblown. One carefully manicured hand—the pink nails the same girlish shade as her bright lipstick—had reached up to brush an errant lock from her eyes.

In the hands of a less skilled photographer, the image might have appeared deliberately posed in poor imitation of some glossy magazine cover. Instead, it looked as if Tera had simply turned in laughing response to someone calling her name, her youthful beauty and exuberance captured forever in that one shot.

Breathtaking, Darla thought with a sudden feeling of dismay that she couldn't quite explain or dismiss.

Hilda, meanwhile, had released her grip on the frame and was handing the photo over to Jake, adding, "Tera gave me that picture just a couple of weeks ago. I-I'd like it back when you're finished."

"Certainly. When we go back down to my office I'll scan it, and then you can take it right back home with you again," Jake assured her as she accepted the photo. "I'm going to make some fliers with her picture on them to start handing out around the neighborhood. I'll leave a stack here to pass out to anyone willing to help, if that's okay by Darla," she added with a meaningful look in her direction.

Darla nodded, concurring with the unspoken suggestion that Reese would be the first recipient of same. In fact, as soon as she had the fliers in hand, she'd give the detective a call.

"Hi, Ms. Martelli," came Robert's voice from behind them. "What's up?"

Using the back of his hand to swipe the last of the crumbs from his mouth, he leaned over her shoulder to see the photo Jake held. "Hey, that's Tera. What are you doing with a picture of her?"

"You know her?" Jake demanded.

He shrugged. "I've seen her around with some of the other girls. I think she's in college."

"Tera is Mrs. Aguilar's daughter," Darla explained with a gesture at Hilda. "She's gone missing, and Jake is trying to find her."

"Oh, yeah? I saw her the other night." He turned and started toward the best-seller display, only to stop in his tracks as he was pelted by a chorus of questions.

"Where did you see her?"

"You're sure it was her? What night, Wednesday or Thursday?"

"Was she all right?"

This last came from Hilda, who hurried over and reached for Robert's arm. The teen swiftly stepped back, holding up both hands in surrender.

"Whoa. Can you, you know, ask me one thing at time?"

"Robert, this is very important," Jake told him, turning the photo so he could see it again. "You're very certain it was this girl you saw, and not some other blonde?"

"Yeah. She's not into the goth scene, so we're not, like, friends or anything, but I've talked to her before. She was standing right under a streetlight when I walked past her."

Jake tucked the photo under her arm and pulled out a notebook and pen from her coat pocket. "All right, we'll assume it was Tera. Which night did you see her?"

The teen squinted in concentration as he counted back on his fingers. "Definitely Wednesday night."

"Good. Now, what time?"

"I don't know. Early. Maybe midnight?" Which time Darla personally wouldn't have classified as early, but then she wasn't eighteen anymore, either.

Jake nodded as she made another note. "Where exactly—I mean, besides under a streetlight—was she when you saw her?"

"She was a couple of streets away from here, near the house where that Curt guy bit it."

"She was near Barry's brownstone?" Darla exclaimed. Then, ignoring Jake's okay-you-can-shut-up-now look, she demanded, "What were you doing there at midnight?"

"I don't know, stuff," was Robert's evasive reply, his expression taking on the same defiant look that Hilda had worn earlier. "It's a free country."

"It doesn't matter what Robert was doing there," Jake broke in. "What's important is what he knows about Tera. C'mon, kid," she urged as he remained silent. "The girl could be in real trouble, and you're the only one so far who knows anything about where she was around the time that Curt, er, bit it. Was she with anyone?"

Robert shook his head.

"And what was she doing, besides standing there? Looking behind her, carrying anything?"

"She was, like, talking on her phone," he replied in an incredulous tone as if to imply, *What else would she be doing?*

Jake nodded again. "Could you tell if she was angry with the person on the other end? How did she seem?"

"I don't know . . . regular, I guess. I didn't stand around listening. That's, like, rude." Another customer walked in just then, and the youth seemed to breathe a sigh of relief. "Sorry, gotta go help the lady," he declared and rushed over to the silver-haired retiree in question.

Darla glanced Jake's way. "I can go wait on the customer. Do you want me to drag him back over for more questions?"

"I've got what I need for now," Jake said and shut her notebook. "If nothing else, we've established that Tera was in the neighborhood the night of Curt's murder. Which doesn't necessarily mean anything," she swiftly reassured Hilda, who had given an audible gasp at that last. "Let's go downstairs so I can scan this photo and get some more info. Darla, I'll be back later with those fliers."

The pair walked to the door, Jake leading the way like the heavy metal version of an avenging angel. Hilda's posture was equally determined, if significantly less intimidating. Darla allowed herself a small smile. Even though she knew that Reese was a good cop, if it came down to betting who would locate Tera first, Darla put her money on Jake.

The question was, would finding the girl also mean that they'd found Curt's killer . . . or was the true murderer still out there somewhere?

Darla pondered this while she made her way upstairs and pulled her turkey Reuben from the refrigerator. She'd carried with her the list she'd started before a disheveled Hilda had come rushing into the store. Between bites, she studied the page again, trying to find another clue in the column of names that she'd written. By the time she'd finished the sandwich, she'd conceded defeat.

"I might as well try a Magic 8 Ball," Darla decided, crumpling her sandwich wrapper and tossing it in the trash.

She nearly threw her list after it but then changed her mind. She'd have James puzzle over the matter later in the afternoon. He'd enjoy the challenge and might well spot something that she had missed. For now, however, she wanted to have a word with Robert regarding his nighttime activities.

Darla made her way down the stairs again, dreading the conversation she was about to have but knowing that the subject would keep gnawing at her if she didn't. Robert lived in the general vicinity, so it wouldn't be unheard of for him to be wandering the neighborhood, even after midnight. But given that he had a job to go to in the morning, the fact that he wasn't home asleep by then raised an unsettling question in her mind: what was Robert doing during his early morning rambles?

"Don't be ridiculous," she said aloud. She already knew he was into the goth scene, which almost by definition required that he engage in dark-of-night activities. And people his age generally treated the wee hours like any other time of day.

But she also recalled the rumor Barry had mentioned that the scrap thieves might be tied to one of the local Russian gangs. Curt had said the last time she'd seen him that the police suspected it was teens doing the deed, particularly since they'd found candy wrappers at some of the scenes. She'd seen for herself that Robert treated candy as one of the primary food groups. He also had bragged about doing construction work for his friend Alex Putin. Could Robert somehow be involved in the recent spate of metal thefts?

And then a far worse possibility flashed through Darla's mind, the thought so disturbing that she halted at the bottom step and abruptly sat down on the stairs lest her legs give out from under her. Try as she might, she couldn't hold back the barrage of questions that abruptly pelted her like an unexpected Texas hailstorm.

What if *Robert* was the scrap thief who stole the copper tubing from Barry's brownstone? And who'd then returned to plunder a second time, only to be confronted by a crowbar-wielding Curt? What if Robert had fought back against the older man and won that struggle?

What if it was Robert—not Tera—who had killed Curt Benedetto?

❚❚ THIRTEEN

HOW LONG SHE HAD BEEN SITTING ON THE STAIRWAY contemplating the possibility of Robert as a cold-blooded killer, Darla wasn't certain. It was only when a member of the store's Friday Afternoon Book Club greeted her with a puzzled, "How have you been, Darla?" and squeezed past her on his way up the steps that she roused herself and headed to the register.

A few of the other club members had trickled into the store as well and were browsing the new releases. While the group had a formal membership of almost thirty—mostly students, retirees, and stay-at-home moms—a core group of about a dozen regulars met every two weeks upstairs in the shop's lounge area. Darla always enjoyed their company and appreciated the recurring business, but today it was the distraction that their arrival offered that earned her gratitude. The conversation level in the store grew louder and more animated as they debated which, if any, of these newcomers might make for good future book club reading.

It took another twenty minutes and a few impulse book purchases before the club members all settled upstairs. Darla had little chance to say anything to Robert as he helped bag the purchases she rang up, and by the time the readers' good-natured arguing had begun drifting down to them, she'd made up her mind to say nothing—at least, not directly to the youth. But as soon as Robert left for the day, she would call Jake for her advice and see if the ex-cop thought that Darla's concerns warranted a call to Reese.

An hour and a half later, the book club meeting upstairs was beginning to wind down. Business had been a bit slow if steady, with one customer seeming to walk in just as another left. James had already arrived for his afternoon shift. After a quick greeting for Darla, he began conversing with Robert regarding the latest shipment of graphic novels from the day before, inventory for which they had a small but devoted customer base. As for Hamlet, he had long since decided that book club day was not his favorite store event and so had spent the past couple of hours safely ensconced atop the history shelf in the back room.

Hamlet rejoined her at the register as Robert stepped up and reached under the counter for his backpack. The sleeping bag was still cinched to it, but now Darla saw more nefarious uses for that piece of camping gear than an aid to making out in the park, as in, something that could be stuffed full of pilfered scrap metal.

"I guess it's time for me to take off," Robert told her, his closed expression reminding her of his attitude the day he'd come in for his initial interview.

Darla did her best to hide her feelings of dismay as she surveyed him. In his short tenure at Pettistone's, the youth had proved a valuable if at times idiosyncratic employee. For now, she simply said, "See you tomorrow. And if you think of anything else that might help Jake or Detective Reese locate Tera Aguilar, you can call me."

He mumbled something that might have been an agreement. Then, with a gentle paw bump for Hamlet and a "See you later" that could have been for either of them, he shouldered his backpack and made his way out.

The book club meeting officially broke up a few minutes later, and James mingled with the departing members. Despite his professed disdain for most modern literature, the ex-professor kept current on both fiction and nonfiction trends. Thus, his opinion was often solicited by the club members, most particularly by the women, several of whom had not-so-secret crushes on the man. Darla was at the register scanning receipts and had just saved off the final tally when the book club's president made her way to the counter.

Martha Washington (*No relation to the late president's wife*, the woman had smilingly assured her on their first meeting) was a slender, mixed-race woman in her late thirties. She wore her multihued hair in waist-length dreads that Darla always found herself envying, and spoke with a clipped English accent that sounded right out of a public television special.

Her pronunciation was no Madonna-type affectation, however, but legitimately earned. Darla knew from their discussions that although Martha's career Army father had been born and bred in Georgia, he'd married an English-woman while stationed overseas. But Martha was definitely accent bilingual. Darla had heard the woman go Deep South in zero to sixty when the topic of conversation warranted it.

"Good afternoon, Darla," she now said, sticking to her precise BBC tones. "Thank you as always for hosting our little group."

"It's my pleasure. Did everyone behave this time?"

Martha grinned at Darla's oblique reference to Mark Poole. One of the group's more vocal members, he'd grown irate with his fellow readers at the last meeting when his interpretation of certain literary symbolism was argued. Finally, knowing he wasn't going to win the point, the man had stomped off before the meeting was over, vowing never to return. It was not the first time Darla had seen a book club member do the real-life version of what online forums referred to as "flouncing." And as typically followed such histrionics, he'd returned for this week's meeting, book under his arm, pretending nothing had ever happened.

"Mark sat quietly and contributed only positive things," Martha assured her. "In fact, before we began, he even offered an apology for his previous behavior."

"Wonderful. So, can I do anything else for you?

"Actually, I found this on the floor back in the reference section and wasn't sure where to restock it for you," she said and held out a magazine-sized graphic novel.

Darla took the softcover book and laid it on the counter. "We just got in a shipment of these yesterday, so this one must have gone astray. Thanks for finding it before it got walked all over."

"Not at all," Martha replied with a smile as she pulled on a long wool coat in the same shades of black and tan and blond as her hair. "Very well, then. See you week after next. We've agreed to skip the planned book and instead discuss that title in the front window."

Darla glanced at the window display. Sure enough, the stack on the red side had dwindled significantly since lunch. With luck, the book club would then choose the blue title as a counterpoint for the meeting after that one. Clutching a tote bag filled with paperbacks, Martha waved good-bye to James and headed for the door.

"Ah, that is the last of them," the store manager declared as bells jingled behind the woman, leaving the store customer free for the moment. "Now that we have Robert, I may need to rearrange my schedule again so that I am off on those afternoons when they meet."

She'd heard that last complaint before and knew that, despite his protestations, he actually enjoyed being in the book club spotlight. But she was more concerned with other issues just now to call him on it.

"Assuming we will still have Robert by then," Darla answered instead.

The comment drew a swift frown from James. "What do you mean? The young man appears to be working out quite nicely despite his, shall we say, quirks."

"I thought so, too, but I fear we might be looking at something worse than a few quirks."

She told him about Hilda's frantic visit earlier that afternoon. She also explained how they'd learned almost by accident that Robert had apparently been in the neighborhood the night of the murder to conveniently witness Tera in the area. Then, feeling somewhat foolish, she showed him the book that had mysteriously fallen to the floor when only she and Hamlet had been in the store.

"*The Man in the Iron Mask*," he said in approval. "One of my childhood favorites. Although I did take issue with Dumas modeling his story on Voltaire's theory that the masked prisoner was actually a blood relative to Louis XIV. I have always leaned toward the Duke of Monmouth as the actual historical figure involved. But what does this have to do with Mr. Benedetto's unfortunate demise?"

While James listened in what could only be interpreted as dumbfounded silence, Darla explained about the bloody paw prints she'd noticed in the basement near Curt's body, and then told him about the swabbing that Jake had done of Hamlet's paws. And she sheepishly explained her theory about Hamlet's book-snagging clues. By the time she had finished, however, James was giving a thoughtful nod.

"I will concede the possibility that Hamlet might well have been the feline that passed through that basement. His propensity for wandering outside this building has been documented. But where I do not follow is how you have determined the killer's identity, when the police apparently are still in the dark on that matter."

Darla flipped open the novel she held and pointed to the summary that she had read that morning. "I thought at first it must be Tera who did it, because I found out from Hilda that Tera's full name is Maria Teresa, just like Louis XIV's wife. But then it seemed too much of a coincidence that Robert, of all people, would be outside Barry and Curt's brownstone the night Curt was killed and just happen to pass by when Tera was standing there."

James gave the page she had indicated a considering look and then shook his head.

"While French literature admittedly is not my specialty, I am fairly confident that the name 'Robert' is not mentioned in this particular novel—nor is 'dude' or 'hoss,' for that matter—which would seem to negate your theory that Hamlet is communicating anything of significance."

But even as Darla conceded that point to herself, he added, "Besides, what motivation would our young employee have for so heinous a crime?"

"He said when I hired him that he does part-time construction work for a guy named Alex Putin, who is apparently some sort of local Russian godfather," she explained. "And Barry said he'd heard that the scrap thieves were somehow connected to the Russian gangs around here. I'm worried that maybe Robert got himself involved in stealing metal for this Putin guy and that Curt caught him that night in the brownstone and came out on the losing end of things."

"An interesting theory. Tell me, what does Detective Reese think about all this?"

"I haven't seen him since last night. I thought I'd ask Jake her opinion before I talked to him."

"Ask my opinion about what?"

While Darla and James had been debating the evidence, Jake had apparently walked in, the chimes unheard by either of them. She was still dressed in her butt-kicking outfit, though now the mirrored glasses were pushed back to the top of her head, and she was carrying a sheaf of papers.

Not waiting for a reply to her question, she plopped the stack on the counter near the register. "Here are the fliers I told you I was making. I've already handed them out around the neighborhood. Do me a favor and hand them out to your customers, too."

"Certainly," James assured her.

"Of course," Darla echoed, picking one up for a look.

The legend in large black letters across the top said *Missing*. Below was the picture of Tera that Hilda had brought with her, along with a description: *Female, 21 years old, dark blond hair, brown eyes, 5' 3", 105 pounds*. It also noted that she'd last been seen in the vicinity of Cheshire Lane—the street where Barry's brownstone was located—and on the prior Wednesday's date. Jake's contact information followed.

"Or call Detective Reese of the NYPD," Darla read aloud as she reached the bottom of the poster, noting that both Reese's phone number and his precinct also were prominently listed. "Uh-oh. I'm not sure Hilda is going to like that."

"Kid, I'm doing what's best for Tera," Jake replied, looking equal parts weary and determined. "I'm worried about her. I don't care that her mother has an issue with the cops. What's important is getting her home ASAP."

Darla nodded her agreement. "Do I need to call him to come get one of these fliers, since Hilda wouldn't give him a photo?"

"Not necessary. I emailed Reese the picture as soon as Hilda left. Now, what's this opinion thing you and James were discussing?"

"We're discussing the possible suspects in Curt's killing. Hamlet's doing his book-snagging routine again, but it's not quite adding up."

"You're pulling my leg, aren't you?" Jake replied with a frown. To James, she added, "Help me out here, would you? It's all well and good playing armchair detective, but explain to your boss that there's a difference between the murder mysteries she sells and the real thing."

"Believe me, I know the difference," Darla shot back before James could take sides. "Or did you forget that Barry and I were the ones who found Curt?" She shuddered. "I even dreamed about dead bodies last night."

"I didn't forget, kid. And you handled yourself really well. But leave the investigating to Reese, would you? I get as much of a kick out of Hamlet's antics as anyone else, but murder is serious stuff. If you do accidentally stumble across Curt's killer before Reese does . . . well, remember, there's no rule that says a murderer can only kill once. Next thing you know, Hamlet might be dancing around in *your* blood."

"Ladies," James interjected in a conciliatory tone, "let us not lose sight of the goal here. We want to find Ms. Aguilar swiftly, and we want to bring Mr. Benedetto's killer to justice. What harm can there be in approaching both problems from multiple angles and see where they intersect?"

"Fine time to play peacemaker, James," was Jake's wry

retort. Then she sighed and said to Darla, "You win. Go on, let's hear Hamlet's list of suspects."

"It's still a work in progress," Darla loftily informed her as she reached for her page. She gave Jake a two-sentence recap of Dumas's tale—a skill she'd developed during her tenure working at the store—and then began reading her the short list.

"I figure we can leave off the musketeer names," she conceded once she ran through those names, "but then we had Maria Theresa, as in Louis XIV's wife. It's a little too coincidental that Tera's full name is—"

"Maria Teresa," Jake finished for her.

"Then there's the author's first name, Alexandre Dumas, which is sort of like Alex Putin."

"*The* Alex Putin? As in, the czar-father of the local construction business?" Jake considered this a moment and then shrugged. "His hands are clean, meaning no arrest record around here, but the rumors fly. The thing is, a run-of-the-mill bashing on the head is a bit understated for those guys, if you know what I mean. They tend to go for something more spectacular, lots of blood spatter, to send a message. But might as well leave him on the list. Who else you got?"

"Robert."

"Robert? You mean, ex-goth-kid-who-works-here-now Robert? You really think he has something to do with this?"

Darla took a deep breath and reluctantly nodded.

"It's possible. I can't picture him deliberately hurting anyone," she said, recalling the story of how he'd defended the girl at the porn shop, "but he is the only person so far who saw Tera after she left her mother's house on Wednesday night. And then he was evasive about what he was doing there that late."

"Well, he does live in the vicinity, doesn't he?" was Jake's reasonable reply. "And you know kids that age. They can stay out all night and still make it to work or school the next day. Loitering doesn't equal murder, so I'd say that's a bit of a stretch, too."

"Sure. But how many kids his age are also best buddies with Alex Putin?"

Jake gave her a sharp look. "You're saying that Robert is friends with that guy? Tell me more."

"Well, maybe not best buddies," Darla conceded, "but Robert told me he did construction work for this Putin guy on the side. And when a girl was being hassled at his old job, he said he threatened the harasser with Putin's name. But remember the copper pipe stolen from Barry and Curt? If Robert was doing the stealing for the Russian gang people, that could be a tie-in."

"Interesting, but a lot of conjecture, and none of it necessarily incriminating. Still, I'll mention it to Reese. But you've left a few people off your list. What about Hilda, or your boyfriend, Barry?"

"Barry is *not* my boyfriend," Darla shot back, feeling herself blush yet again, "but how can you suspect him? Curt's been his best friend for thirty years. Besides, I was with him when we found Curt. No one could pretend to be that upset."

"Guess you've never been to the movies, kid," Jake said with a grin. "They give out awards for that kind of thing." The she sobered. "And I don't want to think about Hilda being involved, either, but she was not a happy camper when she hired me to dig up dirt on the guy. You talk about Mama Grizzly with these overprotective mothers? Well, let's just say she rates in the Mama T-Rex category. She told me she would do anything to protect Tera, and I damn well believe her."

"So who do *you* think killed Mr. Benedetto?" James wanted to know.

Jake shrugged. "Not my concern. My job is to find Tera. But here's the reality: half the time the killer is someone the victim knows, but the other half of the time he—or she—is some random person that your victim had the bad luck to run across. So take my advice and keep your eyes open, but leave the detecting to Reese."

"I suppose you're right," Darla agreed, crumpling her list. "It just seems like nothing is happening very fast here."

"That's where you're wrong, kid."

Jake dragged the sunglasses off her black curls and ran a weary hand through her hair before settling the mirrored shades back in place.

"Take it from an old dog who's been there, Reese is busting his butt on this. It's the whole tip of the iceberg versus what's under the water . . . you, the public, don't see a fraction of what's going behind the scenes. Remember, he's the one who has access to all the forensic evidence. Who knows what they might have found in that brownstone to tie someone to the crime. And don't forget there are two cell phones involved, Curt's and Tera's."

"I understand about Curt's phone," Darla conceded with a frown. "Reese can download all his calls and phone numbers and look for a pattern or for some new suspects, right? But what good will Tera's phone records do Reese if she's not answering her cell or calling anyone?"

"Ah, yes, I believe it is called cell phone pinging," James answered for Jake. To Darla, who stared at him in surprise, he added, "One can learn all sorts of interesting things watching cable television."

The ex-cop, meanwhile, was nodding in approval.

"One of the little miracles of modern technology. As long as your cell phone is turned on, it sends signals to whatever cell tower is closest to you, twenty-four/seven, even when you're not talking. If you know the location of the cell tower, you know where someone is, within a certain range. Person moves around, she can be tracked by which cell towers the signal is bouncing to. Of course, that's only good for narrowing the location to a few blocks. But now that most phones come with GPS, the police can pinpoint their suspect to within a few feet."

Which, on the one hand, was reassuring if you wanted a loved one found, but also a bit too Big Brother-ish for Darla's comfort. Curious, she asked, "Can you do that, too, as a private investigator?"

Jake nodded. "That's what I was working on this morning. I've got a buddy who handles this sort of thing for me, and I'm just waiting for a call back. Legally, I can't do everything that Reese can—some of it takes a warrant—but I'll only be a few steps behind him. With luck we'll have Tera tracked down by the end of today."

So saying, Jake straightened the stack of fliers she'd set down, and then picked up the novel that Martha Washington had brought to the counter earlier.

"Wow," she commented. "Pretty gruesome stuff for kids they're putting out these days. That's awfully graphic artwork."

"Guess that's why they call it a graphic novel," Darla explained with a reflexive smile. "They're written for adults, not children, and they're illustrated by some of the field's top artists. Think of those old *Classics Illustrated* comic books from a few decades back, except really ramped up."

"Yeah, well that blood-covered ape or whatever it is on the cover sure looks ramped up . . . and that half-naked gal, too."

She turned the book so that Darla could see the cover. Darla bit back a gasp and all but snatched the novel from her friend's hand.

"Look, James, it's the graphic novel of Edgar Allan Poe's *The Murders in the Rue Morgue*," she exclaimed. "Martha said she found this lying on the floor near the reference shelves. No way did it get there all by itself. Someone had to pull it off the shelf and move it."

"Are you suggesting that Hamlet has given us another clue?"

"Why not?" Darla smoothed her crumpled list and grabbed her pen again. "There it is, plain as day on the cover"—she pointed—"the word 'murder.'"

"Yes, but I am sure you will recall that the murders in question were not committed by a human. Do you wish to add an orangutan to Hamlet's list of suspects?"

The store manager's tone was politely inquiring, but Darla swore she heard suppressed amusement in his voice. But this latest clue had just bumped another name to the top of her list.

"I've already got an orangutan," she replied with a triumphant nod. "Porn Shop Bill. Otherwise known as the Not-So-Great Ape to his employees. They call him that because of his long arms and orange hair. Pretty much an insult to all orangutans, if you ask me."

Then another thought occurred to her, and she stared at the pair of them in consternation. "But that's not all. I just remembered something that Robert said. Apparently, one of his coworkers claimed that Bill once attacked a guy with a hammer as repayment for an insult!"

"Better mention that to Reese, pronto, so he can—" Jake began, only to be cut short by the disco strains of the Bee Gee's long-ago hit, "Stayin' Alive," blasting from her cell phone. "Speaking of Reese," she said, and punched the "Talk" button. "Martelli here."

Darla could hear the staccato rhythm of a voice speaking on the other end, though the sound was too faint for her to make out any words. Jake punctuated the one-sided conversation with a few "uh-huhs" before ending with a, "Meet you there in a minute."

"Did Reese find something?" Darla demanded before the other woman had even pressed the "Off" key on her phone.

Jake tucked the cell back into her pocket. Though the ex-cop's expression appeared deliberately neutral, Darla felt her stomach knot as she met Jake's gaze. Finally, Jake nodded.

"You know what I told you about tracking down someone by using the cell tower pings and GPS? Pretty much works every time."

"I presume that means the police have located Ms. Aguilar?" James asked, sounding almost as apprehensive as Darla abruptly felt.

When Jake replied, however, her answer wasn't quite what Darla had expected to hear. "No Tera yet. But we're getting close. Reese has tracked down her cell phone."

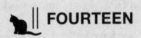 **FOURTEEN**

DARLA HAD HEARD OF DUMPSTER DIVING, BUT WHAT REESE was doing fell into a potentially far more dangerous category.

Leaving James and Hamlet to mind the shop, Darla had accompanied Jake over to Barry's brownstone. There, they found the detective, the battered tan four-door that was assigned to him while on duty parked halfway onto the curb. Barry, wearing his usual gray hooded sweatshirt, sat on his stoop, his expression unreadable as Reese stood waist deep in the rented roll-off Dumpster that Barry and Curt had been using for their construction debris. Stripped down to his dress shirt and trousers, he wore leather work gloves and clutched a large black flashlight, which he was using as both a light source and a makeshift pry bar.

Darla stared uneasily at the container and tried to ignore her lurching stomach. Though no one had said anything aloud, Darla realized chances were that wherever Tera's phone was found, she would be, too. And that did not bode well at all for the girl's continued welfare.

Shakily, Darla settled onto the stoop beside Barry and wondered what in the heck she was thinking, tagging along with Jake to the scene. Darla had had the noble idea of offering Barry some sort of moral support. But now, given that she might well be about to witness discovery of a second crime, she fervently wished that she'd stayed back at the shop with James and Hamlet.

But finding anything inside the weather-beaten red container might take a while. It was full of broken plywood and plasterboard, all of which stuck out from its open top. Discarded paint rollers and empty plastic and metal buckets, caked with plaster and paint, were sandwiched among the debris, while a pile of filthy pink insulation took up a good-sized section near the rear. A dirty ribbon of fluorescent yellow plastic that Darla recognized as crime scene tape dangled from one corner of the Dumpster and flapped like a discarded party streamer with the slight breeze of the late afternoon.

While Jake went to join Reese, picking her way through the random scattering of two-by-fours the detective had apparently already tossed out of the Dumpster, Darla gave Barry what she hoped was a comforting smile.

"So much for a tidy work site," she ventured.

She earned a polite, momentary flash of white teeth for her attempt at a joke. Then Barry fixed what appeared to be an angry gaze on the Dumpster again. "I thought the police were finished here, but he had a warrant and everything."

"I hope he had a tetanus shot, too," Darla answered, cringing a little as she heard Reese curse and then shake one gloved hand like he'd been injured. "There are probably all kinds of nails and stuff in there."

"Nails, wire, insulation, linoleum." Barry shrugged in agreement. "You name it, we tore it out of the place. Any idea what's he's looking for?"

Darla glanced at him in surprise. Apparently, despite the warrant, Reese had mentioned nothing to the man about Tera or her cell phone. Recalling the lecture that she'd received from Reese the last time that she—as he had so bluntly put it—had blabbed, Darla prudently shook her head.

"I'm just here with Jake."

Besides, it could all be a false alarm, she reminded herself. No need to distress the man unduly until there was good reason. Then, taking a deep breath, she added, "Sorry about the other night when you stopped by. You took me by surprise. And that whole hiding-out-in-the-powder-room thing was Reese's idea. He sprang that on me after I'd already buzzed you in. I was kind of caught, and I didn't know what to do, so I went along with it."

"Yeah, well, it did feel kind of like an ambush, but I understand where you're coming from. A cop tells you to jump, you do it."

Which sounded a bit like Hilda's attitude, Darla thought, wondering where Barry had gotten *his* jaundiced view of the police. Then he added, "The thing is, I got the impression you know this cop personally, too."

Darla blinked. Could Barry be, well, jealous? A bit cheered, she replied, "He's Jake's friend, and ex-partner, but that's as far as it goes."

"Okay. I just wanted to make sure you weren't seeing him or anything." Barry gave another small smile, but this time it appeared genuine. "It's not a good move, trying to ask out a lady who's already dating someone . . . especially a cop."

"Guess not." Darla smiled a little, too. "But to answer your question, no, I'm not seeing Reese or anyone else at the moment."

"Great. Then maybe you'd have dinner with me tonight after you close the bookstore. You know, to take our minds off what's happened."

Darla considered the offer for a moment. Should the worst happen and they find Tera, she'd need a lot more than a nice meal to get over it. But she'd worry about that when—if—it happened.

"I guess we could do that," she agreed. "You've seen that Greek restaurant a few doors down from the Thai place? I could meet you there at eight."

"Eight is good."

His gaze lingered on her long enough for her to feel a bit uncomfortable under his scrutiny. Turning her attention back to the Dumpster, she watched in unwilling fascination as Reese made his way section by section through it.

At least it wasn't a regular garbage Dumpster he was searching, she thought, or he'd need to be wearing a hazmat suit. Still, it was likely that Reese's shirt and trousers would be the worse for wear by the time he finished with his hunt. Jake was assisting him, although she'd wisely remained outside the container. Standing on an overturned bucket, she was taking the sections of plaster and board Reese was methodically handing to her. Given the effort they were making, Darla hoped that Reese was pretty darned sure the phone—and perhaps, by extension, the girl—was actually inside the Dumpster.

"Got it!"

The muffled shout came from Reese, who had been almost out of view from Darla's angle, digging in the container's depths. Beside her, she felt Barry go tense, his expression grim. Slowly, he rose, seeming to forget Darla was standing beside him. She gazed up at him uncertainly. Had he guessed what Reese was looking for?

Now, Reese popped up again clutching something in one gloved hand, and Darla reflexively jumped to her feet as well.

"What? What does he have?" Barry asked, but Darla was already trotting over to the container.

She halted next to Jake, who apparently now traveled about with small paper bags the way some people carried chewing gum. Carefully holding what Darla saw was a bright pink cell phone in two gloved fingers, the ex-cop slipped it inside the bag she'd pulled from her coat pocket. She sealed its top while Reese extracted himself from the tangle of lumber and broken plasterboard and crawled out of the Dumpster.

"Good job," Jake congratulated him with a grim smile as she handed the evidence to him. "And thank God Tera wasn't in there with her phone."

"Are you sure?" Darla protested in a shaky voice. "I mean, could she possibly be . . ."

"Don't worry, Red, she's not in there," Reese assured her. "I crawled in there pretty sure we were going to find her, but I dug through the whole container, and there wasn't anything the size and shape of a body that I didn't pull open. Wherever she is, it's not here."

"Thank God," Darla echoed Jake's sentiment. "But I guess we should let Hilda know about the phone so she doesn't waste her time trying to keep calling Tera."

"We?" Reese said, and Jake coughed and gave Darla a look. "I'd prefer you not discuss anything you know concerning the case with anyone else," Reese replied, his formal manner suddenly all cop. "I'll handle any necessary communication with Mrs. Aguilar. Darla, I'm asking this as a favor to me."

Which, translated from cop-speak, meant that even though he was asking politely, he expected her to keep her mouth shut.

Which further translated to mean Hilda was what the CSI shows called a "person of interest" in regard to Curt's murder.

"Sure, Reese, no problem," she managed, feeling her chest tighten.

Until this moment, she'd never truly believed that the elegant

Hilda might have been the one to wield the lethal crowbar. But it seemed that Reese had some reason to suspect her. Darla frowned. What had happened to Porn Shop Bill as a suspect? And what did that mean regarding Tera's disappearance? If Hilda had killed Curt, could Tera have witnessed the crime and then fled lest her mother turn the same weapon on her?

And, most important, what the heck was Tera's cell phone doing in the Dumpster, when apparently Tera was still out there somewhere walking around?

"Mr. Eisen, thank you for your cooperation," Reese was now saying to Barry, who had joined them. "We may need to search this container again, so I ask that you not arrange for its pickup without clearing it with me first."

"Um, sure," Barry agreed, and then gestured to the debris that Reese and Jake had dragged out of the container. "But what about this stuff? Are you going to put it back where you found it?"

"Sorry for the inconvenience, sir, but I need to get this evidence logged in," the detective replied, indicating the bagged phone he held. Turning to Jake, he said, "Why don't I give you a ride back to your place?"

"Sure, if you don't mind a little cigarette smoke." Sliding her mirrored sunglasses back into place, she said to Darla, "You don't mind going home alone, do you?"

"I'll manage," she replied, feeling like she had in high school when a friend would ditch her to hang out with a cute guy.

So much for *dancing with the one that brung you*, she thought with an inner shrug at that old Texas saw as the pair headed toward Reese's city-issued car. She had seen the look the two had exchanged and understood what was going on. Reese wanted to confer with Jake out of civilian earshot, and that could only happen if Darla hoofed it home alone. Still, she couldn't let Reese go without mentioning that other bit of information that she'd learned about Bill.

She raced after them, catching the cop as he was sliding into his seat behind the wheel. Swiftly, she repeated the rumor Robert had told her that about the porn shop owner having once attacked a man with a hammer.

When she'd finished, Reese nodded. "Thanks for the tip, but I already pulled Ferguson's rap sheet. Just a couple of assault charges that were pleaded down. Don't worry, though, the guy is still on my list. And feel free to call me if he shows up at your shop again."

"I will. But, Reese, about Tera's phone . . . why would it be in the Dumpster?"

"Good question, Red. That's what I plan to find out."

He and Jake pulled away from the curb, leaving Darla alone with Barry and the mini–disaster area around them. For the moment, there was nothing she could do about the Tera situation. However . . .

With a rueful look at Barry, she said, "Why don't I help you clean up this junk before I go? It will be getting dark soon, and you don't want to accidentally trip over something."

Then, when he didn't immediately reply, she reached for his arm and gave it a tentative shake. "Barry, are you all right?"

Barry had been silently staring at the Dumpster. Now, looking rather stunned, he turned and focused on her. "I'm sorry, what did you say?"

"I'm offering you free labor," she replied. "I'll help you toss all this junk into the container before I leave."

Seeming to gather his wits, he managed a feeble smile for her. "What do you think they were looking for besides a cell phone? Whose is it, anyhow?"

She hesitated, Reese's warning against blabbing ringing in her ears. On the other hand, he'd been speaking about Hilda, not Barry. And despite this unsettling turn of events, he was apparently in the clear regarding Tera, since Reese had no qualms about leaving her alone with the man.

"You know Tera Aguilar, who was dating Curt? They traced her phone to your Dumpster, and I guess Reese thought he might find her in there, too."

"Tera, in the Dumpster?" Barry shot her an incredulous look. "What would she be doing in there?"

"She's gone missing, and the last time anyone saw her was the night that Curt was killed. There's a chance that the same person who murdered him did something to Tera, too."

"Unless she was the one who clubbed him over the head, and she's on the run now."

His tone held a bitter note. Apparently, he hadn't forgotten the phone argument he'd heard between his partner and the girl. Darla nodded. Then, recalling his original reaction, she asked, "So what did you think Reese was looking for?"

Barry sagged a little and gave her a sheepish look.

"I'd really appreciate it if you didn't say anything, Darla, but some of that stuff we're tossing isn't exactly legal to dump. I figured the building inspector had already been poking around here when we saw him yesterday, and he found something he didn't like. So he called the cops on me."

"Illegal?" Darla gave a doubtful look at the debris scattered around the container. Great, last thing she needed was to be handling toxic waste. "Um, maybe I should rescind my offer about helping you pick things up."

"Actually, I'd appreciate the hand. And I swear, the only thing there's a problem with is that stack of floor covering."

He pointed to a small pile of what was arguably the ugliest kitchen linoleum that Darla had ever seen. "Given its age, there's a good chance that the backing is made with asbestos, but we didn't take the time to test it. But we did handle it real carefully and cut it up with knives, so there isn't any dust or fibers."

When Darla gave him a stern look, he sighed and added, "How about I do it by the book? I'll bag up the pieces and pay a guy I know to come get it, okay?"

"Forget the asbestos. My eyes will never be the same again now that I've seen this stuff. It should be stored in one of those secret government warehouses so it never sees the light of day again," she replied with another disbelieving glance at the flooring. Seriously, who in their right minds could have thought that pink and purple squiggles on a background of grayish-green made for an attractive pattern?

Barry grinned. "Thanks for understanding. I'm all for safety, but sometimes Big Brother goes a bit overboard, and you get tempted to take a few shortcuts. Now, let me see if there are some extra gloves lying around that will fit you."

While he went back inside the brownstone to search, Darla stood on tiptoe and gingerly peered inside the container, even though Reese had assured her that Tera's cell phone was the only thing inside it connected to the girl. The immediate sight of a long and quite body-shaped form wrapped in heavy black sheeting almost gave her a heart attack, until she noticed that the plastic had been pulled open to reveal several more strips of pink insulation. Looking more closely, she could see that Reese apparently had torn into anything that wasn't solid, for several other bags and bundles of trash had spilled their contents, too.

"Find anything else?"

The sound of Barry's voice unexpectedly behind her made her yelp in surprise; then, feeling sheepish, she turned to meet his wry gaze.

"Just putting my mind at rest," she told him as she took the gloves he held out to her and pulled them on. And then, abruptly, she felt a few tears slip down her cheek.

"Sorry," she added, swiping away the unexpected moisture from her face. "I didn't know Curt all that well, but this whole thing—his death, Tera going missing—has had a real impact on me. And you probably think I'm just being some sort of drama queen, since you're standing there all stoic, and you're the one who was Curt's friend."

To her relief, Barry smiled and shook his head. "Frankly, I'd think a whole lot less of you if you didn't care."

Darla managed a smile back. "I guess I just need to know that whoever killed him will be punished, and I need Tera to come home safe and sound again. And I'm not sure that's going to happen . . . not for either of them."

She gave an idle kick at the nearest pile of debris. "Here, let's get this cleaned up. I left the store in a bit of a hurry. If I'm not back soon, James will be tracking *me* down on my cell."

Together, they began picking up the scattered construction leftovers. They were making swift progress loading the trash back into the Dumpster when a flash of pink wedged in a splintered board caught Darla's eye and made her pause. Barry didn't notice she had stopped, as he was wrestling with a heavy coil of electrical wire that had come undone and turned into what looked like an oversized spring toy.

Frowning, she extracted what appeared to be a broken piece of pink plastic about the size of a dime that had been caught in crack in the wood. It was the same bubblegum shade as Tera's phone and looked like it had probably come from one of those plastic snap-on protectors. The piece she held could have broken off when something heavier landed on the phone. She almost tossed it back into the Dumpster but then shrugged and tucked it into her pants pocket. It probably wouldn't do Reese any good, but it seemed like evidence. She'd hang on to it anyhow and give it to him next time she saw him.

A few minutes later, they had finished the cleanup and were both sweating despite the coolness of the late afternoon. Barry tossed a final paint roller into the container and then whipped off his gloves to swab his gleaming forehead with the back of his hand. "That's all of it. Let's get you back to the store so I can head home for a shower before we meet tonight."

Darla pulled off her own gloves and used them to slap at

the plaster dust that now clung to her blue corduroy pants. "I need to clean up a little, too, after our workout," she assured him with a smile.

A short time later, she was back at the bookstore. After reconfirming the time for their date and making her hasty good-byes to Barry, she rushed into the store. "Sorry for leaving you in the lurch," she told James, surprised when she glanced at the wall clock to see that she'd been gone for almost two hours. "I stuck around to help Barry clean up after Reese tossed a Dumpster's worth of junk into his yard."

"And what of Ms. Aguilar and her phone?"

"Believe it or not, Reese found the phone in all that mess. Thank God he didn't find Tera in there, too. But still, I don't have a good feeling about this."

James gave a thoughtful nod. "I agree, the situation is not promising. Do you know if Detective Reese thinks the girl has come to harm?"

"He's not saying, as usual. The only one he'll talk to is Jake, and she's got that whole code-of-silence thing going on, too."

Idly, she picked up the graphic novel copy of Poe's work that she had left on the counter in her rush. "Hamlet's the only one besides the killer who might know what happened, and he's not talking, either . . . at least, not so I can understand him. How does this"—she waved the novel in her manager's direction—"tie in with *The Man in the Iron Mask*?"

James had just assumed the supercilious look of a self-satisfied professor preparing to launch into another lecture, when the shop door jangled and Mark Poole—he of the recent book club flounce—strolled back in. "Hi, Darla . . . hi, James," he called, "I, er, forgot to pick up that romance novel that my mom wanted. But I can't remember the title. Maybe you can help?"

"Ten to one he's buying it for himself," Darla murmured to her manager while giving the customer a friendly wave.

Then, in a normal tone, she added, "I'll go take care of Mr. Poole. Why don't you take your break now, James, and I'll keep an eye on things. But let me know if you think up any clever theories while you're at it."

She tossed the graphic novel back on top of the copy of the Dumas book. Passing by Hamlet, who was lounging, paws in the air, atop the green beanbag in the kids' section, she told him, "Feel free to use the keyboard and just type out a name anytime now."

Hamlet flipped over onto his side and gave her a cool green look as if to say, *I've done my part, clueless human. Now go prove why you're supposedly the dominant species.* Which wasn't much help at all.

Once Darla had rung up her customer and James had returned from his break—minus any additional literary insights, as he made sure to inform her—they agreed he could finish out the shift alone. Darla headed back upstairs to her apartment to shower and rest before her date with Barry later that night.

What she didn't tell James was that her plans for the evening also included keeping an eye on the store's security cameras throughout the night. For it had occurred to her that afternoon that maybe she'd given over the henhouse to the fox by leaving Robert in charge of reviewing the previous night's videos. Much as she hated to suspect the teen of anything, she couldn't dismiss the unsettled feeling she had that something was going on with Robert. She needed to reassure herself that he wasn't wandering around her place or the Plinskis' building in the dark of night looking for scrap metal to steal.

And part of that reassurance meant that before she called it a day at the store, she was going to reset the two exterior cameras.

FIFTEEN

IT WAS QUARTER TO EIGHT WHEN, AFTER SWITCHING ON THE television to the pet channel, she left behind a decidedly peeved Hamlet and started in the direction of the Greek restaurant, the modestly named Greek Restaurant. Though darkness had long since fallen, the streetlights and passing traffic served to illuminate her way. That, and plenty of early evening foot traffic—it was Friday night, after all—made the walk one she normally would not have hesitated over. But the fact that an as-yet unsolved murder had occurred only two blocks away kept her looking over her shoulder more than usual during the short walk.

And she was not the only one, she noticed. Word of the murder had traveled quickly around the neighborhood, and she noticed her fellow passersby scuttling along at a faster pace than she was used to seeing. Greek Restaurant, like similar establishments she'd seen in the city, resembled an authentic taverna with a whitewashed exterior and rough wooden benches set beneath window boxes filled with flowers—obviously artificial, given the time of year, Darla thought with a smile.

Barry stood at the head of a small line that had formed outside the wooden doors as the would-be diners waited to get in. Instead of his usual plaster-streaked jeans, tonight he wore brown dress slacks, and his gray hooded sweatshirt had been replaced by a blue and brown tweed sport coat over a beige shirt. At the sight of him, she was glad that under her own lightweight black wool coat she'd opted for a soft, calf-length knit dress in forest green topped by a fringed Spanish shawl in jewel tones, rather than her go-to fall work uniform of slacks and bulky sweater.

"Perfect timing," he greeted her, his gaze appreciative. "And I really like your hair all pinned up and poufy like that." Then, with a gesture at the door, he added, "Let's hope the food is as good as it smells from out here."

It was. Half an hour later, Darla was blissfully making her way through a salad of red onions, black olives, tomatoes, and cucumbers topped by an herb-encrusted slab of feta. When Barry playfully made as if to steal one of her stuffed grape leaves, she wielded her fork like a tined sword and warned him, "Don't even think about it."

The entrée was even better. After some debate, they had decided to share a platter of dolma, spanakopita, souvlaki, broiled scampi, and mousaka. Darla considered saving a shrimp to bring home to Hamlet as a peace offering for leaving him on his own. After a second glass of a soft red wine, however, she decided the heck with it and finished the final piece herself.

Their dinner conversation was deliberately light, with both of them avoiding the subject of Curt and Tera. Darla regaled Barry with the seamy underside of selling books, while he obliged with bloodless horror stories about his previous career in banking. And again, Darla found herself thinking that Barry was what they called "a nice guy," and that nice was a pleasant change from what she had lived with in the past. It wasn't until they were walking back toward Darla's place a couple of hours later that talk turned to the subject of that afternoon's find.

"So, have you heard anything back from that detective about the phone in my Dumpster?" Barry asked when they paused for a stoplight.

Darla shook her head, the pleasant light-headedness she'd been feeling from the wine wearing off with this turn of conversation. "No, nothing," she assured him. "Besides, he wouldn't discuss an active case with me anyhow."

Not that she hadn't given Jake a call earlier that evening to see if the older woman would at least give her an idea of what was going on. But Jake had been either legitimately busy or else deliberately avoiding her calls, for both attempts had gone to voice mail.

Barry let the subject drop, and their conversation for the remainder of their walk was of pleasant inconsequentials. But as they reached the stoop leading to Darla's private entrance, he said, "Just so you know, I'll be heading out on Sunday morning for Connecticut. Curt's funeral will be on Monday, and I want to be there beforehand for his mom and sister."

"I'm sure they'll be glad of your support. Is there anything I can do for you while you're gone? Water a plant, feed a fish?" she offered before she realized she had no idea where the man actually lived.

To her relief, he shook his head.

"No plants, no fish," he replied with a slight smile, "but I appreciate the thought. But let me know if you hear anything about that business with the phone. I'm not counting on your detective friend to keep me in the loop."

"Sure, but I'll need your number," she reminded him.

He smiled and pulled his phone out of his pocket. "Sorry, I forgot," he said and hit a button that caused Darla's phone to ring a moment later.

She shot him a look of surprise as she pressed the "Talk" button and then shut it off again. "How did you get my cell number? I only ever give out the store number to customers."

"Oh, that." He gave her a wry look. "Actually, I got it from Curt a while back . . . you know, just in case. I hope you're not mad."

She considered that for a moment. Apparently, the whole time she'd been wondering about him, he'd been thinking about her.

"Hey, at least you didn't hang some huge 'Darla Will You Date Me?' sign on my door. That definitely would have rated stalker." Smiling back, she slipped her phone into her pocket. "Anyhow, I guess I've got your number now."

"Guess you do," he answered, and leaned forward to kiss her.

A bit later, as she let herself back into her apartment, she reflected that the kiss—like Barry—had been nice. Not earth-shattering, and not off-putting, but somewhere pleasantly in between. Which was all right for a first date . . . and which boded well for a second.

"Hamlet, I'm home," she called as she set down her bag and hung her coat on the peg.

Hamlet did not reply, which was par for the course. As she made a quick sweep through the apartment, she did not find him in any of his usual lounging spots. She realized with a growing sense of unease that he was not anywhere inside, meaning he had either slipped downstairs into the store or had once again fled the building completely.

"Glad I didn't bring you that shrimp," she said to his absent self as she went into her bedroom to change. Her blue and gold comforter—the one she'd bought upon moving in because of its calming vibe—bore no cat-shaped wrinkles. Only a scattering of black hairs indicated that Hamlet occasionally took a nap there.

"Fine, run away from home just like Tera," she added as

she changed into sweats, "but don't expect me to hire Jake to find you. And I'm not leaving the lights on, either."

The one-sided conversation reminded her to check the security cameras. Maybe now with the camera angle rearranged, she'd get lucky and spot where the crafty feline was sneaking out. She glanced at her watch to see that it was almost eleven p.m. Even if she didn't spy Hamlet skulking about, at least she could reassure herself that things in the vicinity of Pettistone's Fine Books were quiet for the night.

Returning to the living room and the rolltop desk where she kept her laptop, Darla turned on her computer and pulled up the security program. *So far, so good*, she thought with a look at the live camera shots. She'd take a quick look at what had been recorded so far and then check periodically through the night on the live action.

But the two glasses of wine from dinner combined with the stress of the past few days began to take a toll on her. She found herself nodding off as she stared at an unchanging screen. She had reached the point of dragging herself off her chair for a dozen jumping jacks every few minutes just to keep herself awake, when an image flashed on the courtyard camera that abruptly brought her to full wakefulness.

Swiftly, she backed through the video and played it again, this time at half speed so that she wouldn't miss anything. The first indication anything was amiss was when a dark figure scaled the courtyard gate. He shifted something on his shoulder—a backpack!—and then swiftly moved to one side, as if he knew the camera would catch his movements should he walk straight ahead. But what the intruder didn't know was that the cameras were no longer at the same angle they'd covered the previous night.

Which also meant that Robert had no idea he'd been caught on video unrolling his sleeping bag and heading toward a corner spot right outside the shop's courtyard door.

Heart pounding, Darla hurriedly switched the courtyard camera back to live mode. She had finally replaced the burned-out lightbulb in the exterior fixture, which she routinely left on overnight, so that a dim glow illuminated much of the bricked patio within those walls. Now, the courtyard appeared empty. But she knew that even though she had repositioned the camera earlier that day, small blind spots still existed to either side of the door. And she'd seen Robert, sleeping bag in hand, heading toward one of those corners.

The question was, was he still there, hidden now from camera view?

She flipped the view to the playback and swiftly checked the date stamp. Sure enough, the digital time stamp on the video showed that Robert had climbed over the gate but a few minutes before she and Barry had parted company at her front stoop. With the store long since closed for the day, he had no legitimate reason to have returned . . . certainly, no legitimate reason to climb over a locked gate and prowl about her courtyard!

If she hurried downstairs, Darla thought in outrage, she might still catch the teen in the act of whatever it was that he was doing. She stuck her keys in her pocket and then grabbed her cell phone, ready for confrontation.

Abruptly, the image of Curt lying dead in the basement flashed through her mind. He had been unarmed when he had encountered someone—perhaps Robert?—on his property in the middle of the night. If Curt, who had been a good six inches taller and eighty pounds heavier than Darla, had not been able to defend himself, then what were the chances she could?

"So call Jake for backup," she told herself and quickly dialed.

Once again, however, the call went directly to the ex-cop's voice mail. "It's me, Darla," she said in a rush. "I think Robert is downstairs in the courtyard, maybe trying to find something he can sell for scrap. I'm going down there now."

And if things go badly, she grimly told herself, *at least Jake will have a record of my last minutes without having to rely on Hamlet for clues.* Darla glanced around the living room and spied the clublike rain stick that Great-Aunt Dee had brought back from Chile still propped in the corner. Once before, she'd grabbed it up, prepared to defend herself when she thought an intruder had broken into her apartment. It might not be as effective a weapon as a crowbar, but it was better than nothing.

A few moments later she had let herself into the store via the hall entry door, quickly shutting off the alarm. As always, the shop was dark save for a single light she kept on over the register. Silently as possible—though surely no one in the courtyard could hear her footsteps—she made her way to the back door, debating as she did so the best way to handle the situation. She could shut off the alarm and stealthily crack open the door for a cautious look . . . or she could fling open the door and use the element of surprise to her advantage. So what would Jake do in that situation?

Element of surprise, she decided.

Setting down the rain stick next to the door, she turned on her phone and punched in three numbers. That accomplished, she picked up the stick again and tucked it under one arm before gently turning the dead bolt. The lock made a quiet metallic click as it released, and she winced, certain the sound could be heard in the courtyard. She waited a moment, hand on knob, for the scramble of feet beyond; then, when all remained silent, she took a deep breath and pulled the door open.

"I've dialed 9-1-1, Robert," she called out, holding up her cell in one hand and clutching her makeshift club in the other. "You've got one second to tell me what you're doing here."

"Mmmph?" came a groggy answer from the shadows, followed by, "Hey, Ms. Pettistone, please don't call the cops! I can explain."

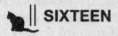 **SIXTEEN**

DARLA GLANCED ABOUT, UNABLE FOR A MOMENT TO TELL where the voice, which was obviously Robert's, had come from. Then she looked down.

In the shadowed corner of the courtyard to the right of the door, she spied something tucked away behind the bistro chairs and table where Darla and her staff often took their lunch. Robert lay huddled on the bricks in his sleeping bag, his head propped on his backpack as a makeshift pillow. That alone was enough to make her eyes widen in surprise.

But what truly startled her was the fact that the AWOL Hamlet lay stretched atop Robert's shoulders, serving as an equally makeshift blanket. The feline raised his head, and his green eyes caught the light. From his casual yet protective pose, she swiftly caught the vibe from him, *It's all under control.*

Leaning the rain stick against the doorjamb, Darla

promptly hit "End" on her phone and hurried down the two steps that led to the patio.

"Robert, what's wrong? Why in the world are you sleeping out here in the cold?" she demanded, her previous outrage replaced by a wave of concern.

Robert, meanwhile, was dragging himself into a sitting position. In the process, he dislodged his feline guardian angel, who slipped off the teen's shoulders and landed neatly on the brick. While Hamlet paused for a quick paw lick, Robert managed to extract himself from the sleeping bag and scramble to his feet.

"Sorry," he mumbled through a yawn, scrubbing the sleep from his eyes with one hand, while with the other he clutched his sleeping bag to him like a security blanket. "I just needed a place to crash. I'll go find somewhere else."

"You'll do no such thing," came Darla's stern reply. "Come inside right now where it's warm and explain to me what's going on."

He meekly followed her inside, trailed by Hamlet, who did not look meek at all. Darla saw that he—the teen, not the cat—was wearing the same clothes as he'd had on earlier that day, though now the garments were notably crumpled. Shaking her head, she locked the door again and led Robert back to the register where the light above illuminated that portion of the counter. She pointed him to the tall stool there and said, "Sit."

He did, while Hamlet lightly leaped onto the counter for a better view of the action. Once they both were settled, she said, "Now, talk. How come you're not at home where you belong?"

"I, um, don't have a home anymore," he said, not meeting her gaze. "My dad, he, you know, tossed me out as soon as I turned eighteen back in the spring."

"Your dad threw you out?" Darla stared at him in shock. "Why, you were still in high school then, weren't you?" At his nod, she went on, "What, were you doing something illegal, and he didn't want you in the house?"

"No! I was making all A's in my classes and everything. It didn't matter to him. He said his time was up, he wasn't responsible for me anymore. He said his dad threw him out at eighteen, so he was, like, returning the favor."

"But what about your mother? How could she allow that?"

"She's somewhere in California. I haven't heard from her since I was eleven."

The youth's matter-of-fact tone affected Darla more than any bitterness or anger. How could a parent do such a thing to his or her child? If the youth had been sitting around the house unemployed and using drugs, maybe that would have been different, but he'd been in school and then holding down a job of one sort or another ever since graduation. Apparently, his only transgression had been having a birthday.

Darla shook her head in disbelief. Even though she'd lived in the New York City area for only a short while, she knew full well how hard it was to make rent there. With only a high school education, and working jobs that paid little more than minimum wage, no way could Robert support himself on his own or even scrape together enough to get himself somewhere else.

"We'll talk about this some more tomorrow," she told him. "For tonight, why don't you go up to the lounge upstairs and sleep on the couch? You can use the shower in the little bathroom up there in the morning, and I'll bring you down some breakfast around nine o'clock. And then we can figure out what to do."

She paused, dreading the next question but knowing she

needed to ask it. "And Robert, about seeing Tera Aguilar the other night . . . tell me, what were you really doing out on the streets that late?"

"I was, you know, heading back here," he said, clutching his sleeping bag more tightly to him. "Sometimes my cousin lets me crash at his place, but he wasn't home, so I thought I'd stay in the courtyard here. I figured it was, you know, safer than the park."

"That was all? Do you promise you're not the one going around the neighborhood stealing scrap metal to sell for cash?" she asked, though knowing his circumstances as she did now, she'd be hard-pressed to judge him too harshly.

Robert, however, gave his head a vigorous shake.

"No way, I don't steal. Besides, Alex . . . Mr. Putin . . . is pretty mad about whoever's doing that. I don't want to get on his bad side."

"I'm glad to hear that," she replied, relieved to realize that she believed him. Though, of course, one final question remained. "And you don't know anything about who killed Mr. Benedetto, either?"

He shook his head again, though this time he was stifling a yawn, as well. "No clue. I just hope they catch him soon. It's kind of, you know, creepy being out there at night thinking some psycho dude might be running around."

"Well, you don't have to worry about that tonight," Darla assured him. "Like I said, you can stay upstairs. Now, get moving, so we can both get some rest."

"Sure. And, uh, thanks for not being, you know, mad."

He slid off the stool and started for the stairs, looking so young and vulnerable that she wanted to run after him and give him a motherly hug. She suppressed the impulse, however, and merely watched to make sure he made it up the stairs safely. Hamlet, meanwhile, rose and looked from her to the departing teen.

"Go on ahead," she softly told the cat. "I think he could use a little company."

Seemingly agreeing with her assessment, Hamlet slipped down off the counter again and padded his way up the steps. Darla gave them a moment to get settled in; then she let herself out the side door again and headed up to her apartment. Once there, she sent a quick text message to Jake—*All OK ignore voice mail I'll explain tomorrow*—and then took a quick look at her computer screen. All stations were quiet once more. Leaving the program open, just in case, she flipped out the lights and then headed off to her bedroom.

One potential suspect in Curt's death had been ruled out, at least to her satisfaction, she decided as she shed her sweats for an oversized T-shirt and settled beneath her comforter. The teen's explanation regarding his involvement—or rather, the lack thereof—with the scrap metal thieves had the ring of truth. As for the actual murder, so far as she knew, Robert wasn't anywhere on Reese's radar. James would be equally glad to learn that Robert had nothing to do with either the Curt situation or the scrap metal thefts. But the older man would likely be as distressed as she to know of the teen's homeless plight.

Once again, Darla's redheaded temper simmered at the thought of Robert's father callously throwing out the boy to live on the streets. If not for her changing the cameras and thereby catching him, how long might Robert have spent sleeping in the bookshop's courtyard? And what would have happened once winter truly hit, when the temperatures dropped well below freezing and snow filled the walled-in terrace? Hopefully James could help her figure out a solution to Robert's situation.

But even with Robert now accounted for, that still left Curt dead and Tera missing.

Darla groaned and pulled the covers over her head. She'd

try again tomorrow with Robert's and James's help to puzzle out an answer to Hamlet's cryptic clues. And maybe by then Reese would have learned something of value from Tera's cell phone records and messages.

Which reminded her that she still had that piece of plastic in her corduroys that she needed to give to Reese.

Which also reminded her that, despite all the unpleasantness of the past few days, at least she'd had a very pleasant meal with a very pleasant man.

She smiled to herself in the darkness. *The proverbial sterling lining to the cumulonimbus*, as James would put it. For the dinner with Barry *had* been fun, and she was looking forward to a second time out with him. She suspected that he was looking forward to it, too. And she could even overlook the slightly underhanded way he'd managed to get her cell phone number.

Of course, the big question was, did he like cats . . . and more important, would Hamlet like him? She couldn't recall seeing the two of them in the same room together, and so the feline's opinion of the man was an unknown at this point. But she rather suspected the two would get along well enough.

After all, if the persnickety Hamlet could become BFFs with a goth teen, then anything was possible.

"WHAT DO YOU MEAN, YOU'VE NEVER HAD BISCUITS AND GRAVY FOR breakfast before? What kind of uncivilized place is New York, anyway?"

Smiling, Darla set down a basket of fluffy biscuits in front of Robert, followed by a bowl of white sausage gravy, and then sat beside him. They were upstairs in the bookstore lounge, which up until a few minutes ago had been Robert's temporary sleeping quarters. Today, he was wearing what she could only term a mod black turtleneck over his fashionably skinny black jeans. He'd tied the look together with yet another vest, this one made of some shiny silver fabric with a distinctly futuristic vibe to it.

By the time she'd come upstairs, he was folding the blanket that normally was tucked beneath the oversized coffee table that anchored the sofa with a pair of wingbacks. The coffee table served equally well as a dining table, which was a good thing, since Darla had decided to indulge her inner country cook that morning and go with the works.

First, however, she'd had to feed Hamlet, who had been sitting in her kitchen as usual, awaiting his kibble and fresh water. Apparently, his teen-sitting duties extended only through nighttime hours. While he crunched away at his breakfast, Darla gave him a few "atta kitties" for watching out for Robert overnight. And, to make up for the shrimp she'd not brought home for him from the Greek place, she'd cooked a small chunk of thick-sliced maple bacon just for him. Hamlet had finished off the crispy slab in a couple of appreciative bites and favored her with a *meow* of enjoyment in return.

At nine on the dot, as promised, she'd made her way down to the shop carrying the essentials of a good southern breakfast. In addition to the biscuits and gravy, she'd scrambled a few eggs, which she topped with cheddar, and cooked several slabs of the same kind of bacon that Hamlet had just enjoyed. To counteract all the heart-clogging grease, she had also carried down a carton of orange juice, all packed into an old picnic basket of Great-Aunt Dee's. The coffee was already taken care of, as she'd recently splurged on one of those single-cup brewers and installed it in the lounge.

Now, Robert picked up a biscuit and stared at it in bemusement. "Don't you have any, like, grape jelly?"

"Jelly is for toast. No, no, don't dunk it like a donut!" she exclaimed as he attempted to dip the biscuit into the gravy bowl. Picking up a biscuit of her own, she went on, "Hold your horses, and I'll show you how to do this right."

Though, of course, doing it right meant you also needed to follow said breakfast with a five-mile run so as to unclog any arteries that had become dangerously plugged up during the course of the meal.

"First, you tear the biscuit into little pieces that you put on your plate. Or, if you want to be formal about it"—she paused and grabbed a second biscuit—"you can slice it like a muffin and put both halves like so," she explained, arranging top and bottom alongside each other to form a flaky figure eight. "Now take your gravy and pour it over the biscuits. And I don't mean little dollops. Drown those suckers."

Still looking doubtful, Robert followed her lead, pouring until his biscuit halves were swimming in the creamy sausage and gravy mixture. "Now what?"

"Now eat it and thank God you're a country boy," she told him, grinning at the John Denver reference that she was pretty sure went straight over that city boy's head.

He took a tentative bite and swallowed. "Not bad." And then, while Darla watched in amusement, he went on to polish off four biscuits topped with gravy, most of the scrambled eggs and bacon, and half the carton of juice.

They weren't kidding about a teenaged boy's appetite, she thought, suddenly understanding why her contemporaries with high school–aged children were always complaining about their grocery bills. Her amusement faded, however, when it occurred to her that in addition to lacking a regular place to sleep, Robert might be missing a few meals as well.

Finishing off her own two biscuits, and vowing to have nothing but salad for lunch and supper as penance, she settled back in her chair and fixed him with a serious look. "All right, that's taken care of. Now, do you feel like telling me how you've been getting along these past few months? You said you stay with your cousin sometimes?"

"Yeah, except when he, you know, has a girl over. Or when he lets some other friend stay there. He's only got, like, one room, so I can't live with him permanently."

"So what do you do when you can't stay with him?"

"I stay with a friend, sometimes, or else in the park. And this girl I know who works at a gym, she sneaks me in some mornings so I can use their shower and washing machine. And I can lock one of the dressing rooms and sleep in there for a while, too."

He paused and took another swallow of orange juice. "Oh, I almost forgot. A couple of weeks before he fired me, Bill found out I needed a place and let me stay in his basement. He only charged me, like, a week's salary. I mean, there was a cot and a dresser and this old TV, and except one time when it leaked after it rained real hard, it wasn't too bad. But after what happened, I had to pack up again."

She wanted to ask him if he'd considered finding someplace where he could split the rent with a friend. But then it occurred to her that in this part of town it would probably take four or five friends to afford anything that wasn't another Bill's basement.

"I tried a homeless shelter one time," he went on, "but it was, like, kind of sad. Old dudes and ladies with kids, mostly. I figured they needed the space more than me, so I didn't go back. I mean, I'd feel bad if some five-year-old little dude had to sleep on the sidewalk because of me."

"But aren't you ever scared out there alone?" Darla persisted, recalling horror stories she'd heard about life on the streets.

He shrugged. "It's okay. Except one time two guys jumped me and, you know, stole my phone. Oh, and my shoes. But nothing, like, bad ever happened. I can take care of myself."

His tone as he related all this had been matter-of-fact, but now Darla saw a brief flicker of uncertainty in his expression that belied his air of unconcern. By her calculations, he'd been homeless for maybe six months, long enough that any feeling of adventure at fending for himself had likely been replaced by a growing sense of hopelessness. But if she had anything to say about it, last night's courtyard campout would be his last night on the streets.

Not wanting to push the subject, however, she turned the conversation back to southern cooking while they drank their coffee. Finally, glancing at her watch, she told him, "It's almost ten. Go ahead and stack all these dishes in the picnic basket while I get the register set up. If you think you can hold down the fort by yourself for a bit, I need to run down and visit with Jake."

She'd had a text message from the ex-cop waiting for her when she got up that morning: the words *cryptic much* followed by several question marks. She'd grinned a little at that virtual jab and texted back half a dozen exclamation points followed by *will stop by @ 10*. After all, given the number of times that Jake had left her hanging, a little payback was in order.

A few minutes after opening, Darla left Robert and Hamlet—who'd wandered down in search of more bacon—to talk to Jake. Besides needing to explain the Robert situation and perhaps get some advice, she still had the bit of pink plastic to pass on to Reese. She also wanted to know if there was an update on Tera. The fact that Jake had not been answering her phone last night might mean some new developments. On the other hand, she was almost certain that Jake's breezy text indicated that nothing earth-shattering had occurred in the interim.

Even before she knocked at Jake's door, Darla could hear the faint echoes of distorted guitar licks and throbbing bass drifting up from the basement apartment. Not exactly the sort of music she'd expect to hear playing at that hour of the morning, but then, she'd seen Jake's music collection before. Save for a scattering of jazz and classical, everything in her library was 1980s or earlier rock, emphasis on guitars, bass, and drums, from bands with names that included words like "death" and "black." Since Darla's own music tastes ran more toward light rock, with an occasional segue into country or New Age for variety, the two of them had agreed to disagree on that particular subject.

Figuring she'd never be heard over the headbanging if she knocked, Darla opened the door and walked on in.

Jake sat at her table typing at her computer, her mane of black curls bobbing in time to the music. She might have passed for a college student studying for a final save for the reading glasses, which Darla had never seen her wear before, perched on her nose. Jake glanced up at Darla's approached, waved her in, and snatched up a small remote control. The music promptly quieted from an unholy roar down to a breathy growl.

"Sorry," she said, plucking off the glasses and giving Darla a grin. "After yesterday, I had this urge to play a little music from the good old days."

"Which days were those, the Inquisition?" Darla replied with an answering smile. "Talk about torture, having to listen to that. What is it, grunge?"

Jake shook her head in mock dismay. "You really did lead a sheltered life back in Dallas, didn't you? Well, let me give you a little music education, kid."

She assumed an exaggerated storytelling tone, as if she were trying out for the Jersey version of *Faerie Tale Theatre*.

"Once upon a time, somewhere between the long-ago embarrassment that was disco and the current abomination that is Britney Spears, lived a genius of a musical genre

known as heavy metal. Their name is legion—Black Sabbath, Metallica, Judas Priest. And, of course, Iron Maiden,
which is playing for your listening enjoyment as we speak.
Some of these groups have spent thirty years on the charts,
which I kinda doubt Britney is gonna do. And these guys"—
she pointed in the direction of her very 1990s stereo—"are
as old as me and still putting out new albums and touring. So
listen and learn."

"Thanks, but no thanks. I value my eardrums and my
sanity." Darla plopped herself into one of the chrome chairs.
"Besides, I'm here to tell you about last night."

While Jake listened attentively, Darla recounted how
she'd found Robert and Hamlet sleeping in the courtyard,
and the teen's explanation as to how he'd become homeless.
When she was finished, Jake shook her head.

"I hate to tell you, but I've seen that happen more times
than I care to count. Not that the other extreme where you let
your kid live with you until he's forty is much better, but you
just don't toss a teenager into a city like this without any
money or life skills or some kind of plan. At least Robert has
a good head on his shoulders and has managed to take care
of himself to this point, but most of those kids aren't as
savvy as he is. They're out there looking for a place to live,
needing something to eat, wanting a little cash in their pockets. Pretty soon they've hooked up with a gang or a pimp or
a dealer, just to survive. And that's why the teen crime rate
is so high, and the teen victim rate is even higher. And don't
even get me started on teen suicide statistics."

"So what do we do with him?" Darla asked in concern.
"He can't sleep in the bookstore lounge indefinitely. And I
don't have room in my apartment for him."

"What about the Plinskis? Didn't Mary Ann say she was
looking for a new tenant?"

Darla nodded. "Actually, I thought about that on the way

down here, but no way could he afford the place working part-time hours here and for Putin's construction business. And I don't think the Plinskis would be too keen on a whole herd of teenage boys living in their garden apartment, which is what it would take to make the rent."

Then she brightened. "Maybe James has a spare room, at least temporarily until we figure something out."

"Yeah, I like how they have that whole father-son look going with the vests these days," Jake replied with a snicker. "Or maybe Reese would know a place."

"Reese! That reminds me."

Darla stood and reached into the pocket of her slacks to pull out the small plastic ziplock bag where, in emulation of Jake, she'd carefully placed the found piece of pink plastic. "When I was helping Barry clean up after Reese dumped all the construction junk onto his lawn, I found this caught in a piece of wood. It must have broken off the plastic case on Tera's phone. I don't know if it will do him any good, but I thought I should give it to him."

"Good work, kid. You never know about stuff like that."

Turning in her chair, Jake opened one drawer of the file cabinet behind her and pulled out a pair of long curved tweezers. Then, setting a clean sheet of paper on the table, she opened the small plastic bag and carefully shook out the piece of pink plastic onto that page. Putting on her reading glasses again, she used the tweezers to pick up the fragment and studied it with a frown. Finally, she set it down again and gave Darla a sharp look.

"I hate to break it to you, kid, but what you've got here isn't part of a cell phone case. It's a fingernail."

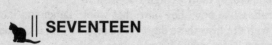

SEVENTEEN

"A FINGERNAIL!?"

Darla shoved back away from the table with the same sense of revulsion as if Jake had announced that she'd been carrying around an actual finger in her pocket. Jake, meanwhile, had used the tweezers again to pick up the bit of evidence and reseal it inside the bag.

"Actually, it's one of those acrylic nail tips," the ex-cop clarified. "You know, the kind you pay big bucks for at the salon. And once they're on, they're on. It takes a lot of work to pry those suckers off again."

Abruptly, Darla recalled the picture of Tera that Hilda had brought in the day before. A few of the fliers that Jake had made from the photo were still sitting on her table. Hands shaking, she snatched one up.

Jake had printed the poster in color. Despite the photo's small size, Darla could make out quite clearly the girl's manicure, her fingernails the same vibrant shade of pink as the nail tip that Darla had found. A sense of foreboding gripped her, and she could almost feel the warm biscuits and gravy that she'd enjoyed less than an hour before congealing into a cold lump in her stomach.

She looked up to see Jake nodding.

"Yeah, I'd put money on it that the nail tip belonged to Tera," the older woman said in a flat tone. "The question is, how did it—and Tera's phone, for that matter—get into the Dumpster?"

When Darla waited expectantly for an answer, she sighed and went on, "All right, I can think of a couple of possibilities. Number one: the fingernail fell off when she tossed the phone in there herself."

"But why would Tera throw her phone away?"

Jake gave her a hard look. "We've got to face it, Darla, there's a chance that she was the one who killed Curt. Maybe she planned it; maybe it happened in the heat of the moment. Either way, she wouldn't want anyone tracking her down. If she's like most kids her age, she would know about cell phone pinging from those detective shows on television, or maybe the movies. She runs out of the building, stops to toss her phone into the container, catches one of those fake nails on a piece of lumber, and pops it right off."

"And if she didn't kill Curt?"

"Then we move on to possibility number two. Maybe Tera had the bad luck to walk in on the killer as he was whacking her boyfriend, and gets killed, too, but taken elsewhere, and the murderer tosses her phone in the Dumpster."

Darla sat silent for a moment, grateful for the music that filled the unsettling gap in their conversation. She wasn't sure which scenario she found more comforting: Tera, alive but a murderer, or Tera, dead but an innocent victim. "I think I prefer possibility number three, whatever that might be," she finally said, drawing an answering nod from Jake.

"Yeah, me, too," the older woman said with a weary sigh. "So try to keep a positive attitude. Right now, this bit of plastic isn't anything more than another piece of evidence for Reese. I'll give him a call and let him know what you found."

Darla nodded, not trusting herself to speak for a moment. What Jake had said earlier about homeless teens like Robert could apply equally well to Tera. She might have an indulgent mother and a nice roof over her head; still, she was young and likely as naïve as most twenty-one-year-old girls. If she'd hooked up with Curt—who might have had his own share of shady acquaintances—who knew what sort of situation she had stumbled into by proxy?

While she considered this, a lyric from the music Jake was playing knocked at the door of her subconscious and then all but slapped her to full attention. Darla sat up straighter in her chair. The mournful introductory instrumental passage that had gone on for a good minute had given way to fast, pulsing lyrics. She could have sworn the lead vocalist had just rasped out the words "Murders in the Rue Morgue."

"This song . . . what's playing right now?" she demanded, straining to catch more of the spill of words.

Jake shrugged. "It's still Iron Maiden. I told you, that gruesome graphic novel you had on the counter yesterday made me remember this album of theirs. This cut is called 'Murders in the Rue Morgue.'"

The chorus repeated, and to Darla's surprise Jake joined in singing. *"Murders in the Rue Morgue, running from the Gendarmes, Murders in the Rue Morgue, running from the arms of the law."*

As the ex-cop continued singing along with the next verse, Darla stared openmouthed at her. "The Man in the Iron Mask . . . Murders in the Rue Morgue . . . Iron Maiden," she murmured while Jake sang along. "Could they all be related? But how?"

The song ended just then, and Jake shut off the player with her remote. "I'm heading out to meet Reese in a few," she said. "I'll let you know later if he has any ideas about Robert's situation. In the meantime, try not to worry about Tera. That's my job."

"I can't help but worry, it's in my DNA." Darla managed a small smile as she said that, but in truth she was more than a little fearful that the search for the missing Tera was not going to end well. As for learning the identity of the person responsible for Curt's death—and, possibly, Tera's fate—it seemed that Hamlet was still the only one with any insight into that. But as soon as she got back to the bookstore, she was going to start flipping through the clues he had left her and figure out what she'd missed.

"I SUGGEST THAT WE RETURN TO THE GRAPHIC NOVEL, *THE MURDERS IN the Rue Morgue*," James said soon after he arrived for his two o'clock shift. "For starters, I would make note of the fact that the title says 'murders,' meaning multiple. And if you will recall the particulars of the story, the two victims were mother and daughter."

"As in, Hilda and Tera?" Darla speculated before shaking her head. "Except that Hilda isn't dead. And hopefully Tera isn't, either."

Despite her resolution to work on Hamlet's clues first thing, the bookstore had been busy as usual on a Saturday morning, leaving her no time for detecting. But now that James had arrived for his afternoon shift, Darla had pulled out her list from the day before and was making new notes. James, after hearing about her Dumpster find and the interesting coincidence regarding the heavy metal song title, had agreed to contribute his own opinions.

And Darla's quick dismissal of his first observation did not go unchallenged.

"I will concede the fact that at least one of the pair is demonstrably still breathing, so perhaps we should view it as a symbolic death. The death of trust, the death of innocence, the death of—"

"Fine, I get the picture."

Darla added a second column labeled *Murders in the Rue Morgue*, under which she wrote the names *Hilda* and *Tera*, each followed by a question mark. "And don't forget our perfect tie-in to Porn Shop Bill. He's got the orangutan looks and the motive and bad temper to make him a killer. He definitely stays on the suspect list," she said, circling his name for good measure.

Though, to be fair, Reese had said that the man had only ever been convicted of assault, she reminded herself. Still, who was to say he didn't up the ante with Curt?

"Now, about the song." She wrote the words *Murders in the Rue Morgue (song)* over a third column, and beneath that added *Iron Maiden*.

"That's two 'irons,'" she pointed out, underlining the words in question, "plus a 'man' and a 'maiden' . . . and as you said, we've got the word 'murders' twice."

She underlined the rest of the words and then looked up at James, stricken. "It sure seems like the clues all tell us that Tera is dead, too. You've got a man, Curt, and a maiden, Tera . . . and two murders."

"Remember, Darla, it is *all* speculation at this point. Before we jump to more conclusions, perhaps we need to try our hand at word association."

James's words were calm, but Darla had seen a flash of dismay in his expression. No doubt he was struggling not to concede that she most likely was right. To keep up both their spirits, she decided not to harp on the theory.

"Fine. Let's start with Iron Maiden. What else do you think of when you hear those words besides a heavy metal band?"

"For the record, that would not have been my first association," James replied with pointed look. "I would go with the medieval instrument of torture, although I have read speculation that the Maiden never actually existed but was something of an archeological hoax."

Hoax or not, Darla reluctantly added *torture* to the list. "All right, what else?"

"The former British prime minister, Margaret Thatcher," was James's second response. "She was nicknamed the Iron Lady. And, if memory serves me correctly"—he paused and typed in a few swift words on the computer—"yes, it does appear that the prime minister's middle name is Hilda."

"You're kidding."

Darla peered over his shoulder at the official biography that he'd pulled up online. To her amazement, she saw that the British politician's middle name was indeed the same as that of the missing Tera's mother. Shaking her head, she added Hilda's name to the song column.

"Okay. What else do you think of when I say 'iron'?"

"How about, you know, Iron Man?"

The question came from Robert, who apparently had finished the task Darla had assigned him of stacking cartons of books upstairs and had wandered back down to the shop floor again. When she and James both turned slightly dumbfounded looks on him, the teen rolled his eyes.

"Don't you ever, like, go to the movies? The comic book guy in the red metal suit. His real name is Tony Stark."

"I saw the movie," Darla loftily informed him. "It's just that some 'comic book guy' sounds so, well, random."

"No more random than a British politician," James interjected, defending his protégé.

Darla shrugged. "All right, I'll give you that one. Maybe Curt knew a guy named Tony," she agreed and added that name to her growing list.

Robert was looking over her shoulder as she wrote. "Oh, I forgot to tell you. The theme song to the movie is called 'Iron Man.' It's by this ancient metal band called Black Sabbath . . . you know, the one with that guy that, like, eats bats. He's got a reality show or something on cable."

"Ozzy Osbourne," Darla supplied, feeling unduly proud to realize that she knew something about a band that an eighteen-year-old did not.

Then she frowned. Black Sabbath had been one of the names that Jake had mentioned in her paean to heavy metal music. Could this all be mere coincidence? It was as if anyone and everyone might have had a hand in Curt's murder.

"We're still missing some vital clue," she said, setting her pen down and trying to tamp down the frustration she could feel welling inside her. She glanced around for Hamlet, who'd been keeping himself scarce since breakfast. If he could snag one more book for her, maybe that would somehow make the connection clear.

James picked up the list and perused it for a moment. "It would seem we have sufficient data but, as you say, no logical tie. I fear that Hamlet is falling down on the job as a detective."

"Hamlet solves crimes?" Robert asked, eyes wide. "Hey, sweet!"

"I swear, we're not a bunch of crackpots," Darla said, "but Hamlet does seem to have a special knack for this detecting thing." She gave him a quick rundown on how Hamlet had helped solve crimes in the past. "But for heaven's sake don't say anything about Hamlet's book snagging to our customers," she warned him. "Who knows what people would think? Besides," she joked, "we don't want to be overrun with crazies wanting Hamlet to solve Jimmy Hoffa's disappearance and the Kennedy assassination." *Though the wily cat likely has insights into both crimes*, Darla wryly told herself.

Robert pantomimed zipping his lips. "Don't worry, I won't tell. And I'll keep an eye out for books on the floor."

"You do that. So, you feel like working a full shift today?"

The offer was not entirely altruistic. While the extra hours would give a small boost to the teen's paycheck—and the work would keep him off the streets for a few hours—she had another reason to hold him there. She wanted to pay another visit to Hilda to see if she could learn a bit more about the woman's relationship with her daughter. Maybe she'd be more forthcoming with Darla than with Reese or even Jake.

Robert, meanwhile, was eagerly nodding. "Yeah, sure. I'll stay."

"Perfect. James, Robert is going to finish out the shift with you. And I'm going to take off an hour or so to run an errand."

Once she was sure the pair had things under control, she grabbed her coat—the temperatures hadn't climbed above the midfifties, which was brutally cold as far as she was concerned—and started down the street. Mary Ann was on her stoop sweeping, and Darla paused for a quick greeting. After a few words about the weather, which the native New Yorker Mary Ann referred to as simply "mild," the old woman asked, "Did you get a chance to ask Detective Reese about the neighborhood watch yet?"

"Sorry, Mary Ann, he's been busy with the murder investigation, so I didn't want to call him. But I did send him a text, and I promise I'll ask next time I see him."

"Well, you can let him know that I have my baseball bat ready. Oh, and I found a set of walkie-talkies that Brother used to use back when he would go hunting with his friends. Perhaps they will come in handy."

Darla nodded, picturing the brick-sized walkie-talkie units of a couple of decades past. They'd likely be more useful as weapons, she thought as she smothered a smile. Hit someone over the head with one of those babies, and it would be lights out for a while.

They exchanged a few more pleasantries, and then Darla continued on. What exactly she would say to Hilda, she wasn't sure. To her relief, Great Scentsations was open. She'd half expected the door to be locked, but doubtless Hilda preferred keeping busy to sitting home in an empty apartment hoping for her missing daughter to return. Still, the atmosphere inside the shop was far different than the spalike mood the place usually evoked.

Instead of the usual New Age music, Gregorian chant greeted Darla as she stepped inside. And rather than the usual candle scent of the day, the sweet aroma of incense—frankincense, perhaps, overlaid with sandalwood—clung to the air. In fact, the shop smelled and sounded more like a cathedral—or perhaps even a funeral parlor—than a trendy body and bath store. And, for the first time since Darla had ever been inside the place, no customers browsed the aisles or waited at the register.

"My customers, they sense it."

Hilda's voice drifted to her, the tone oddly lifeless. Concerned, Darla headed for the back, where she spied the woman seated behind the register. Unlike the other day, Hilda had made a halfhearted attempted at styling her hair and had put on a bit of eye shadow and lipstick. But the makeup was too bright for her coloring—in fact, Darla suspected that the products might have belonged to Tera—and gave her skin a gray appearance that aged her a good ten years.

Not needing to feign concern, she asked, "What do they sense, Hilda?"

"Death."

The single flat word sent a small shiver down Darla's back. If this was the sort of vibe Hilda gave off to everyone who entered, then no wonder the store was empty. In fact, she might have hightailed it out of there herself save for the fact that, having seen Hilda in her current state, she was now concerned what the woman might do if left to her own devices.

"Hilda, the police are working very hard to solve Curt's murder," she assured her. "And both Jake and Detective Reese are doing their best to find Tera. You must be patient."

"You don't understand, Darla. If they do find her, it will be only to give me her body so I can bury her."

"Don't say that, Hilda. You mustn't give up hope. She's only been gone a few days. For all you know, she got mad and ran off to Atlantic City for a breather."

"Without her phone?" At Darla's look of surprise, the woman gave an emotionless chuckle. "Oh, yes, your Detective Reese came by this morning and told me that they found Tera's phone in the trash outside that Curt's house. And he didn't say, but I know he thinks I know how it got there."

"And do you know?" Darla asked, not sure she wanted to hear the answer.

Hilda gave an elaborate shrug. "Everything is in God's hands now. All I want is justice for my daughter."

Darla hesitated. Was Hilda simply a grieving mother fatalistically accepting what was the most likely outcome to Tera's strange disappearance, or was she a desperate woman coolly hiding something that she knew about Curt's murder?

Keep her talking, Darla told herself. *Maybe she'll let*

something slip that could help Reese, or even connect Hamlet's cryptic dots.

"If there's anything I can do to help you through this, Hilda, let me know," she said, meaning it. "But for now, remember those eye compresses you told me about? I think I should try those."

"Certainly." Hilda rose and gave her a jaundiced look. "And perhaps you could use a new foundation. Those freckles are charming on a young girl but, woman to woman, you're a bit too old for that look."

Biting back a retort—did anyone ever tell Julianne Moore or Bryce Dallas Howard that *she* should cover *her* freckles?— Darla followed the older woman toward the front of the store again. While Hilda lectured on tinted organic moisturizer and concealers, Darla found her arms filling with pricey jars and bottles. Just as she was beginning to fear she'd need to take out a small loan to cover it all, she heard the shop door open and the sound of a familiar voice.

"Hello, Mrs. Aguilar," Reese said as he strode down the aisle toward them.

Just as two nights ago when he'd shown up at her apartment, he was wearing his official prepping-for-the-promotion outfit of slacks, dress shirt, tie, and sport coat topped by the trench. Once again, it was belted behind him to swing wide open, and this time she could see his gold shield clipped to his belt. Definitely on official business.

He gave Darla a sidelong glance and added, "Darla, why don't you do me a favor and step over to the register for a minute?"

"Uh, sure."

She made her way to the front again in time to see a uniformed police officer about Reese's same height—though twenty years older and at least that many pounds heavier— enter the store. Darla watched as the officer lurked just inside the doorway, his expression impassive behind mirrored sunglasses. His stance, however, reflected alertness as he kept his gaze fixed on both Hilda and the detective.

Darla set down her would-be purchases on the counter and tried to ignore the sense of foreboding that had gripped. From the look of situation, she might not be finishing her transaction . . . good news for her bank balance, but potentially disturbing news for Hilda. Maybe they'd located Tera and were bringing her home, she tried to tell herself, though surely Reese would look a bit more cheery if the girl was all right. Or maybe the police had found Tera and instead were holding her for questioning in the matter of Curt's murder, and had come to inform her mother of that fact.

Of course, there was another, far more awful possibility that Darla swiftly dismissed from her thoughts even as she strained her ears to catch every bit of any conversation that might ensue. Said conversation, however, proved surprisingly brief.

"Detective Reese," Hilda greeted him in a frosty tone that out-chilled the weather. "Unless you have news about my daughter, I have nothing more to say to you."

"Well, ma'am, for the moment we're finished talking."

He reached under his coat, and Darla saw in shock the gleam of metal as he pulled out a pair of handcuffs. It took her a moment to register what the detective was doing, for this was one scenario that she'd never actually believed would happen. She still didn't believe it even when she heard Reese tell Hilda, "I'll need you to turn around, ma'am, so I can place these cuffs on you."

Hilda took a step back, the look on her face one of pure outrage. "How dare you say such a thing to me in my own store! What do you think you're doing?"

"What I'm doing, ma'am, is arresting you for the murder of Curt Benedetto."

EIGHTEEN

DARLA WATCHED IN DISMAY AS, WITHIN THE SPACE OF A FEW moments, Reese had handcuffed Hilda and, accompanied by the uniformed officer, was walking her toward the front door. After her first protest, the woman had made no sound, until they reached the register.

"Wait, my shop, it's all I have left," she cried, her Cuban accent once again slipping past her usually crisp tones as she dug in her heels and halted in midstep. Catching Darla's gaze, she went on, "*Dios mío*, I can't just leave like this! I'll be robbed blind. Please, Darla, can't you take care of things for me?"

"Ma'am, I need to ask you to come along," Reese told her. "We can send an officer back to lock up later."

"Reese, please let me handle this for her," Darla urged. "I'll close the place and set the alarm. You know the problems we've been having in this area."

The detective gave her a hard look but finally nodded.

"All right, ma'am," he told Hilda, "you can let Ms. Pettistone know where to find your keys."

In a choked voice, Hilda told her where to find her purse in her tiny backroom office and then gave her the alarm code. "It's 0-6-1-1 . . . Tera's birthday. The keypad is there by the front door. All you have to do is put in the code and press 'Enter,' and you'll have ten seconds to go out the door and lock it behind you."

"Don't worry, Hilda," Darla assured the distraught woman, though her own voice was trembling almost as much. "I'll take care of things here, and I'll let Jake know what happened, too. She can help you arrange bond or find an attorney."

"My purse . . . I'll need it."

"Better you leave your bag with Darla, ma'am," Reese told her. "I'll give you a minute to let her find your cell phone and stick a few dollars in your pocket so you'll have cab fare when you make bond, but the less you have to check in at the property desk, the better."

Remembering how the woman carried half her life around in her purse, Darla was in total agreement with that. She rushed to the back room and secured the woman's designer bag, found her phone, and then rifled through her wallet and counted out what she judged would be sufficient for a taxi ride. Returning to the front again, she tucked the cell and the cash into the pocket of Hilda's suit jacket. She'd give the purse and keys to Jake later to hold for the woman.

By that time, Hilda appeared past speaking; still, she gave Darla a grateful nod as Reese and the officer walked her out the door. Darla followed after them in time to see the uniformed cop loading the woman into a police cruiser. Reese's own beater was double-parked in front of the shop with one of those flashing lights on its dash. The sight of both vehicles with their strobing lights had drawn a small crowd of neighbors and passersby. Though Hilda had held her head high until the patrol car's door closed after her, Darla knew that the proud woman must be feeling thoroughly humiliated by the situation.

That was, if she was innocent.

Darla waited until the patrol car with Hilda inside had pulled away from the curb before she rounded on Reese. "Seriously, you're arresting Hilda for murder?"

"No, Darla, this was just a joke," he shot back, irritation obvious in his tone. "I like going around pretending to arrest people for crimes they didn't commit. In fact, I consider it a bad week if I don't fake arrest at least one innocent person in front of all their friends and neighbors for no good reason."

"Sorry, that came out wrong," she replied in a humble tone, realizing that she'd just questioned his professional competency. "I know you wouldn't arrest her without good cause. I just can't believe that Hilda could be capable of killing another person."

"Yeah, well, that's pretty much what every friend and relative of every murderer I've ever arrested says."

Then his expression softened. "Believe me, the circumstantial evidence on this one is pretty damning," he went on. "Pictures, phone messages, that sort of thing. I can't tell you much, but let's just say that your buddy Curt had a thing for serial dating mothers and daughters. And I don't think that Mama Aguilar was too pleased about sharing, if you get my meaning."

Mothers and daughters?

Abruptly, Darla recalled the last time she'd seen Curt alive. While discussing Tera, he'd made a winking reference to putting the moves on Hilda as well. At the time, she'd dismissed his comments as simply one of Curt's crude attempts at humor. But if what Reese was saying was correct, then the man's sly comment about Hilda had actually reflected a previous relationship with the woman. Could jealousy have been Hilda's motive for murder?

"What about Tera?" Darla asked, more unsettled by Reese's words than she wanted to let on. "Do you think Hilda . . . that is, could Tera's own mother actually . . ."

"Do you mean, do I think Mrs. Aguilar killed her daughter, too?" He sighed and scrubbed a weary hand over his face. "I'm not sure. And you might want to remember that we still don't have any proof one way or the other that the girl is even dead."

"But what about Tera's phone that you found in the Dumpster, and the fingernail I found later on? Isn't that evidence pretty convincing?"

"Just because those two items were in the container, it doesn't necessarily follow that there isn't a less sinister explanation," he replied.

Darla shook her head, recalling how she'd had the identical conversation with Jake just a few hours earlier. Maybe Reese could supply possibility number three.

"So how did the fingernail and the phone get into the Dumpster, then?"

"My best guess at the moment is that Mrs. Aguilar walked in on a little rendezvous between her daughter and Curt there at the brownstone. She'd had it up to there with the two-timer, went ballistic, and offed Curt with the crowbar . . . you know, your typical scorned woman."

Ignoring Darla's sharp look at that last sexist observation, Reese went on, "Then she struggles with her daughter—maybe trying to kill her, too, or more likely just trying to calm her down—which is when Tera loses the phone and the fake nail. The girl breaks loose and goes running into the night to escape Mommy Dearest. Hilda spots the phone and fingernail lying on the ground and has the presence of mind to toss them into the trash before she hotfoots it out of there."

"So you think Tera may still be alive?"

"I hope so, Red." He glanced at his watch and then gave her

an encouraging pat on the shoulder. "I've got to head down to the precinct now so I can chat with our suspect some more."

Then, as Reese headed toward his car, another thought occurred to her. "Wait, what about Barry?" she called after him.

He turned and quirked a brow. "What about your boyfriend?"

Something in his tone made her take on a defensive air as she answered, "Any reason I can't let *my boyfriend* know that someone has been arrested for his friend's murder? You know, common courtesy and all that? He's headed out to Connecticut tomorrow for the funeral on Monday, and I'm sure he'll want to update Curt's family on the situation."

"You might want to hold off on saying anything," was Reese's equally cool reply. "Mrs. Aguilar has been arrested, but she's not officially charged with anything yet. You never know, some judge might decide there's not enough of a case against her and dismiss the warrant. No need to get the family's hopes up yet."

All of which made sense, Darla decided as she watched Reese drive off into afternoon traffic. Even so, his brusque manner rankled. She could only hope that poor Hilda could hold her own against him. For despite the detective's claim that the circumstantial evidence was significant, something told her that Reese had arrested the wrong person.

She went back inside Hilda's shop, locking the door behind her lest an unwitting customer drop in before she could finish closing the place down. Then, realizing that she'd been gone longer than she'd planned, she pulled out her phone and called James.

"An unsettling turn of events," was his determination once she'd told him about Hilda's arrest. "I must say, I would not have anticipated this end. Is Detective Reese very sure about this?"

Darla snorted. "Well, he about bit my head off when I asked him the same question. So I'd say yes."

Letting James know she'd be back once she closed down Hilda's shop, she hung up and went on to the first order of business: locating the audio system and shutting off those chanting monks. Then she followed her nose to the source of the incense. It had almost burned itself to ash; still, as a precaution, she covered the small ceramic bowl with its matching lid. She left the products that Hilda had loaded her down with before Reese's untimely appearance for another time. All that remained was to check on the back door and shut off the lights before setting the alarm and heading out the front door again.

Without the mumble of the monks to add ambient noise, Darla's footsteps on the sleek wooden floors echoed in the small shop as she made her way to the office. She confirmed that the rear door was locked, and went to turn off the light, only to hesitate with her hand on the switch. Near the door sat a small wicker trash can, empty save for what appeared to be several torn photographs. On impulse, she stooped and plucked the handful of ragged-edged scraps from the can and carried them to the small desk.

It took but a few moments to piece together what proved to be four different photos. Surprisingly, all appeared to be taken in the same parklike setting as the now-poignant shot of Tera that appeared on Jake's missing-person flier. And as with that photo, these obviously were of professional quality, so crisp were the colors and so perfect was the lighting. One pose immediately caught Darla's eye. In composition, it was almost identical to the Tera photo, with its windblown subject gazing over her shoulder and coyly smiling at the unseen photographer.

The major difference was that the woman in that and the other three ravaged prints was not Maria Teresa Aguilar.

Darla turned over the pieces of that particular photograph one at a time until she found what she'd suspected might be there. Written across one back corner in pencil—for the photographer would have known better than to use anything else—was a single charming, if highly unoriginal, phrase: *You are so beautiful to me.* The penciled date was almost three months earlier. The sentiment was signed *Curt.*

Darla sighed a little as she flipped the pieces faceup again. Carefully, she fit the jigsaw puzzle that was the torn photo back together once more. Had the picture been ripped at a different angle, it might have been salvageable. As it was, the subject's elegant beauty now was marred by a tear in the photo paper that divided her pale features perfectly in half from top to bottom.

Too bad, she told herself, for she suspected it would be a long time before Hilda ever looked this happy again.

"*YOU ARE SO BEAUTIFUL TO ME.* YEAH, PRETTY CHEESY SENTIMENT," Jake agreed that evening as she and Darla sat together over a glass of wine in Darla's apartment while discussing Hilda's arrest. "I didn't tell you before, but Curt wrote the same thing on the back of the picture of Tera that Hilda gave me. I noticed it when I took it out of the frame to scan it. Hilda said Tera gave the framed photo to her as a gift, so Hilda probably didn't even know the writing was there."

Darla raised her brows in surprise. She had carried the torn photo back with her when she'd left Hilda's shop, virtuously telling herself that she wasn't protecting the older woman, but simply preserving evidence. After all, she had rationalized, what if Hilda had a cleaning service? They might come by and tidy up the place—including disposing of the trash—before Reese obtained a warrant to search the store for evidence to back up his arrest. Feeling only a bit guilty, Darla had turned over the pieces to Jake, who had sighed and muttered a few things about chain of custody before putting the torn photo in an oversized envelope to give to Reese later.

"But that's what I don't understand," Darla persisted. "Curt had been dating Tera for at least a month before he was killed. From what everyone indicated, the whole thing was going down right under her mother's nose. Why would Hilda wait so long to finally go bat-poo crazy and kill the guy?"

"Maybe because she really, really wanted the slimeball back? I hate to say this, but I think the dirt I dug up on him was what convinced her that wasn't going to happen."

"Dirt?" Darla echoed, trying not to sound too eager for an accounting of said grime.

Jake stared into her wineglass for a long moment, obviously debating with herself. Finally, she snorted and shook her curly mane. "Since Curt is dead and Hilda is currently in jail, I guess it can't hurt to tell you. But I need your word that nothing leaves this room. Breathe anything to anyone, and I'll take a crowbar to you myself."

Darla nodded her agreement and did Robert's zipped-lips pantomime. "Spill away. I'm all ears and no mouth."

"Apparently, that was Curt's thing, seducing mothers and daughters. His ultimate goal was a ménage à trois, but he was okay with sleeping with them one at a time, too. I managed to track down a couple of his previous girlfriends"— she gave that last word finger quotes—"and they were pretty explicit about how he went about finding and managing his victims. One of his hobbies was photography, and as you can see, he actually was pretty damn good at it. That was his usual 'in,' so to speak."

"Creepy," Darla said with a shudder of distaste.

Jake nodded. "I'd say he's definitely in the running for Jerk of the Century in the posthumous category. He targeted Hilda first. She was a willing enough victim on her own—

apparently, the jerkoid could be pretty charming when he wanted to be—but she didn't really get what it was he was after. For all her sophisticated air, I have the impression that she's pretty naïve when it comes to sex. Even when I explained it to her, she had a hard time understanding that's how he liked his relationships . . . and then, you should have seen her face. Mama T-Rex on the loose!"

"What about Tera?" Darla asked, something more than the prickly surface of her horsehair sofa making her shift uncomfortably in her seat. "Was she into that threesome scene? I mean, why would she want to date a guy who'd dated her own mother?"

"Who knows? Maybe it was one of those one-upsmanship kind of things . . . you know, proving she was hotter than her mom. Or maybe she was so thrilled at the idea of an older guy hitting on her that she didn't care. Anyhow, I think it had reached the point that both of them were ready to give him the heave-ho."

Darla nodded, relieved. Not that her acquaintances' sex lives were any of her business, but it was good to know that the two women had had some standards, even though both had stooped to dating Curt. "So what happens to Hilda now?"

"She called me this afternoon from the jail, and I arranged for a bail bondsman I know to work with her. Since you brought me her purse, I had her credit card number, which made things easier. With luck, Luis will spring her in the next few hours, and she can spend most of the night in her own bed."

But where, Darla wondered, would Tera be spending the night? And that brought to mind something else . . .

"At least I've got one bit of good news," Darla told her friend. "James agreed to let Robert stay with him for the next few nights, until we figure out a permanent place for him to stay."

"You mean, as in a forever home?" Jake asked with a

smile, using the familiar pet-adoption term. "Poor kid, you make him sound like he's a stray dog."

"Well, given what his father did, he might as well be," Darla replied, unable to hide a note of bitterness in her voice. "But James is putting out the word to some of his friends at the university in case they know any new graduates looking for roommates."

"Tell Robert to check out the bulletin board at the deli, too. That's as good a place as any to get the word out. And speaking of word"—she paused and gave Darla a significant look—"with all the hoopla, I never did hear word one about your date with Barry. C'mon, kid, your turn to spill."

Feeling herself blush a little, Darla recounted the evening out for her, up to and including the good-night kiss. Jake listened with a maternal look of satisfaction on her face. When Darla had finished, the other woman gave her a small toast with her now-empty wineglass.

"Good for you for finally getting back on the horse," she said with approval as she set down her glass and poured them both more wine. "Do you think you'll go out with him again?"

"Probably. I won't see him for a few more days, though. He said he's headed out first thing tomorrow for Connecticut. Curt's funeral is on Monday, and he wants to spend some time with the family helping them through this."

"That's decent of him. This has got to be almost as tough on him as it is on them. I just hope none of Curt's exes show up for this eulogy. That could get pretty nasty."

Fortified by their second glass, the two of them devolved into an exchange of black humor regarding some of the speeches that might result from outraged female funeral crashers. They were still laughing when Jake's cell phone let loose with the nasal falsetto of Barry Gibb. "Hi, Reese," she said as she pressed "Talk" and silenced the "Stayin' Alive" ring tone. She listened a moment and said, "Actually, I'm up in Darla's apartment. Do you want me to come meet you?"

Darla strained her ears to hear the other end of the conversation, but to no avail. Then, with a final, "Sure, see you in a bit," Jake hung up.

"That was Reese," she said unnecessarily as Darla gave her a questioning look. "He needs a hand on something related to the case, so I'm going to meet him down at Teddy's."

Which was, Darla had only recently learned, a smoke-filled bar frequented mostly by cops and ex-cops. She'd first heard about the place from Jake when the eponymous owner of the place had been threatened at gunpoint by a drug-addled thief intent on robbing the crowded place. The would-be robber had promptly found himself the target of two dozen or more gun-wielding patrons whom he'd discovered to his detriment were off-duty police officers. The incident—surprisingly, not the first in the bar's history—had made the papers and likely would earn the man a stiff prison sentence as well as the scorn of his fellow criminals.

"What about Hilda?" she wanted to know. "What if she makes bail before you get back home again? You've got her purse and house keys."

"If Hilda calls before then, I'll have her come here. You don't mind hanging on to those things until I get back, do you?"

Actually, Darla did. She privately suspected that she was the last person Hilda would want to see. After all, Darla had been a witness to the woman's arrest. Moreover, if Hilda had indeed taken a crowbar to Curt—no matter the provocation—she was not someone that Darla cared to be alone with in close quarters, either. Still, she could always have the woman wait outside while she handed her the bag from the safety of the foyer.

Thinking fast, she answered, "I'm not going anywhere else tonight. But why don't you leave her bag in the downstairs foyer behind the lamp table? You have the key to the building. That way, if you get home late you can pick it up without having to call me, and if Hilda gets here first, I'll just meet her downstairs." Jake agreed to the plan and a few minutes later had left to meet Reese, leaving Darla alone with Hamlet.

Or rather, she had assumed Hamlet was there until another hour had passed and he still hadn't come out to join her on the couch.

By ten p.m., she had begun to have serious concerns as to where the stubborn feline had gone. With Robert safely at James's place, there was no need for Hamlet to be wandering down to the courtyard or up to the lounge to keep the youth company. And Robert had taken pains to inform Hamlet of the change in plans before he left with the store manager.

Hey, little bro, I'm rooming with the Big Hoss tonight. That means you be sure to stay in your apartment where it's, like, nice and warm, he'd told the cat. Hamlet had *meowrmph*'ed in reply to indicate message received. Why, then, had the furry beast gone AWOL again?

"He'll be back," she declared in her best Ah-nold tone, trying to reassure herself. Hilda had not yet phoned, either. A quick look downstairs indicated that Jake had not returned, since the purse was still in the foyer where she had left it. With things so unsettled, she'd stay up awhile longer, she decided as she put down the best seller she'd been reading and flipped on the early news.

Unfortunately, the lead story was "local woman arrested in the bludgeoning murder of Brooklyn man." A photo of a grinning Curt, complete with gold chain, flashed on the screen, followed by a video taken earlier that day of Hilda doing the perp walk. Darla groaned and promptly flipped the station to the animal channel for a bit of respite, only to find that a repeat of a shark special was playing. She clicked through the channels again and settled on an infomercial featuring an over-the-hill action star hawking a piece of exercise equipment. But his nasally twang was soothing, reminding her of the folks back home, and before she knew it she'd fallen asleep.

When she awoke, it was to find herself curled uncomfortably on the sofa with another infomercial—this one for the Eggspert Egg Slicer—winding down. Hurriedly, Darla checked her answering machine and her cell phone in case she had slept through a call. Finding that neither Hilda nor Jake had phoned while she slept, she wearily made her way downstairs to check on the purse. It was gone, meaning that Jake had made it home and retrieved the bag for later.

She had just started up the stairs again when her sleep-fogged brain cleared enough for her to realize that the entry-way lighting seemed strange somehow. She could see flashes of blue and red, almost as if a police car was parked right outside her door. Fully awake now, she hurried back to the door and peered past the curtains covering the glass. She gasped to see, not a police vehicle, but an ambulance parked on the street in front of her building.

Swiftly, she unlocked the front door and stumbled out into the cold night. Jake, dressed in her long black leather duster over gray sweats, was standing near the Plinskis' stoop, a protective arm around Mary Ann. The old woman was dressed for sleep in a long pink flannel nightdress. She'd wrapped herself in a thick gray shawl the same pewter shade as the single long braid that hung past her thin shoulders.

"Mary Ann . . . Jake . . . what's wrong?" Darla called as she rushed down her steps to join the pair.

Mary Ann turned toward her, and Darla saw that tears streaked her wrinkled cheeks. In a quavering voice, the old woman cried, "Darla, it's Brother. I-I think he's had a heart attack."

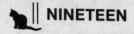# NINETEEN

"OH, THANK GOD! I'M SO GLAD TO HEAR THAT. RIGHT, SEE YOU soon."

Darla hung up her cell and turned to James and Robert. They had been leaning against the bookstore counter listening to her side of the conversation with matching expressions of hopeful concern. It was an improvement on the gloomy looks that the pair had worn ever since she had given them the lowdown on the previous night's medical emergency when they arrived at the store. Robert, in particular, had taken the news hard.

"He's, like, the only grandfather I have," the teen had mumbled, looking dangerously close to tears. "If he needs, you know, blood or something, I'll donate."

Darla hadn't had the heart then to explain that his impulsive offer wouldn't be needed for the old man's particular condition. She tucked the phone back in her pants pocket and gave the pair a big smile.

"That was Jake. The doctor just checked in on Mr. Plinski again, and he's doing fine. Jake will be bringing Mary Ann home in just a bit, and her brother should be out of the hospital in another day or so."

"Ah, then apparently the diagnosis of a minor heart attack that the emergency room physician gave last night was correct," James said with a satisfied nod.

For his part, Robert let loose with a fist pump and a fervent, "Sweet!"

"Sweet is right," Darla agreed, sitting down on the register stool and giving an audible *whoosh* of relief. "I have to admit, I was pretty worried last night. When the paramedics carried Mr. Plinski out on that wheeled stretcher, he looked in pretty bad shape."

In fact, Darla had feared the old man was already dead, recalling the small, still figure that she'd seen strapped to the gurney. But then he'd momentarily lifted a wrinkled hand in his sister's direction, indicating he'd not yet gone to that big antique store in the sky. Mary Ann, of course, had wanted to jump into the back of the ambulance with her brother, but Jake had gently dissuaded her.

"That's no place for you," she had said as the paramedics loaded the old man into the EMT rig and then, lights still flashing, pulled away from the curb. "The ride is bumpy as hell, and the paramedics will be busy taking care of your brother. You don't want to end up all bruised. I know which hospital they're taking him to. We'll get you there another way."

"We can take Maybelle," Darla had promptly volunteered, speaking of the old Mercedes sedan that Great-Aunt Dee had left her. The vehicle was parked in a garage perhaps five minutes' walk away. "Jake, why don't you take Mary Ann back to her apartment so she can put on some proper clothes. I'll go back inside for my keys and then go get Maybelle."

Normally, Darla would have been leery about running

through the darkened streets at that hour of the night, but concern gave her feet what James would call the proverbial feathered appendages. She jogged her way to the garage and, almost hyperventilating, took the elevator up to where her car was waiting. As always, it turned over with a single twist of the key, and a few minutes later she was parked at the curb of the brownstone while Jake helped a distraught Mary Ann down the concrete stairs.

"We can't all go," Jake was quick to point out. "I haven't heard from Hilda yet, and we can't leave her stranded if she gets out before we're back from the hospital."

Darla had considered that a moment and then quickly tossed the car keys in Jake's direction. "You go. You know where the hospital is, and you're better in an emergency. But be sure to call me when you know something, no matter what time it is."

She'd given Mary Ann an encouraging hug and helped her into the passenger side, where the frail woman barely made a dent in the padded leather seat. She waited until Jake had made a thoroughly illegal U-turn before heading back inside her own apartment again.

It had been almost five in the morning before Jake had awakened her from a restless sleep with a call telling her Mr. Plinski's condition was serious but not dire, and they'd know more soon. Barely had she drifted back to sleep again, however, when Hilda called saying she was waiting downstairs.

Feeling punchy from her erratic night of missed sleep, Darla had grabbed her spare key to Jake's garden apartment. Groggily, she had gone down to retrieve the woman's handbag while Hilda waited in the taxi that was idling at the curb.

Hilda had looked as haggard as Darla felt. Her words of thanks had been brief as she reached through the cab window for her purse and then waved the driver to go on. Darla had chalked that brusque reaction to a combination of embarrassment and exhaustion. With a shrug, she had taken a moment to call Jake at the hospital and let her know that Luis had managed to spring Hilda and that the woman had reclaimed her bag and keys. Then, praying no one else would disturb her for a while, she had returned to her bed for a few more hours' sleep before the store's usual Sunday opening time of noon.

When she'd awakened, it had been very close to that hour. She'd had time only to hop into the shower and then pull on jeans and a bright yellow sweater. Since she didn't have time to tame her hair, which had frizzed into an auburn cloud overnight, she'd twisted it into a quick bun, which she'd secured with a pair of wooden hair sticks. She'd made it downstairs just in time to see Robert and James, wearing matching green plaid vests, come walking up the stoop.

And now, while Robert and James celebrated the good news about their elderly neighbor with fist bumps and high fives, Darla was unhappily considering the fact that not everything was all right. Hamlet had never shown up that morning for his breakfast. And now, at almost half past twelve, the inconsiderate feline still was missing.

"James, Robert . . . I'm worried about Hamlet. I didn't get to tell you earlier in all the excitement about Mr. Plinski, but the cat has been gone since sometime last night. The last I remember seeing him was when the two of you left the store."

"What?" Robert demanded, his grin fading. "Like, no way. I told the little bro to stay here."

"I know you did, but seriously, when I see that little so-and-so again—"

"I am sure you looked everywhere," James smoothly interjected before Darla could finish her threat, "but maybe we should make another sweep through the store in case he is simply being stubborn about joining us."

The three of them promptly spread out in different directions. Darla knew that it wasn't unusual for Hamlet to be discovered curled up in some out-of-the-way nook, or else for him to be found lounging atop a bookshelf that appeared inaccessible. But what *was* unheard of was for the cat to skip his breakfast. Hamlet did not operate well on an empty stomach.

A few minutes later, they regrouped at the register.

"No Hamlet," Darla said with a shake of her head. "I even checked that little gap between the bookshelves near the heat register, but no sign of him."

"I looked upstairs in the lounge and out in the courtyard," Robert offered, "but he wasn't, like, there, either."

"And I, too, had no luck . . . although I did find this on the floor near the reference area," James said and handed Darla a thick paperback with a tricolor binding of black, red, and yellow.

"English-German, German-English Dictionary," Darla read from the cover without much enthusiasm before tossing it onto the counter. "I guess that will come in handy if we want to say *Where the hell is the damn cat?* in German."

"If I recall from my studies many years ago, that would be *wo die Hölle die verdammte Katze ist,*" James replied in a passable Teutonic accent. "But I agree, that is not much help under the circumstances."

"Maybe he was, you know, worried about Mr. Plinski," Robert suggested, sounding pretty concerned himself. "I'll go check their stoop."

He was back in a few moments shaking his head. "The little dude isn't there."

"I'll check the apartment again," Darla decided. "You know how he is. He probably snuck back in already and is up there laughing at us dumb humans."

But Hamlet wasn't upstairs, nor had he made an appearance by the time Jake and Mary Ann arrived back at the brownstone an hour later. The old woman looked surprisingly alert for someone who had spent most of her night sitting in a hospital waiting room.

"My dear, I am so grateful to you for lending us the car," she exclaimed to Darla as Jake helped her out of the Mercedes. "I used to ride around in Maybelle with Dee quite often. That made the trip to the hospital rather comforting, like my old friend was watching over me."

"I'm glad I could help in some way . . . though, of course, Jake is the real champ here."

Mary Ann nodded and gave the ex-cop a teary smile. "I must confess, I phoned Jake even before I dialed 9-1-1. I was so flustered when I woke up and heard Brother calling to me. He said he'd been in pain for a good half hour before he finally decided that something was wrong. The nice doctor who took care of him said things could have been much worse if he'd waited any longer."

"All of us were relieved to hear that he should be fine," Darla assured her. "And we'll all lend a hand if you need help while Mr. Plinski is laid up." Turning to Jake, she added, "You look beat. Why don't you get Mary Ann settled and then get some rest yourself. I'll take Maybelle back to the garage."

"Thanks, kid," Jake replied with a tired smile that suddenly showed her age. Tossing Darla the keys, she admitted, "Now that the worst of it is over, I'm about ready to drop."

Darla assumed her friend meant the medical emergency with Mr. Plinski. The specter of the missing Tera, along with the fact that Hilda had been charged with the brutal murder of a man they all knew, loomed large still. And that didn't even count the situation with Robert. He still needed, as Jake had so wryly put it, his "forever home." But for the moment, her most immediate concern was finding Hamlet.

Darla went back into the shop for her phone and coat. "I'm taking Maybelle back to the garage," she announced. "And I'll walk back the long way just in case Hamlet is doing a little Sunday stroll out there."

"Take your time," James urged her, "and I will be certain to call you if he shows up while you are gone."

On the brief drive to the garage, Darla kept a keen eye out for a sleek black flash. As was to be expected, the missing feline was not to be found among the shoppers and walkers all out enjoying the crisp weather. She reminded herself that it was afternoon, which equaled prime catnapping time. Wherever Hamlet was, he likely was snoring away as he rested up for the arduous journey back to the bookstore.

She didn't dare consider the alternative, that he'd had a run-in with a vehicle while roaming and that his sleep might be of the permanent sort.

By the time Maybelle was safely parked, Darla had mapped out a search route in her mind to include one particular place: the brownstone belonging to Barry. It had occurred to her that Hamlet, for reasons known only to his wily feline brain, might have made another trip to the basement where they'd discovered Curt's body. With Barry on his way to Connecticut, she wouldn't be able to go inside, but she could walk around the place and peer through the basement windows.

She did not slack on searching along the way, though. She peered behind garbage cans in alleys and behind decorative floor pots lined up along storefronts. She even made her stealthy way down to a few garden apartments to peek behind the bicycles chained securely at the bottom of their entry steps. Once, a sprawl of black fur atop a short concrete column sent her hurrying to check out a stoop halfway down one block. Unfortunately, the feline sunning itself there proved to be female and of the tuxedo variety—definitely not Hamlet.

"As soon as I find you, I'm going to slap a GPS collar on you," she threatened, drawing a disdainful look from the tuxedo cat, who likely assumed the words were meant for her.

Shoving her hands deep into her coat pockets—as usual,

she had neglected to bring gloves—Darla continued in the direction of Barry's brownstone, one block over from where the tuxedo cat lived. Her pace was faster now, but she warned herself not to get her hopes up. Chances were he wasn't there, either, and she'd just have to wait until it pleased His Furry Highness to come home.

Her next stop on the way, however, was one she hadn't planned. Having made a detour down a street she'd never traveled before, Darla walked past a dingy shop front and then did a literal double-take. The neon sign in its window proclaimed in large red letters, "Bill's Books and Stuff." And, even worse, as she halted for a moment in startled confusion—his nasty porn shop was located this close to her nice store?—the shop door opened and Bill himself lumbered out into the daylight.

He recognized her almost as quickly as she recognized him, and he sneered.

"Whaddaya doing in front of my shop?" he demanded, his simian jaw thrusting in her direction. "No, don't tell me. You're looking to steal another one of my employees."

"I most certainly am not," she choked out, even as she reminded herself she didn't owe the man an explanation.

His sneer morphed into a cold leer. "Well, then, let me guess. I know, you're here to buy yourself one of those ladies' toys. A single gal like you, all alone at night . . ."

He trailed off suggestively, and Darla felt heat flame her cheeks. She'd thought Curt with his extracurricular activities was bad, but Bill the Porn Shop Owner made him look like the model of civility. Thank goodness poor Robert didn't have to suffer under this jerk's influence anymore!

Fleetingly, she considered a few responses of the anatomically impossible kind and then decided dignified silence was her best resort. Given Robert's accounts of the man's foul temper, taunting him would be foolish at best . . . and dangerous at worst. Turning on her heel, she hurried on in the direction that she'd been going, trying as she did so to ignore the man's mirthless laugh and his parting crude comment, "Hey, c'mon back! We got a two-for-one sale going on!"

A man like that definitely bore watching, she thought in outrage, though her burst of anger was swiftly replaced by an unsettled feeling. Why, she might have been standing within a few feet of Curt's murderer. Reflexively, she glanced over her shoulder, suddenly fearing that the man might have followed her. Had Reese questioned him at all, she wondered, or was the cop so set on pinning the crime on Hilda that he'd overlooked someone who was, in Darla's view, a far more likely suspect? Either way, she'd be steering clear of that particular block in the future.

She only hoped that Hamlet would do the same!

Just to be careful, she took a slightly circuitous route away from that neighborhood, checking another time or two behind her and breathing a relieved sigh when she saw no sign of Bill's apelike visage leering after her. It wasn't until she reached Barry's brownstone a few minutes later that the heat in her face finally faded and her heartbeat was back to normal. Even though it was still midafternoon, the angle of the sun through the surrounding buildings left this portion of the block in early shadow. She shivered a little as she surveyed the house from the sidewalk. Without Barry there to lend his placid company, the feel of the building had changed. Something about the place now set off her hinky meter.

No longer was it simply a once-charming Greek Revival bravely holding up under the excesses of time and the previous owners' careless remodeling. Instead, the building had assumed an air of cold abandonment that dared anyone to cross its threshold. It wasn't simply that a murder had occurred on its premises, though that was bad enough! Wrapped in afternoon shadows, it hunkered behind its single shielding oak, its few unboarded windows seeming to watch for the errant passersby who strayed too close and needed to be taught a lesson.

At that last thought, Darla gave herself a firm mental shake. Shades of *The Haunting of Hill House*, she told herself with grin at her overwrought imagination. The place might be a dump in its current state, but Barry had mentioned nothing about any sinister history connected to it. The only thing that walked in that house was a mouse or rat or two—and possibly a certain black feline.

She softly groaned. *Way to psych yourself up, kid,* would have been Jake's grinning response to the situation. But Darla cheered herself by remembering that she needed only to do an exterior search. Barry would have locked the place before he left. With that thought, she stepped around the woven construction fencing and made her way to the basement windows. There, she knelt in the damp earth. Clutching the security bars, she peered through the dirty glass into the darkness.

Or, rather, what should have been darkness. From what little she could make out through the layer of black grime coating the window, most of the basement was cloaked in deep shadow, save for a small light that seemingly had been left burning in one corner beyond the boiler. She frowned, scrubbing at the glass with her hand in an attempt to clean it.

She succeeded only in smearing about the dirt so that her view of the basement was even murkier, if that were possible. Had the crime scene investigators forgotten one of their flashlights? Or else maybe neglected to turn off one of Barry's clip-on lamps? But the light meant that if Hamlet was in the basement, with luck she would spy him, or, at least, maybe a stray beam would catch his wide green eyes.

"Hamlet! Hamlet, are you in there?"

She strained her ears for some sound in reply; then, hearing nothing, she scooted over to the next window. Squatting in front of the glass, she tried again. "Hamlet! Kitty, kitty, kitty! Come on out!"

Barely had the words left her mouth than she thought she saw through the window's veil of dirt a shadow move within the deeper darkness of the basement. "Hamlet," she called again, reaching through the bars to rap at the window, "are you in there? Come out like a good cat, would you?"

The shriek of metal hinges nearby made her jump. She gave a reflexive shriek of her own and fell backward, landing with an ungraceful *thud* into a sitting position there on the grass. Heart pounding wildly, she shot a quick look toward the porch. Someone was hanging out at what was supposed to be an empty brownstone!

Her view of the door was blocked by the pile of brick and its wrapping of orange construction fencing, so her imagination—already running full bore—had a few fleeting moments to conjure various scenarios. Perhaps she'd stumbled upon the scrap thieves in their work, and they didn't want any witnesses. Maybe Bill had guessed she suspected him of Curt's murder and followed her, planning to drag her into the empty house and kill her, too. Or it could be that Curt's ghost was lonely with Barry out of town and was looking for some company.

She scrambled to her feet, not liking any of these possibilities and poised to take off at a dead run. If Hamlet was in the basement, he'd just have to fend for himself until she could return with reinforcements—the kind wearing badges and carrying guns! But the adrenaline that had been rushing through her veins slammed into a figurative wall of confusion when she saw just who was standing on the porch staring down at her.

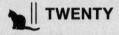 **TWENTY**

"BARRY? I-I THOUGHT YOU WERE IN CONNECTICUT," SHE exclaimed as she self-consciously brushed the dirt from her pants. Not that he looked any better. His faded jeans were streaked with dirt, as were his well-worn running shoes, while the tattered plaid jacket he wore over an equally dirty T-shirt likely had never seen the inside of a dry cleaner's. If it weren't late fall, she would have guessed from his appearance that he'd been gardening.

Barry, meanwhile, was observing her with a look of surprise that seemed tinged with something very close to anger.

"Darla? What are you doing here?"

"Looking for Hamlet. The little wretch ran off again, and I was afraid he'd sneaked back into your basement." She gave him a quizzical look of her own. "What happened to Curt's funeral?"

Barry shook his head in disgust.

"There was a problem with the family," he said with a

dismissive wave of his heavy work gloves. "They couldn't decide whether to bury Curt or have him cremated. He didn't leave any instructions behind—hell, who expects to die at our age?—and it was turning into this whole family feud between his sister and their mother. I called this morning, and all the plans were still up in the air, so I figured I'd get some work done today and head out tomorrow."

"I'm sorry to hear that. There's nothing worse than when a death touches off a war within a family."

"You're telling me." His expression hadn't lightened any. "So, about Hamlet . . ." He trailed off questioningly, and Darla realized that, for all intents and purposes, she was trespassing on the man's property.

"Sorry," she said, feeling unaccountably guilty. "I don't normally go around looking in people's windows, but he's been missing for almost a day now. We've looked everywhere else for him, so your place is kind of my last hope. Cats are creatures of habit. I thought there was a good chance he'd be here."

Barry shook his head. "I was just down there putting a part on the boiler, and I didn't see hide or whisker of him. But I'll be glad to call you if he turns up."

"Oh." Darla didn't bother to hide the disappointment in her voice. "Listen, would you mind very much if I took a look inside to satisfy myself? If he's there, he might be afraid to come out if it's just you."

The man hesitated. Finally, he nodded, though she heard a note of reluctance in his tone as he replied, "I don't mind if you take a look in the main house, but I really wish you wouldn't go in the basement."

"But that's probably where Hamlet is, if he's here!"

"Darla, I told you I didn't see any sign of him down there, and I've been working in the basement for a couple hours now."

He paused and spread his gloved hands in a helpless gesture. "I've got the boiler taken apart, and I had to move a few things, so it's not easy walking around. Beside, with that whole Curt situation, I don't like the idea of anyone going down there anymore. In fact, I'm thinking really seriously about plastering over that door."

Then, when Darla stared at him, he added with a deprecating smile, "I know it sounds superstitious, but I don't think I can keep working here in the house otherwise."

"Sure, I understand," Darla said with a sympathetic nod. "I'll just take a look around the main floors and call for him for a few minutes, and then I'll let you get back to work."

He nodded and stepped aside so she could enter in front of him. Darla wrinkled her nose. It was obvious that no one had been there for the past few days. The place had taken on a stale and faintly unpleasant smell, as if the rats had had a field day in Barry's absence. Opening the windows wasn't an option, since all but those of the upper floors were boarded up.

"I have to say, I sure was relieved to see it was you on the porch," she told him to break what once again had become an awkward silence between them. "While I was out looking for Hamlet, I ran into my employee Robert's old boss, a guy named Bill Ferguson, who knew Curt, too. He owns an adult bookstore a few blocks from here. Maybe you know him?"

Then, when Barry gave her a surprised look, she realized how that must have sounded. "I didn't mean to imply that you hang out at adult bookstores," she hurriedly corrected herself. "I just thought that since Curt knew him, you might have run into him before."

"Can't say I have." Then, with a frown, he added, "But what would this guy be doing at my place?"

"Maybe following me?"

The likelihood of such a scenario sounded pretty weak

now that she said it aloud; still, considering how neatly Hamlet's clues pointed to the porn shop owner, she forged on. "The last time Curt was in my store was when Bill came by to harass Robert. He didn't hide the fact that he and Curt had some bad blood between them, which I mentioned to the police. So if Bill picked up on the fact that I think he might have been involved in Curt's death, he could be gunning for me, so to speak."

"Really?" His expression sharpened, and he gave her a quizzical look. "But I heard on the news that they arrested Hilda Aguilar for murder . . . not that your cop friend bothered to mention that little fact to me."

"Reese did arrest her," she agreed, relieved that Barry knew that much, so that she wouldn't have to break her word to Reese about keeping her mouth shut. "I'm sure he planned let you know. But Hilda is out on bail now." Darla paused and shook her head in dismay. "I don't know what sort of evidence the police think they have, but I just can't see Hilda murdering anyone."

"Yeah, upstanding citizen and all that. The problem is, you never know about people, do you?"

His tone held a note of bitterness now, though she couldn't really blame him. He'd just lost a friend that he'd known for almost a lifetime, and the person arrested for the crime was someone he knew, at least peripherally. Which, she assumed, must be almost worse than a random killing by a stranger. Feeling again like an intruder, although Barry had invited her in, she decided to get on with looking for her lost cat and then get the heck out of there.

"Hamlet, here kitty!" she called, poking her head into each of the downstairs rooms for a look. In between shouts, she listened, hoping for the sound of an imperious *meow*. Each time, she heard nothing.

She tried the next floor as well, carefully skirting the

holes in the subfloor that were still to be repaired. Her search there and on the third floor yielded no results. Discouraged, she made her cautious way back downstairs to where Barry waited for her.

"No cat?" he asked.

She shook her head. "Nope, no cat. I just don't know where he could have taken himself off to."

"Maybe you should call the humane society in the morning. Animal control might have picked him up."

Privately, Darla doubted that any animal control officer would be able to snare the wily feline, but she nodded. "If he's not back by morning, that's what I'll do."

"All right, then."

The words hung awkwardly between them, and Darla realized that he was looking for a polite way to tell her to go. So she would be polite and not make him say it out loud. "I've taken up too much of your time. I guess I should head back to the store now."

"Probably. Sorry, I didn't mean that like it sounded," he added with an apologetic smile, looking more like the old Barry she knew as he pulled off his gloves and stuffed them in the back of his belt. "Normally, I'd be thrilled to have your company, but I've got things I need to finish before tomorrow, since I'll be gone for a few days."

"And daylight is burnin', like my dad always says," she answered with a smile of her own. "Don't worry, I understand."

Before she could wish him a good trip for yet a second time, however, her cell phone rang. She pulled it from her pocket gave a quick look at the caller ID.

"It's James. Maybe he's calling to say that Hamlet is home." Pressing the "Talk" button, she eagerly answered, "Hello, James. I'm still here at Barry's place. Did you find Hamlet yet?"

"No, I am afraid he is still missing. But that is not why I am calling."

"James, hold on a minute. Barry," she said to the man before her, "James says that Hamlet's still not back yet. Do me a favor and keep an eye out for him, just in case he does head in your direction, okay?"

"Darla?"

James's voice was soft in her ear, his tone suddenly urgent. "I'm going to ask you a question. Don't answer anything besides yes or no. Do you understand?"

I'm going to ask you a question. Don't answer anything besides yes or no.

Darla abruptly frowned. For the first time since she'd know him, Professor James T. James was speaking in—dare she say it?—contractions. Something serious had to be going on, indeed.

"Yes," she replied, turning a little so that she wasn't facing Barry.

James's voice was still soft but direct as he asked, "You said you're at Barry Eisen's place. Is he by chance standing there with you?"

"Yes."

"All right, Darla, I want you to listen very carefully. Pretend I'm talking to you about the store, and step away from him as if you need a little privacy. We can't afford for him to overhear anything. And whatever you do, don't react."

"Yes?" she answered, feeling her heart rate beginning to increase as she gave Barry an apologetic shrug—*Sorry, it's business*—and walked a few feet from him. Obviously, this was something very, very bad.

"Do you recall before you left the store that I found the German-English dictionary lying on the ground?"

"Yes."

"I suspect that Hamlet must have pulled it down before he

ran off. And I am embarrassed to say that I didn't make the connection until just now, while Robert and I were looking at the other two books of Hamlet's."

"Yes?" she persisted, impatience and concern warring within her. Would the man just get to the point!

"The one word connecting all of Hamlet's clues is 'iron.' *The Man in the Iron Mask*, *Murders in the Rue Morgue*, or rather, the song of the same name as sung by Iron Maiden. Do you know what the German word for 'iron' is, Darla?"

"No."

"*Eisen*. The German word for iron is *Eisen*. Darla, I think Hamlet is trying to tell us that Barry Eisen murdered Mr. Benedetto."

Barry a murderer!?

Darla's grip on her cell tightened as she struggled not to physically react to the fact that her store manager had just informed her that she was standing within arm's length of a cold-blooded killer. Assuming, of course, that James was correctly interpreting Hamlet's clues, she faintly reminded herself. For even if Barry had killed his friend, the question remained . . . why?

"Darla, did you hear me? Darla?" came James's voice in her ear, sounding oddly distant.

She gave herself a mental shake. *Don't go to pieces . . . not with Barry standing right there.*

"Yes, James, I heard you," she managed, assuming the tone of a serious shopkeeper who had learned that something was amiss at her store. "I'll head back to the shop right away."

"You're sure you can leave without his suspecting anything?" James persisted.

She glanced at the front door. The path to it was clear, and though the hinges stuck a little, she could manage it. All she needed to do was walk right out, just as she had been in process of doing.

She nodded, though of course James could not see her through the phone. "I was just telling Barry good-bye, anyhow. Try to keep everyone there happy, and I'll be back soon."

"I shall be timing you," he warned, returning to his usual precise tones, "and if you are not here in a reasonable few minutes, we shall come looking for you. In the meantime, I shall notify Jake so that she can contact Detective Reese regarding the situation."

"Sounds good, James. Bye."

She hung up the phone and stuck it back in her coat pocket; then, with an effort, she looked up to meet Barry's politely questioning gaze. No way he was a killer, she told herself. She'd gone out on a date with the man, had even kissed him!

Darla took a steadying breath. James—and Hamlet—had to be wrong. After all, she'd been with Barry when they'd discovered Curt's body, and she'd seen his stunned expression at the sight of his dead friend. No one could be that good of an actor. Could they?

Guess you've never been to the movies, kid, she could hear Jake telling her the first time Barry's name had come up in connection with Curt's murder. *They give out awards for that kind of thing.*

Fearing she'd need to give an award-winning performance right this moment, she managed a smile. "Sorry, a little disaster at the store, gotta go," she said in a rush. "I'll see you when you get back."

"Sure thing. I'll walk you to the door."

Darla did her best not to flinch as he lightly caught her arm and escorted her. She hadn't realized before how strong his grip was. She remembered, too, how he'd talked about playing baseball in high school, and later in college. It occurred to her now that there couldn't be much difference between swinging a bat and swinging a crowbar.

Quit thinking about it, and just get the hell out of here, she told herself.

Once she was out the door and out of his sight, she'd do the high-school-athlete thing herself and break a few cross-country records on her way back to the store. Anything after that was Reese's problem. She breathed a quiet sigh of relief as Barry reached for the doorknob, and the familiar earsplitting shriek of rusted hinges rang out.

Except that he hadn't yet turned the knob, and the shriek wasn't from the hinges.

"Hamlet!" she cried, abruptly forgetting that she was trying to make good an escape. "That was my cat. He's in here somewhere, and he sounds like he's hurt. Hamlet!"

Had she tried to describe the sound, it would be the piercing cry of a screaming baby overlaid by the nerve-tingling scrape of chalk on a board. It sounded angry . . . and frightened. Pulling away from Barry's grasp, she ran to where the foyer and narrow hall met, frantically listening for another feline screech. "Hamlet, where are you?"

"Me-ooooooooow!"

"There," she cried, pointing to the closed basement door. "He's down there."

"Darla, no! Don't go down there!"

His expression anxious, Barry raced toward her, but she had already jerked open the door and was rushing down the steps. The faint light from the corner was enough to guide her down and bright enough to show her that Barry had left his big flashlight on and sitting on the bottom step. She grabbed it, shouting, "Hamlet, where are you?"

"Me-ooooooooow!"

The sound was coming from the boiler area. She moved forward, swiftly picking her way through a path of disassembled boiler parts, and shined the light in that direction, aware of Barry's heavy footsteps pounding down the stairs after her. Hamlet screeched again, sounding this time more demanding than frightened, as if he'd been waiting impatiently for her to find him.

"Hamlet, I'm coming! What's wrong?" she called as she reached the unlit boiler and shined her light behind it.

Her beam illuminated a pair of golden green eyes that seemed to be floating well above the height of an average cat. Moving closer, she saw in relief the familiar silhouette of Hamlet, apparently unharmed. He'd stopped his unearthly crying, but as Darla watched he began pawing at something beneath him. She aimed the flashlight beam lower and then bit back a scream at what she saw.

Hamlet stood balanced atop what appeared at first glance to be a roll of black sheeting, rather like the plastic she'd seen outside in the roll-away container. But this bundle had been tied at intervals, giving it an unsettlingly familiar shape. As her beam swept farther out, Darla could see where someone had pried up the century-old brick flooring next to it and had been digging in the damp soil. A shovel had been thrust into the small pile of dirt that had already accumulated, as if the digger had stopped in his task but intended to return.

And then she noticed something else. At the spot where Hamlet had been pawing, what appeared to be a hank of long blond hair snaked out from the end of the bundle.

Oh my God, Darla thought. *I've found Tera!*

▌ TWENTY-ONE

"I TOLD YOU TO STAY OUT OF THE BASEMENT, DARLA."

Barry's voice was almost in her ear, startling her so that she jumped and dropped the flashlight. The long silver cylinder rolled lazily across the brick floor, its white beam rising and falling against the far wall. Unhurried, Barry went to retrieve it and then turned and shined the light in her direction.

"It's not what you think, Darla," he said in an oddly conversational tone. "Well, actually, I suppose it is. And I guess your next logical conclusion would be that I must have killed Curt, too."

That conclusion James and Robert had already reached. With an effort, Darla tore her gaze from tail of blond hair, which looked almost white beneath the flashlight beam, grateful that the rest of Tera was hidden away beneath the black plastic.

"That's why my manager called me," she replied in a

voiced that sounded strangely detached, even to her own ears. "He and Robert already figured it out. If I'm not back at the bookstore in a few minutes, they'll be coming here for me . . . after they call the police, of course."

"Really?"

Now, Darla heard a note of amusement in Barry's flat tone.

"Last I knew, Curt's murder was pretty much solved. The police already have their man . . . or, rather, woman. So what proof are your friends going to bring to them to show that I had anything to do with all this?" he demanded with a gesture that encompassed the basement.

Iron.

Hamlet for a witness.

Not enough to exactly hold up in court without her testimony as to what she'd seen and heard. Darla gave another reflexive glance at the wrapped body lying beside what was obviously meant to be grave, and then drew a deep breath. If she couldn't get out of that basement, chances were Barry would soon be digging a second hole alongside the first.

"It doesn't matter," she bluffed. "The point is, they know."

This time, Barry laughed aloud.

"Good try, Darla, but what you're saying is that your friends don't have squat. Add that to the fact I have no apparent motive for either of the killings, and the police have zero evidence to pin on me. Of course, now there's you"—he paused and shrugged—"but I think I can solve that little problem."

"Please, Barry, don't do this," she choked out, putting out a hand in a reflexive attempt to ward him off. "Everyone knows I'm here. It-it won't gain you anything."

"Did I ever tell you that besides pitching for my high school team, I was captain of the debate team for three years?" he asked in a conversational tone, as if she hadn't spoken. "I always did have a knack for bringing people around to my point of view."

With those words he started toward her.

For a terrible instant, Darla's only thought was that this was like every lame cliché in every bad movie she'd ever seen: the soon-to-be murder victim just standing by helplessly while her would-be killer advanced on her. *Go, go, go!* the voice in her head screamed, but her legs would not respond. She was paralyzed, caught in a waking nightmare, and unable to flee her pursuer. Being "frozen in fear" really wasn't just a casual expression, but a cold reality. And it seemed that she was having the very bad misfortune to learn this firsthand.

"Me-ooooooooow!"

The high-pitched shriek, like the battle cry of some demon feline, abruptly shattered the wall of fear surrounding her. Darla turned to run, but not before she saw Hamlet launch himself from his post atop the plastic-wrapped body. Claws fully extended, he flew right into Barry's face.

The man screamed in pain and shouted a stream of obscenities as he attempted to dislodge the cat from his upper body. Darla didn't wait to see what happened next. Adrenaline coursing through her, she sprang toward the stairs.

Fast as she ran, however, Barry was quicker. He'd managed to dislodge the attacking feline and had rushed after her, catching her arm before she could take the first step. His fingers bit through her coat sleeve, holding her in a grip from which she could not break free.

"Where in the hell do you think you're going?" he gritted out, his face inches from hers, flashlight clenched in his free hand like a club.

She could see blood freely welling in the trio of claw marks that ran down one side of his neck. Hamlet had done some damage, she saw in terrified satisfaction. But what had happened to the brave feline?

She found out an instant later when Barry gave another shout and let go of her arm. This time, Hamlet had gone into stealth mode, silently leaping up and sinking his formidable fangs into the man's shoulder. But Barry was wearing a jacket, and in a swift move the man slipped out of the coat and flung it to one side, taking Hamlet with it. Cat and jacket rolled across brick and plywood as the feline attempted to detach his claws from the fabric. An instant later he was free, and like a small black panther came charging forward yet again.

This time, however, Barry was prepared for him. With a growl of his own he flung the flashlight with unerring aim in Hamlet's direction. Darla screamed a warning, but it was too late. She heard a soft *thud*, and the cat dropped like a stone.

"Guess I still have the old pitching arm," Barry said, grim satisfaction in his tone as he strode over to where the still black form lay sprawled on the brick.

Dead?

Darla stared in shock, unable to believe that the valiant feline had not risen for another attack. But Hamlet didn't move, not even when Barry picked him up by the scruff of the neck and carried the cat's limp body to the boiler. To Darla's horror, he yanked open the firebox and tossed Hamlet inside, then slammed the rusty iron door shut.

"I don't think you'll be trying that trick again," he said with a humorless laugh. "Now, Darla, where were we?"

Where Darla was, was halfway up the stairs. Gasping for breath, she shoved through the basement door and shut it behind her, then made a beeline for the front door. She twisted the ornate knob and yanked, but the door remained stubbornly closed.

"No, no, no!" she shrieked. How could the door suddenly

be stuck like that? It had opened fine just a few minutes before.

Locked!

Barry must have taken a moment to lock the front door before following her down to the basement. Almost sobbing now, she flipped the latch and gasped in relief when the knob turned freely. She was almost home free. All she had to do was reach the street. But barely had she dragged the reluctant door a few inches open when it slammed shut again.

"You're worse than that damn cat of yours, the way you just won't quit!"

Arms on either side of her, Barry held her pinned against the door, his breath now coming in angry, ragged gasps.

"You know, I felt kind of bad about this at first," he went on in the same outraged voice. "I really liked you . . . not like that bitch Tera. But now, you've really pissed me off. I think I'm going to enjoy getting rid of you after all!"

Later on, Darla realized that this should have been her moment of greatest terror. Instead, something had kick-started her redhead's temper into overdrive, enveloping her in white-hot fury, the likes of which she'd never before felt. Maybe it was hearing Barry's total disregard for his victims, or his casual assumption that he would kill her, too. Or maybe it was just recalling how he had tossed away the fearless Hamlet like so much garbage. Whatever the cause, she knew with sudden certainty that she wasn't going down without a fight.

And with that flash of emotion came something just as useful: the memory of Robert's eager comment from the previous day. *Those fancy chopstick things in her hair? Those would make, like, really sick weapons, just like in the movies.*

With a scream of pure fury, Darla smashed her foot onto Barry's sneakered instep; then, as he stumbled back in pain, she snatched the hair sticks from her bun and stabbed him.

Had this been one of Robert's movies, each carved stick would have plunged with painful accuracy deep into Barry's chest, immediately taking him out like a staked vampire. The reality was that he easily blocked the first attempt, catching her wrist in his hand and squeezing it so tightly that her makeshift weapon dropped from her suddenly nerveless fingers. Her second attack was more successful, with the hair stick driving a good inch into his bicep. If far from fatal, the effort was enough to gain her a momentary advantage.

Barry gave a wordless, agonized shout and promptly released her. And in that instant while he was yanking the stick from his injured arm, she was free again and running, her red hair sailing about her shoulders.

Her options for what to do next had long since flashed through her mind, the first two already considered and dismissed in the space of a heartbeat. Her first escape route was the front door, but Barry—though momentarily distracted by the pain of her attack—still blocked that way. The rear door was of no use, for the stack of lumber she'd seen on her last visit still blocked that exit. Her last chance at escape, then, was through one of the unboarded windows on an upper floor.

Which was how she came to be halfway up the stairs when Barry recouped from his shock and turned to pursue her.

Holes in the floor, watch out for holes in the floor!

Remembering from last time that portions of the subfloor had been sawed through, Darla dodged the first hole she encountered, only to stumble into the sawhorse barricade surrounding the next one. She flung herself to one side and narrowly avoided dropping through the woman-sized gap, though the sound of something clattering past the sawhorses and landing on the floor below told her how close she'd come to disaster.

Scrambling to her feet again, she ignored her bruised elbows and knees and barreled up the second flight of stairs. Now, her breath was coming in strangled gasps, while sweat born of fear trickled from her armpits and down her forehead. Swiping her tangled hair from her face, she ignored the missing handrails and spindles that under other circumstances would have slowed her progress as she struggled with acrophobia. The familiar fear of falling had nothing on her newfound fear of being caught by a murderer!

Once on the third floor, she bypassed the first room and ducked into the second, praying that she had guessed correctly. Rushing to the window, she saw directly below what she was looking for: the construction Dumpster. Jumping into it would be risky, potentially even deadly—sharp wood and rough plasterboard outweighed soft insulation—but it was a chance she had to take. Catching hold of the window frame, she struggled for a few precious seconds with the sash.

Painted shut, she realized in true panic when the window, despite her best efforts, refused to budge. She swung around, wildly looking for something to break the glass. She was running out of options, and, like poor Hamlet, chances were she wouldn't be able to manage a second attack on Barry.

Barry!

He stood in the doorway now, blocking her only way out again and looking strangely unhurried as he watched her frantic struggle. The upper portion of one denim shirt sleeve was bloody, and his mouth turned down in a pained grimace, but otherwise he appeared unhampered by her previous attack. It was like smacking a grizzly on the nose, she realized with a return of her earlier hopelessness. She might have pissed him off, or even hurt him a little, but no way was that going to stop him.

Her heart beating so loudly she knew he must hear it, Darla looked again for something to break the windowpane, or failing that, something with which she could defend herself. But the room was empty of all but a few metal paint buckets and rolls of paper tape and duct tape.

Think of Curt . . . of Tera . . . of Hamlet.

But that first wave of adrenaline that had crashed through her veins had retreated just as quickly, leaving her sapped of energy. Try as she might, Darla could not summon back what had felt for those few moments like supernatural fury.

Barry must have seen the sudden despair in her expression, for he gave her a cold smile. "Looks like you made a little tactical error. What's the expression, Darla . . . trapped like a rat? Or maybe a cat?"

She took an uncertain step back. *Think!* There had to be another clever trick she could try, even something as simple as . . .

The phone! Frantically, she reached into her coat pocket, searching for her cell. It would take an instant to dial 9-1-1, and surely she could shout her location into it before Barry tried to wrestle it away. But where was it?

"Looking for this?" he asked and held out the missing cell.

Belatedly, she recalled the clatter when she'd stumbled and nearly gone through the hole in the second floor. The sound she'd heard must have been her phone slipping out of her pocket and tumbling through the gap. Now, as she watched in dismay, he let the phone drop to the floor and deliberately crushed it beneath his heel.

"Don't want to make that same mistake twice," he said with a cold smile. He bent to scoop the shattered phone into one of the empty metal paint cans and then replaced the lid, pounding it tightly shut again with his fist.

"So, as you were saying, you were here, and then you left.

And when someone asks what happened after that?" He trailed off on a mock-questioning note and shrugged. "Sorry, Darla, but it's not like I'm your boyfriend. No one expects me to keep track of your whereabouts.

"And here's something you probably don't know," he went on as she struggled not to break down into desperate sobs. "I overheard Tera telling Curt that her mother had bought a gun. Your detective friend must have figured that out for him to arrest her. Apparently, Hilda had plenty of opportunity and a whole boatload of motive. Hell, if I'd been a little more patient, I could have let her to do the job for me."

"B-but, he is—was—your friend." *Keep him talking. Buy some time.* "Why would you kill him?"

"Let's just say that my old buddy Curt found out that my relationship with the building inspector's office was a bit more . . . involved . . . than he thought. Toby and I had a few profitable little projects going on the side that didn't include him. Curt wanted a cut, and after all the work I'd put in, I wasn't inclined to share. Things got out of hand after that."

"But why bring me here so I could find Curt's body?" she pressed him. "Why not bury him in the basement, too?"

"Because it was a hell of a lot easier to have him found murdered with you to back up my story than to try to hide the body."

Barry gave his head a disgusted shake.

"Unfortunately, that kind of plan only works well once. Oh, and thanks for the tip about Bill Ferguson. If the police decide they don't have enough evidence against Hilda, I'll be sure to tell your detective friend that I overheard Bill threaten Curt more than once. With any luck, maybe we can pin your disappearance on him, too."

With that, he made a show of glancing at his watch and added, "Like you said before, daylight's burning, so why don't we get this over with? Remember, I've got a funeral to go to in Connecticut."

Once again, he advanced on her with grim purpose. Limbs quivering, Darla stubbornly began moving in a circle away from him while trying to avoid yet another hole cut through the subflooring. She vowed as she did so that first thing tomorrow—if she made it to tomorrow—she was signing up for self-defense classes. But for now, her only strategy was to keep the man from backing her into a corner. Pinned against the wall, she would be helpless. If she could keep on moving, just like in a chess game, she might still be able to slip past him and avoid a fatal checkmate.

Barry, however, knew what she was doing.

"You're not going to win this one, Darla, I promise you. The harder you keep fighting, the worse it's going to be for you—"

He broke off with a curse to dodge the roll of duct tape she had snatched from the floor and flung at him. The tape merely bounced off him, but she didn't care. She took her chance and dashed toward the door. He made a grab for her arm and caught her coat sleeve, but an instant later she had pulled the same trick he'd done with Hamlet and shrugged out of her coat, free again. She was almost to the door, and out of arm's reach now.

All except for her hair.

As she flew by him, Barry snagged his fingers in the long locks and jerked, stopping her short with a painful snap of her head that made her stumble against the doorjamb. He jerked her again, and this time her temple smacked squarely against wood. Momentarily stunned, she almost fell.

And then she was choking, her fingers helplessly scrabbling at the hands that were wrapped around her throat, cutting off any hope of screaming, any chance of breathing. Barry had won, just as he'd promised. Before the day's end she would be joining the luckless Tera in a shallow hole that would be covered again by bricks and plywood.

Unless James managed to convince the police that Barry had something to do with her disappearance, then that would be the end of it. Once Reese and his people searched the basement and found nothing, Barry would be free to plaster over the basement door as planned, guaranteeing that no one would find them, or discover Hamlet's battered body stuffed away in the ancient boiler. Barry would finish his remodel and sell the place to someone else . . . someone who would not know that a man had once been murdered within those damp subterranean walls, and would never guess that two women had followed him there in death.

But as she teetered on the last edge of unconsciousness, accepting her fate, the pressure abruptly released, and she dropped to the ground.

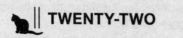 **TWENTY-TWO**

DARLA FELT THE SPLINTERED FLOOR PRESSING INTO HER cheek as she struggled for air, her vision little more than a red blur. Through the sounds of her gasps, she was aware of a distant pounding that wasn't just her throbbing head, and then ripping sounds.

"You were right, your friends have come looking for you," she heard Barry's furious voice from what seemed a long way away. He loomed in suddenly to slap something cold and sticky over her mouth before wrapping her wrists and ankles together with something that held them immobile.

"You wait all nice and comfy here. I'll talk to them and then be back to deal with you in a minute." Then he was gone, shutting the door after him and leaving her lying in a heap.

"Hang on, I'm coming," she heard Barry's voice drifting up to her through the holes in the floor.

Get up, the familiar voice in her head shouted, though it was hard to hear it over the roar of blood in her ears as her pulse raced. She tried to force her body to comply, dragging her knees to her chest so that she could shift her bound legs beneath her and prop herself into a sitting position. But even that small effort made her head spin.

Through the haze she heard the now-familiar shriek of hinges that was the front door opening and realized she had only a few moments to try to pull herself together.

Focus! James knows something is wrong . . . that's why he's here . . . don't let him leave without finding you!

Her vision began to clear, and she realized in relief that while Barry had used duct tape to bind her wrists, in his haste he'd left her arms in front. She could rip the tape from her mouth and scream for help . . . or could she? As her dizziness subsided, she saw that the tape covered not just her wrists but her hands as well, plastering them together in a prayerlike pose that left all but her fingertips immobilized.

Frantically, she began scrabbling with her fingernails at the edges of the silver tape on her face that stretched almost from ear to ear. As she did so, she was aware of voices drifting up to her, the holes in the floor channeling the sound to her as clearly as if she was in the same room.

"Uh, hi," she heard Barry say, his tone one of friendly bafflement. "I wasn't expecting guests."

"We are looking for Darla," came James's chilly response. "I spoke to her on her phone less than thirty minutes ago. She said she was here, and that she was on her way back to the store. Unfortunately, she never arrived."

"Well, I—"

"Quit stalling, Mr. Eisen."

This voice was Jake's. Thank God James had had the sense not to come alone!

"You've got about three seconds to tell us where Darla

is," she threatened, lapsing into cop mode, "and then I'm calling 9-1-1 and Detective Reese, in that order. One, two . . ."

Darla could hear the steel behind her words and knew that Barry had met his match. But the man didn't seem inclined to admit it.

"Wait a minute," he replied, sounding confused. "Darla was here, yes. I heard her talking to you, Mr. James. But then she left in a hurry. Didn't she call to tell you what happened?"

"I tried calling her on the way over," James replied, "and I got no answer."

Darla had finally loosened a corner on the tape gag. Now she began tugging on it, tears springing to her eyes as the top layer of her skin seemed to pull off with every inch of tape that she managed to dislodge. Had she been able to get a better grip, she would have ripped it away in a single agonizing motion. Instead, she was forced into this slow torture.

"Mr. Eisen, you look like you've been in a fight." This was Jake's voice again, sounding colder still. "You mind telling us how you got blood on your neck and your shirt sleeve?"

"I'm trying to explain."

Now, Barry sounded politely exasperated, and Darla could picture him giving them a deprecating shrug.

"Darla came over here looking for her cat. She got a call from you"—Darla assumed he was indicating James—"and said it was an emergency at the store. But as she was leaving, we heard a cat meowing out by the Dumpster. We ran to check, and it was Hamlet. He was injured. His back leg looked pretty messed up. We assumed he'd been hit by a car and crawled there to hide, like cats do."

"Hamlet's, like, hurt?" The incredulous voice belonged to Robert, who had apparently rounded out the posse that had come in search of her. "Where is he now? Where's Ms. Pettistone?"

"She took him to the emergency vet. I had to crawl between the container and the house to get him out, and that's how I got scratched up."

Barry's voice was rueful, the nice guy who'd tried to help out and gladly paid the price for it. And even worse, Darla thought in despair, the ex-debate captain's story sounded reasonable.

"I told her I'd call a car service so she could take him to the vet, but she said her own car was parked in the garage nearby, and it would be faster for her to go get it."

"Why didn't you go with her?" Jake's tone was accusatory, disbelieving. "How was she going to drive and carry a hurt cat all at the same time?"

"I told her I'd go. Hell, I volunteered to drive her car. But the cat was going crazy. I guess I caused him some pain when I pulled him out from where he was stuck, and he didn't want me anywhere near him. Darla said it was better for me to stay here. I should have thought to call you, Mr. James, but she said she would phone you as soon as she got to the vet."

"I have Dr. Birmingham's phone number in my contacts," James said. "Let me phone her now and see if Darla is there."

"I'll try Darla on her cell," Jake said. There was a pause, and then Darla could hear Jake's voice again, saying, "It goes straight to voice mail. James, did you get the vet?"

"I reached a recording saying that the vet's offices are closed on Sunday, and it gave an emergency number to dial. If what Mr. Eisen is telling us is indeed the truth, then perhaps they have sent Darla elsewhere."

Darla barely heard this last, however, for she had finally tugged off the final bit of tape. Though the delicate flesh around her mouth burned painfully now where she'd lost skin in the process, her emotion was one of triumph. It didn't matter that her hands and feet were still bound. All she needed to do was scream and her friends would come racing to her rescue. She took a swift breath and let it out again in what she meant to be a primal cry for help.

But what came out of her ravaged throat was nothing more than a whispered croak.

Horrified, Darla tried again, but with the same results. Though it had been brief, the pressure of Barry's hands around her throat apparently had been sufficient to do some damage. In fact, the pain that somehow had stayed on the fringes of her consciousness now swept over her. Her throat felt scraped raw and was painfully swollen, the sensation far worse than the time she'd been rushed to the emergency room as a child when the strep throat she'd contracted had set fire to her tonsils and made breathing almost impossible. And that didn't even count the raging headache from where she'd struck her head on the doorjamb.

Think! If she couldn't make some sort of noise, Jake and James and Robert might well leave without finding her. And that meant Barry would return upstairs to finish what he had started.

Trying to hold back a wave of dread at the thought, she pounded her bound hands against the wooden subfloor. The resulting sound, however, was muffled by the tape, and the vibrations absorbed by the floor's surface. At this rate, she'd never catch anyone's attention two stories down. If only she had a hammer, or something with some weight behind it!

She frantically scanned the room for something mallet-like, even though she knew all Barry's tools were downstairs. She heard Jake say, "I think I should call Reese, anyhow. And we can send Robert over to the garage to see if Darla's car is still there."

"I agree with your suggestion," James said. "In fact, I—"

"Now wait a minute."

Barry's voice had cut James short, and Darla could hear the anger in his tone.

"I don't mean to be rude, and I don't want to make it sound like I don't care about Darla or her cat, but I've got some projects I have to finish here. I was supposed to be in Connecticut for Curt's funeral, but one of the building inspectors was giving me a hard time about the wiring we just did. So I really need you people to leave right now so I can finish this project and get on the road."

"We won't be in your way," was Jake's flip reply. "Go on with what you were doing. I'm just going to call Detective Reese."

"Call him," Barry said, no longer bothering to sound like Mr. Reasonable Guy. "I'll mention to him that you guys were asked to leave and you won't. I think it's called trespassing, and probably harassment, too."

Darla, meanwhile, had spied another of the empty gallon paint cans lying near the closest wall. Not a hammer, but better than nothing. She began wriggling her way over to it, careful to avoid the hole in the floor. If this didn't worked, as a last resort she could fling herself through that opening. Her body hitting the floor below would cause enough ruckus to bring someone running—and the fall couldn't be any worse than what Barry had planned for her.

"Maybe we should leave, Jake," James was saying now, and his suggestion sent a wave of panic through her. Had Barry actually convinced them that he was hiding nothing? "If Mr. Eisen wants us off his property, I think we are obliged—"

"Hey, look what I found behind the door," Robert cut him short, his tone excited. "They look like the sticks Ms. Pettistone had in her hair this morning. And this one looks like it has, you know, blood on it!"

Blood from where I managed to stab Barry, she thought

in satisfaction as she inched her way closer to her goal. Surely the sight of blood would convince them that something was wrong there.

"Remember, I told you the cat was hurt," she could hear Barry counter reasonably. "We tried to make a splint with those hair things, but it didn't work. That's where the blood came from. She must have dropped them there."

At his words, a shudder went through her. Once again, the man had come up with a plausible argument for another uncomfortable question. Plausible enough that the trio might finally give up and unknowingly leave her behind. She couldn't let that happen. She had to get to that paint can before they marched back out the door again!

But this time, it seemed that her friends weren't buying what Barry was selling.

"That story is, in the parlance, bullshit," James replied, much to her relief. "In fact, I am beginning to think you are keeping something from us. Darla, can you hear me? Are you somewhere in this house?"

"Darla! Darla, are you here?" Jake echoed. "Damn it, Barry, you'd better spill your guts now, or I'll let Robert use that bat of his on you!"

Barry began to argue the point, and James to counter him, but Darla didn't need to hear any more. The important thing was that her friends didn't believe him!

By now, she had reached the paint can and dragged herself to her knees beside it. The sweat from her palms had seeped into the adhesive of the tape, loosening its grip on her skin. Now, she could use both hands to readily grasp the bail on the paint can. Holding it by that wire handle, she raised the empty can shoulder high and then smacked it against an exposed stud in the wall.

To her surprise, the can gave off a hollow bong, almost like a bell.

Encouraged, she raised the can and swung it against the stud again, and yet again. Each time, the dull rings were louder, reverberating in the empty room.

"Wait!" Jake's voice rose above the small hubbub that had been going on below. "What in the hell is that sound? It's almost like a cowbell ringing."

Darla raised the can to strike it again; then, recalling something Jake had said a few days earlier, she changed her mind. Grabbing the metal container by its edge now, she used it like a mallet against the floor to beat out a familiar two-part rhythm.

Shave and a haircut, two bits. Shave and a haircut, two bits.

"Oh my God, it's Darla," she heard Jake's stunned cry. "Did you hear that? She's the only one I know who does that stupid knock."

"It sounds like it's coming from, you know, upstairs," Robert added. "Here, I'll go look for her. Ms. Pettistone! Where are you?"

"Give me that bat, Robert. I might need it. James, go with him," Jake snapped. "I'll keep an eye on Mr. Eisen until Reese and his team can get here."

Darla could hear feet pounding up the first flight of stairs, heard James and Robert call her name as doors flung open. She rang her makeshift bell again, and then again, doing her best to guide them her way. And finally, a lifetime later, the door to the room where she was huddled burst open.

"Ms. Pettistone?"

"Darla?"

Both men stared at her with looks of shock, as if they'd not really believed to find her there, and in such a state. By that point, the energy she'd summoned to drag herself across the floor and play bell ringer had begun to seep away, so that she could do little more than raise her bound hands in a semblance of a greeting.

"Watch out for the hole," she croaked and then slipped into a state of semiconsciousness.

Vaguely, she was aware of the pair tearing the tape from her wrists and ankles, and then James carrying her down the two flights of stairs, Robert hovering protectively in front of him and carrying her jacket. They set her down again in the foyer, well away from Barry—though she had seen with surprise that he was facedown, with Jake standing over him and wielding what appeared to be a Louisville Slugger.

"Jake, any trouble here?" James wanted to know as he took off his coat and carefully covered Darla with it.

The ex-cop gave him a cool smile.

"Nope. Reese and the ambulance should be here any minute." Then, with a glance at the prone figure at her feet, she added, "Oh, him? I had to give our friend a little pop behind the knees with Mary Ann's bat when he tried to take off. Unfortunately, he smacked his head when he fell, so he's feeling a little woozy right now. Robert, come stand guard a minute. I need to talk to Darla."

Handing off the weapon to the teen, who promptly shouldered the bat as if he were at home plate, she hurried over to where Darla lay, her throbbing head pillowed by her coat.

"Hey, kid, you look like hell," she said with small smile, joining James in kneeling beside her. She brushed Darla's tangled red hair from her face in a motherly gesture. "Are you up to telling me what happened? James told me on the way over that he and Robert were certain Barry was responsible for murdering Curt. Given what happened to you, I'm guessing they were right."

Darla tried to nod, and then winced as her head began pounding again. "He killed Curt," she managed in a ragged whisper, "and Tera, too."

"Tera?" Jake's dark eyes opened wide, while James gave an audible gasp. "You're sure of that, kid?"

"All I saw was blond hair, but I'm sure it's her. She's in the basement."

Struggling into a sitting position despite James's protests, Darla pointed in the direction of the basement door. Her voice still hoarse, she added, "Jake, she was an innocent victim. She saw Barry kill Curt, so he killed her, too."

"Oh my God."

Jake's words were little more than a whisper, and her olive cheeks went ashen. She sunk back on her heels and slowly shook her head. "Tera's dead. Damn it, she was just a kid, too. I don't know how I'm going to break it to Hilda."

Then, with a sharp look in Barry's direction, she added, "It's a damn good thing there are plenty of witnesses here, or I might be telling Reese how I had to defend myself with a baseball bat against that son of a bitch when he attacked me."

"Swing away," James said in hard voice Darla barely recognized. "I will be happy to testify as to an unprovoked attack and a necessarily prolonged attempt at self-defense."

"Yeah, me, too," Robert chimed in and raised the bat in a threatening gesture over the prone Barry.

Jake, however, shook her head. "Satisfying as it might be, I won't have you guys perjure yourselves over that piece of garbage." Then, turning her attention back to Darla, she said more softly, "You said she's in the basement. Can you tell me where, so I can show Reese when he gets here?"

"Behind the boiler," she whispered, swiping at a tear that had rolled down her cheek. "She-she was wrapped in black plastic, like she was trash."

She paused, wishing she could forget that horrifyingly poignant sight but knowing she never would. Even though she had suspected all along that harm might have befallen the girl, she had continued to hope until that last moment for her safe return.

"He told me he was going to Connecticut today," she went

on, "but instead he stayed behind to take care of Tera. He was digging a hole in the basement floor to bury her, and then he was going to plaster over the door so no one would ever go down there again. But I messed up his plans when I came here to look for Hamlet."

"Yeah, where is he? Where's Hamlet?" Robert demanded.

Darla took a deep breath, the pain in her throat intensified by the sob she found herself holding back.

"He was the one who found Tera first," she managed. "I heard him meowing in the basement. I ran down there to look for him, and he showed me where she was. When Barry went after me, Hamlet tried to save me . . . that's why Barry had scratches on his neck. But then Barry hit him with a flashlight."

She paused and then in a rush finished, "I-I think Hamlet's dead."

"No!" Robert's disbelieving cry was that of a young boy. "Hamlet can't be dead. I'm going to go see for myself!"

"Wait!"

Jake leaped to her feet and hurried to intercept the youth. He had dropped the bat and was headed for the basement, tears streaming down his face.

"Robert, I know you're upset, but if there's a body down there, it's a crime scene. I can't let you go trampling around there, even for Hamlet."

"But what if he's not dead? Ms. Pettistone said she didn't know for sure."

"He's right. I-I don't know," Darla choked out, aware that her own tears had begun to spill in a similar storm of grief. "Please, Jake, let him look."

Jake pursed her lips and then nodded. "Can you tell him exactly where you saw Hamlet last?"

"He was lying on the bricks. Barry picked him up and threw him in the boiler firebox."

At her words, Robert's grief-stricken expression turned murderous. He rounded on Barry, who had begun to moan and stir.

"Dude, you'd better hope that Hamlet is all right. My friend Alex Putin . . . he, you know, likes cats," he threatened and ran to the basement door.

"Don't touch the handle of the firebox with your bare hands," Jake called after him as she returned to kneel beside Darla. "Fingerprints! Use your shirttail."

Robert nodded and vanished behind the door. James, meanwhile, picked up the discarded bat and took up position near Barry. Cocking his head in the direction of the front windows, he said, "I believe I hear sirens."

"About damn time," Jake replied. She gave Darla's hand a reassuring squeeze and said, "Hang in there, kid. The paramedics will be here in a minute, and we'll get you to the hospital so the docs can check you out."

Darla hugged James's coat to her like a security blanket. In a small voice that reminded her of herself thirty years earlier, she rocked back and forth there where she sat on the floor and whispered, "I don't want an ambulance. I want my kitty."

As if in answer, a faint shout came from the basement. Darla couldn't guess if it reflected Robert's shock at seeing Tera's body or if it was an indication that he'd found Hamlet. She hugged the coat more tightly, trying to tell herself that she didn't care that all that much, that she'd never wanted a cat.

It didn't work. All she could see in her mind's eye was Hamlet valiantly trying to hold off Barry so that she could escape from the basement, rather than slipping off into the shadows and leaving her alone.

Now, the emergency sirens sounded like they were just outside, so Darla didn't hear Robert come back up from the basement until he abruptly emerged through the doorway.

He was cradling a furry black form that lay limply in his arms, looking like little more than a large black pelt. Darla gasped.

"Is he . . . ?"

Is he okay? Is he dead?

She didn't know which question to ask . . . didn't dare ask either.

And then youth gave a tremulous smile. "He's breathing. But we should, like, get him to the vet."

The sirens abruptly cut off then, and over the shouted commands of the emergency personnel outside, Darla heard a querulous *meow*. The limp black form began to squirm, and a pair of emerald eyes blinked open.

"Hamlet!" Darla cried, or rather, tried to. Instead, what came out was a relieved sob.

Robert, meanwhile, had broken into a grin as the squirming was followed by another, more insistent *meow*. "Hey, little bro. What's the matter? Do you want down?"

Gently, he set Hamlet down on the floor. The feline blinked and gazed around him, as if taking roll of everyone in attendance. Spying a groggy Barry lying several feet from him, he took a step back and gave an evil hiss.

"I think we all second that sentiment," James remarked, and Darla saw him swipe away what appeared to be a suspicious bit of moisture from his eyes.

Darla blinked back her own tears. "Hey, Hamlet, thanks for taking care of me," she croaked. "You're a true cat hero."

Hamlet stared at her, green eyes bright; then, quite deliberately, he padded his way toward her.

It was at that point that the front door burst open, and Reese and two uniformed patrolmen rushed in. One of the latter shouted an all clear, and the paramedics followed inside, their gear clattering as they demanded to know where their patient might be. Jake sprang to her feet and was telling

Reese what had happened, with James chiming in with his own version. At the detective's quick word, the nearest officer slapped a pair of cuffs on Barry and then dragged him to his feet—roughly, Darla was glad to see.

But exciting as it all was, the distraction held her attention only until she felt a soft paw touch her knee. She looked down to see Hamlet gazing up at her, green eyes inscrutable. Then, with the flick of a whisker, he settled himself on her lap and began to purr.

TWENTY-THREE

"HILDA SAYS TO TELL YOU THAT SHE HOPES YOU'RE FEELING better," Jake said as she snapped her phone shut again and leaned against the counter not far from the stool where Darla sat behind the register. Then, setting a gift bag embossed with the Great Scentsations logo on the counter, she added, "And here's a combination thanks and get-well gift from her."

"Well, you deserve as much thanks as I do," Darla protested. Still, she eagerly glanced into the bag to find it filled with several products she recalled from her last foray into Hilda's shop. She smiled wryly when she saw that one was a jar of cucumber eye compresses.

Jake, meanwhile, reached into her jacket pocket and pulled out a familiar, genie-bottle-shaped vial, which she displayed with a satisfied smile of her own. "Hey, I got mine. Oh, and Hilda said she'll email you the names of some ointments that will help fade the rest of that bruising."

Darla put a self-conscious hand to her throat, which was wrapped in a bright blue paisley scarf of Great-Aunt Dee's that she'd found in a box in the back of her closet. She'd donned it less as a wry fashion statement and more to stave off questions and dismayed looks from her customers who might peg her for a battered woman and decide she needed intervention. Of course, the concealing fabric was no defense against the curious shoppers who'd seen the evening television news a few days earlier and already knew her backstory, having caught the report about what Robert had been referring to as the "Showdown at the Brownstone Corral."

The aftermath of that event, while nowhere nearly as dramatic, had been in its own way equally as trying. The ER doctor treating her had insisted that Darla stay overnight in the hospital while they assessed her head injury. *A mild concussion, along with some tracheal trauma*, was the doctor's determination.

Dressed in her green ER scrubs, the young doctor had looked to Darla like a kid who'd escaped a slumber party. Still, her soft voice had an unmistakable air of authority as she reminded Darla that not all her injuries were outwardly visible.

"Let's not forget there's a certain psychological trauma involved with being almost murdered," the woman had added, eyeing her over her clipboard with an expression that seemed to indicate she'd seen a few things in her short tenure. "You don't want to go home and pretend everything's normal, because it's not."

Though Darla had been determined to prove the doctor wrong, she'd not succeeded. Sleep was hard to come by, mostly because her dreams invariably devolved into a hazy re-creation of those frightening minutes when she'd truly feared for her life. And even safely ensconced in her apartment, she found herself jumping at every small noise and constantly looking over her shoulder lest Barry suddenly be there.

Physically, things were only a little better. Four days after her struggle with Barry, the distinct pattern of splayed fingertips was still visible on her pale flesh. The original reddish-blue coloring now had faded to a gruesome-looking combination of green and yellow; still, Jake had warned her that it would take at least another week or more for the bruising to fade completely. And while her voice was almost back to normal—the hoarseness relieved by repeated doses of hot tea and honey—the bruises were a constant reminder of just how close she'd come to being Barry Eisen's third victim.

Which brought to mind the man's second victim . . .

"That's nice of Hilda to think of me, considering what she's coping with right now," Darla said, meaning it. "So how is Tera doing?"

That the missing girl had resurfaced later that same day, while Darla had been recuperating at the hospital, had been the one bright spot in the whole tragic affair. Barely had Darla learned to her immense relief that the body she'd found in the brownstone basement had not been Tera—according to Jake, the victim was instead the blond ponytailed building inspector who'd had words with Barry a few days earlier—than Reese had called her hospital room. Fearing dire news, she'd instead been overjoyed to hear that Tera Aguilar had been discovered alive, and relatively well despite a broken arm, and was being reunited with her mother.

You won't believe this, Red, the cop had told her, *but the whole time she's been holed up with a couple of her girlfriends. And the real kicker? The girls are Alex Putin's daughters.*

The fact that Tera had been suffering from mild amnesia and was obviously in fear of her life had convinced her friends that it wasn't safe for anyone else to know where she was.

This Putin guy made a couple of phone calls and got a doc to patch her up on the QT, Reese had continued. *They figured she was hiding from an abusive boyfriend, so no way were they going to let her out in public. And Tera couldn't remember enough about what had happened to know if it was safe for her to tell her mother where she was. It wasn't until you made the news, Red, that she knew it was okay to come out of hiding.*

"The doctor said whoever set her broken arm did a decent job of it, so she won't need any follow-up surgery once she'd out of the cast," Jake said. "And she doesn't seem to have any lasting damage from the concussion, though she really doesn't remember much of what happened before she crawled out of that Dumpster and went looking for help." Jake shook her head and added, "Too bad we can't say the same thing for that building inspector friend of Eisen's. But if it comes down to a choice between either his or her body wrapped in that plastic, I'm damn glad it wasn't Tera."

"Tell me about it!" Darla agreed with a sigh. "When I saw that long blond hair sticking out of the tarp, I was sure that Barry had killed her, too. It never occurred to me it could have been Toby who had been murdered."

Now, Darla wanted to know, "Did Reese get anything out of Barry that would explain what the heck happened there?"

"At this point, since Tera is still iffy as a witness, it's mostly conjecture," Jake replied, idly playing with the tassels on the display of bookmarks beside her. "Eisen's no fool. He lawyered himself up and isn't talking. But I can make a few educated guesses."

."Go ahead," Darla urged. "I want to hear it."

"Okay. From what Reese pieced together from Tera's statement, she showed up at the brownstone Wednesday night sometime after midnight. That fits in with when Robert said he saw her on the street. Unfortunately for her, she arrives just in time to witness Eisen club her boyfriend with the crowbar. She panics and tries to run out of there. Barry doesn't want any witnesses, so he goes after her and gives her the old crowbar treatment, too. That's how she got the broken arm and concussion."

"But the whole thing about the Dumpster . . . how did Tera end up in there?" Darla wanted to know.

Jake let the tassels fall back into place and moved on to the cartoon pencil display.

"In the heat of the moment, Eisen probably didn't check Tera too closely," she replied. "He just assumed he'd killed her. And then he had the problem of two bodies lying around the brownstone. I'm sure he figured he would be pretty safe in trying to pass off Curt's death as an accident. And if the ME ruled it murder, he'd have the scrap thieves or someone else to pin it on. That's why he made sure that you were there when the body was found, to bolster that story."

Jake gave a humorless smile. "But Tera was one body too many . . . it would be pushing things to have you find both of her and Curt dead. He probably assumed he was safe enough stashing her in the Dumpster for a day or so until the cops released the crime scene. Then he could get a car and dump her somewhere, or else bury her in the basement like he was going to do with the building inspector. Then Reese threw a monkey wrench in his plan by doing a little Dumpster diving before he could move Tera's body."

"Except that Tera wasn't really dead," Darla added, stating the obvious.

This time, Jake's smile held true amusement as she nodded.

"The girl has more lives than Hamlet, and she's just as gutsy. Apparently, when she came to in the container, she managed to drag herself out—broken arm and concussion and all—and get the heck away without Eisen knowing she was gone. But she left behind her cell phone in the Dumpster."

Jake paused and chuckled outright. "Can you imagine what was going through Eisen's head while Reese was digging around in that container looking for the phone? He had to have been sweating bullets the whole time, expecting Tera's body to pop up any minute. And then the only thing Reese found was the cell. The man must have been going out of his mind wondering where she was."

"He did seem nervous," Darla told her, "but when I asked him about it later, he said it was because he was afraid Reese was there to arrest him for illegal dumping."

"Yeah, the guy has an answer for everything, doesn't he? I'm sorry that you got taken in like that, kid."

Darla nodded, not trusting herself to speak on that subject. She didn't want to go there . . . not now. Instead, she asked, "So how did Toby the building inspector fit into this? Why did Barry need to kill him, too?"

"Unless Eisen sings, we might not ever know for sure what really went down. But the police did identify the dead guy as one Toby Armbruster. He really was a building inspector for the city, but let's just say he was putting in some unauthorized overtime. Reese found a couple of complaints against him that raised a few flags."

As Darla listened with interest, Jake went on, "Best Reese can guess, Armbruster would show up at a small restaurant or business, flash his city credentials, and claim to find a problem with wiring or plumbing or something. Then he'd threaten to shut them down if they didn't get the issue fixed, pronto. The next day, they'd conveniently get a visit from Barry Eisen, who would tell them he was an approved contractor for the city. Long story short, Eisen pretends to make the fixes, collects the cash, then Armbruster does a reinspection and tells them they pass. No one's the wiser, and the two of them split the money for work that wasn't ever done."

"And Curt found out about the scheme and wanted in on it," Darla reminded her friend, "which explains how he ended up dead. But wouldn't killing Toby have been killing off the goose that laid the golden egg?"

"That's what I thought, too, so I'm guessing what happened there was semi-accidental. Think about it: Eisen had to have been going crazy over the whole disappearing-Tera situation. Then Armbruster comes poking around the place the other night for some reason. It's dark, and he's probably wearing a coat. Eisen gets a quick look at him, just enough to see that blond ponytail, and he jumps to the conclusion that Tera has come back to blackmail him or accuse him, or something. A quick whack on the head—he used a hammer this time out—and no more Tera. Except it turns out that he offed his partner in crime instead."

Darla gave a sober nod. While the dead building inspector had seemed a particularly unpleasant sort, she still didn't want to see him dead.

Jake, meanwhile, seemingly was ready to move on to a new subject.

"I don't know why you're working today," Jake now scolded her. "Even a minor concussion isn't something you fool around with. You should be resting upstairs."

"I've already done that, and I'm going stir-crazy. But I promise, I'm letting Robert do all the hard work until James gets here." Darla paused and gave her friend a conspiratorial smile. "Don't say anything to him yet, but I've decided to bump Robert up to full-time, at least until after the holidays. So all Hamlet and I have to do is sit here behind the counter and look friendly."

She gave the feline a fond look. He was sprawled across

the counter, taking up most of the spot designated for checkout, where any customer making a purchase would be sure to notice him. Normally, she would have shooed him off to a more convenient location. For the foreseeable future, however, he had a free pass on obnoxious behavior. Besides, he was on convalescent watch, just like her.

From what James had told her later, while Darla was busy protesting being loaded into the ambulance for a ride to the hospital, he and Robert had retrieved her car—the teen, to her surprise, proved to have an actual driver's license—and transported Hamlet to the emergency vet. Fortunately, Hamlet had been merely stunned by the flashlight that had hit him, and his stint inside the disassembled boiler had done him no additional harm. He'd been sent home with a couple of days' worth of pills to soothe the pain of a few minor soft-tissue injuries and a bump on his head.

James and Jake had suggested that while Darla remained in the hospital for observation, Robert should camp out in her living room to keep Hamlet company. Darla had groggily agreed. And she'd been touched to find on her return home that Robert had taken the flowers sent by her family and customers and arranged them in bright bouquets around the apartment.

"Speaking of Robert, what are we going to do about helping him find a place to live?" she asked Jake, lowering her voice, although the youth, who was upstairs busily stocking books, could not hear her. "He can't keep going from place to place each night like he's been doing."

"I know. I put out a few feelers, but nothing's come up that's in his price range. If James is tired of him, I guess he can stay on my sofa for a couple of nights until we think of something."

The bells on the front door range just then. Darla saw

with pleasure that it was Mary Ann walking in, carrying a covered dish. She gave the old woman a friendly wave.

"There you are, my dear," Mary Ann exclaimed, setting the dish on the counter. "I tried calling your home number, and when you didn't answer I took a chance you might be down here. I brought a little something for you so you don't have to cook dinner tonight."

"That's nice of you. I have to admit, I'm pretty tired of soup."

"I'm sure you are, dear. How are you feeling?"

"Much better. And Hamlet is feeling pretty perky now, too."

In fact, the cat had risen and walked over to the casserole dish that Mary Ann had left. He took a sniff and sneezed. Then he did a little scraping motion with one paw, as if he were burying something in his litter box, before turning tail and removing himself a few feet from the offending dish.

"Hamlet!" Darla scolded him. "Mary Ann went to all the trouble of making us food, and you diss it right in front of her."

"Oh, don't worry," the old woman replied with a smile and a wave of one bony hand. "It's a vegetable casserole, which is probably why he doesn't like it. But what are you doing back at work already? Didn't you just get out of the hospital?"

"They only kept me for a night . . . but don't worry, I'm still on part-time duty. I won't be back to working full-time until next week."

"Well, my gracious, don't hurry it. Though I have to keep reminding Brother of that, too." She sighed. "I have to admit, it's been difficult trying to work in the store *and* take care of him. I wonder if it's time for us to shut the place down and retire."

"But Mary Ann, you love that store," Jake protested. "Can you hire some part-time help?"

"My dear, I would love to, but in this economy, people don't really need antiques and collectibles. We're barely scraping by as it is." The old woman gave her head a brusque shake. "Quite frankly, we can't afford to hire anyone. And if we can't find someone to rent our garden apartment soon, we'll surely be in trouble."

Darla hesitated, glancing Robert's way, and then exchanged a glance with Jake. So the apartment was still available. Maybe with a little tweaking and compromise, it could prove a solution to both the Plinskis' and Robert's problems.

"Mary Ann, I have an idea."

Swiftly, she explained Robert's situation. And then, as the old woman *tsk*'d in consternation, Darla told her how she and Jake and James were taking turns keeping a roof over his head while they tried to figure out how best to help him.

"You know how it is, Mary Ann. With needing to scrape together enough money for first and last month's rent, plus a security deposit, there's no way Robert can afford any place that's inhabitable. I know your rent is pretty much what he makes here in a month now that he's full-time, but maybe you can take some of it in trade? We'd have to ask him, of course, but maybe he could work for you a few hours on his days off. And since you know him, maybe you'd be able to waive all the upfront money."

Mary Ann frowned, tapping a finger on her chin.

"Oh, Darla, I'm not sure," she said in a tone of dismay. "That's so much money."

Darla immediately felt contrite. "You're right, I shouldn't have suggested it. You and Mr. Plinski need to do what's best for you. We'll find a place for Robert eventually, and in the meantime he can stay with one of us."

"Oh no, my dear. You misunderstood me. I meant, that's far too much money for me to charge the dear boy for rent."

Then, as Darla stared at her in surprise, Mary Ann went on, "Frankly, I'm quite distressed that you didn't tell me about Robert's troubles before now. I had no idea that he wasn't living with his father anymore."

She assumed a militant expression, her strong gaze as she surveyed Darla and Jake that of a woman half her age.

"Face it, girls, Brother and I are old. And that means we can't do things we used to do, that we have to swallow our pride sometimes and ask for help. And I have accepted this. But some people think that old means foolish. They think that they can take advantage of us just because we don't see and hear as well as we used to. I don't want to be one of those old people who wakes up one morning and finds out that her tenant stole her identity and emptied her bank account. And I don't want to be the old woman who didn't know her tenant was operating a drug lab in her basement."

"Mary Ann, that would never be you," Darla protested.

The old woman gave a firm nod. "And that is because I know that a fat rent check doesn't mean a thing if the person signing it is a criminal. We know that Robert is trustworthy, and we like him very much. And it will be a comfort to have a strong young man around the shop on occasion to do the heavy lifting. So I think you need to call him over so that we can sign the deal."

Darla grinned. "You bet! Robert, come down here," she called upstairs. "Ms. Plinski is here, and she has a business proposition for you."

Robert, dressed in black and wearing a tiger-striped vest, appeared at the top of the stairs. "Yo, Ms. Plinski," he called with a smile and a wave.

Taking the steps three at a time, he landed at the bottom

of the staircase and trotted over to join them. "Hey, food," he said in approval and lifted the lid. "Green bean casserole, awesome! I just ate breakfast, but I can probably eat again."

"That food is for later," Darla admonished him with a smile. "We've got something more important to discuss. Mary Ann, why don't you tell Robert our idea?"

"Of course. Robert, it's like this. Brother and I need a tenant in our garden apartment. You would be doing us a huge favor if you moved in."

"I'd love to, Ms. Plinski . . . but I can't, you know, afford the rent," he protested, looking embarrassed.

Mary Ann shook her head. "Nonsense. We are prepared to suggest a substantial reduction in the going rate in exchange for a few hours of labor a week. I believe the revised rent amount would be within your budget," she said and named a dollar figure.

Robert's eyes widened. "That's not much more than Bill charged me to stay in his basement. Do you, like, really mean it?"

"Certainly. How soon can you move in?"

"I can move in, like, now!" he exclaimed, his tone excited. Then he paused and glanced at Darla. "That is, you know, if Ms. Pettistone says I can leave for a few minutes."

"Go ahead. You can make it up later."

Robert gave a little whoop and reached under the counter for his backpack. Then he put out a triumphant fist to Hamlet, who obligingly bumped.

"Hey, little bro, guess what? I have a home. Maybe Ms. Plinski will let me get a dog or something, so you can have some company."

"Oh dear," Mary Ann said with a shake of her head as she let the youth escort her out, "let's talk about *that* another time."

As the front door closed after the pair, Darla turned to

Jake. "Fist bump for finding Robert a forever home," she said and touched knuckles with her friend. "I think this will work out fine for all of them."

"Agreed," Jake said with a matching grin. Then she glanced at her watch. "Sorry, kid, gotta run. I've got a client meeting in five. Will you be all right alone until Robert gets back?"

"Sure. Thursday is usually a slow day, anyhow. Besides, my official attack cat has my back."

After Jake left, Darla reached under the register for the stack of invoices that had been piling up since her hospital stay. "Might as well work on these while we have some down time," she told Hamlet and reached for her checkbook. But barely had she opened the register when she heard the shop door jangle, and a familiar voice said, "Hey, Red."

▟ ‖ TWENTY-FOUR

DARLA LOOKED UP. "REESE?"

She hadn't seen him since the evening in the hospital, when he had come to take her statement. Jake had assured her that was no reflection on her. After all, she reminded Darla, he had a few other things on his list, like making sure there weren't any other victims of Barry's besides Curt and the building inspector. But Darla couldn't help but wonder if his absence had something to do with the fact that he'd arrested the wrong person for Curt's murder, and that Hamlet had been the one, for all intents and purposes, to solve the crime.

His expression unreadable, he strolled on in. Darla noted that he was back to the motorcycle jacket and jeans look. Either it was his day off, she thought, or he was no longer bucking for a promotion.

"So, holding down the fort alone?" he wanted to know.

She nodded. "Robert is next door with the Plinskis . . . it looks like he's going to rent that garden apartment from them. And James doesn't get here for another hour. So it's just me and Hamlet taking care of business."

Hearing his name, the feline in question opened a sleepy green eye and gave Reese a disdainful look. Apparently, Hamlet was not impressed by his human counterpart's detective work. Not that he and Reese had ever been best buddies; still, the cat tolerated his presence.

Unlike with Barry.

"Oh my God, I just realized something," she said with a small gasp. "Ever since the day Curt was murdered, whenever Hamlet saw Barry or sensed his presence, he would disappear. He didn't want to be in the same room with him. He knew what Barry had done, and he was afraid of him."

"Smart cat," Reese observed.

He hesitated, and then went on, "I don't like telling you this, but you'll find out eventually. It turns out this wasn't the first time the guy has been arrested for murder."

"You mean, Barry killed someone before Curt and Toby?"

The detective nodded. "There was an incident about ten years ago in Connecticut. Similar scenario, though that time the weapon of choice was a tire iron. Unfortunately, there wasn't any physical evidence to tie him to the crime, and the only witness statement got tossed for some reason. But I have a feeling the boys in Hartford will be reopening that case again soon."

"Wow," Darla replied in stunned disbelief. "I guess next time I decide to date a guy, I'd better be sure I get a paw's up from Hamlet."

And then, to her mortification, she began to cry, not stoic tears of fear or confusion, but loud, full-on sobs filled with equal parts outrage and self-pity. Reese handed her a handkerchief but wisely let her keep on crying until the storm subsided and the painful sobs had given way to the occasional sniffle.

"I'm sorry," she croaked out once she'd blown her nose and dried her eyes. "I feel like an idiot. I'm fine, Hamlet's fine, and Barry the bastard is in jail. So I don't know what I'm crying about, except that my head still hurts and my throat looks like something out of a horror movie."

"Don't be so hard on yourself, Red. If you were a cop and this had happened to you, you'd have got some mandatory days off and been sent in for counseling. But being the tough bookseller lady that you are, you're trying to soldier through this on your own. What you're suffering from is survivor PTSD."

"Posttraumatic stress disorder? You mean, like what happens to soldiers?"

"And cops and firefighters and pretty much anyone who gets put in a life-and-death situation and manages to survive it. And a concussion on top of the mental trauma makes it twice as bad. You've got your nightmares, your feelings of helplessness and paranoia."

All of which sounded uncomfortably familiar, she realized, thinking over her mental state the past few days.

He paused and gave her a keen look. "I'm not trying to tell you how to run your life, but you don't do anything about this now, you walk away as a permanent victim. I'll get you the names of a couple of people who know about that kind of thing. You might want to give one of them a call."

"Thanks, I appreciate that."

She took a deep breath and let it out. "All right, no more waterworks, at least for now. So, how's the case going? How long before he goes to trial?"

"Depends on the court's caseload, but it'll probably be a good six months at a minimum. But don't worry," he added when she gasped a little, "no way Eisen is getting out on bail. You won't have to see him again until you testify."

Testify? She hadn't thought about that, but obviously she

was a prime witness in the case. "How about I send Hamlet in my place? After all, he was the witness to the original crime."

"Yeah, about that." Reese gave his head a resigned shake. "Jake told me that all you guys think he solved the case."

"Well, he did. He knew it was Barry, and he told us so."

She went on to explain in detail about the clues that centered on "murder" and "iron," and how Hamlet's final dictionary clued had led James to tie everything to Barry's name. Then, not bothering to hide a small smirk, she finished, "I'm sorry that my sweet little kitty outsmarted you."

"We would have figured it out eventually without him," was the detective's dry response. "But so you know, there was plenty of evidence pointing to Hilda Aguilar. I didn't just pick her name out of a hat."

"The pictures I gave to Jake?" Darla asked, remembering the photos that Curt had taken of Hilda, and how the woman had torn them to shreds.

He nodded, and to her relief didn't mention the whole chain of custody thing. "That, and a series of threatening messages she left on Mr. Benedetto's voice mail that were pretty damn incriminating. And it turns out that her relationship with her daughter wasn't all sweetness and light. She and Tera had been fighting over the past couple of weeks. One of Tera's friends overheard Hilda threatening to hurt her if she didn't break it off with Curt. But the topper was that she'd bought a gun off some street guy."

A gun? So Barry hadn't been lying about that one thing, at least.

"You think about it," Reese went on, "if Eisen had waited just one more day, there's a good chance Mrs. Aguilar *would* have taken care of Benedetto for him."

"Or maybe Bill the Porn Guy would have stepped in," Darla added. "Did you ever find out why he and Curt were feuding?"

Reese nodded. "I dropped by to question him the day we located Tera's phone in the Dumpster. Ferguson wasn't willing to do much talking without a lawyer around, but he did manage to give me a little something. Apparently, Benedetto's photography skills went beyond taking pictures of pretty women in parks."

Darla held up a hand. "Don't tell me. He was photographing all the people going into the porn shop and then blackmailing them?"

"Good try, but you're not thinking like a true bottom-feeder. Turns out Benedetto had modified one of the video booths in the porn shop with a couple of strategic holes in the wall. That way, he could be in there pretending to watch movies, but the whole time he was secretly using his own video camera to record the action that went on in the room next to his."

"That's disgusting!"

Reese grinned. "Hey, it gets better. He owned one of those members-only porn websites. He was posting his home movies there and making a nice chunk of change doing it. Ferguson found out and was pretty ticked . . . but not because of any violations of privacy for his customers. He thought that since it was his place, he should be getting a cut of the action."

"Ugh, bottom-feeder is right," Darla said with a disgusted snort. "I'm seriously considering running background checks on all my customers after this. So what about Barry and Curt's brownstone? What happens to it now?"

"That'll be up to the courts . . . and by the time they figure it out, chances are the city will have already condemned the place and razed it."

"I hope so," was Darla's fervent reply. Knowing that the place where two people had died—the same place from which she had barely escaped with her life—might one day be someone's home or place of business was a chilling thought, indeed.

"And what about the scrap thieves?" she wanted to know. "It's good to know they're not the ones out there murdering people, but it would be nice to know that it's safe to leave my nice metal fixtures where they are outside."

"As a matter of fact, we haven't had any more theft complaints since we arrested Mr. Eisen," Reese said with a shrug. "It might be pure coincidence; maybe the gang found another neighborhood with better pickings and moved on. Or maybe that whole stolen scrap metal thing was another little side business that Eisen and his building inspector buddy had going. Don't worry, I'll let you know if I find out anything on that."

With the subject of murders and scrap thieves exhausted for the moment, an awkward silence fell between them. She abruptly found herself wishing for a customer to conveniently drop in and dispel the mood. When that didn't happen, she began, "So—"

"So—" Reese said at the same time and then broke off at the same moment that she did.

Darla smiled. "Let's try again. You first."

"I was going to say, so, that's all I have," Reese told her with a shrug. "You?"

"Pretty much the same."

The awkward silence fell again. Then Reese said, "Actually, there is just one more thing."

"Isn't that what Columbo used to say?" she asked with a small smile. Then, at his questioning look—surely he wasn't so young that he'd never heard of the quirky television detective before—she shook her head and added, "Never mind. What's the one more thing?"

"I thought"—he paused for a breath—"well, since I kind of barged in on your dinner the other night at your apartment, I thought I could take you out after work, if you were up to it."

"You mean, like a couple of friends going out?" she carefully asked.

He gave a quick nod. "Sure . . . I mean, like you said . . . a couple of friends."

"That would be fun. But not Greek food, if you don't mind," she hurried to clarify.

He looked perplexed but agreed. "No Greek. I was thinking we stick with good old Italian, if that's okay by you."

"It's okay by me. Shall we say seven-ish?"

"It's a date! Well, it is, but it's technically not . . . oh hell, you know what I mean," he answered and beat a hasty exit to the door. "See you later, Red . . . I mean, Darla."

"Red's okay," she heard herself saying, but by then the bells on the door were already jingling behind him.

She smiled a little and then glanced over at Hamlet, who had slept through the entire exchange—or, at least, had pretended to. She saw that both green eyes were open now and watching her. Her smile broadened, and she reached over to scratch him under the chin.

"What do you think, Hammy? He says it's not a date. Should I believe him?" Then, when Hamlet made no reply, she persisted, "How about this? Blink once for yes, and twice for no."

She didn't really expect an answer to that one, either. And so she was surprised when the cat slowly blinked once.

Yes, believe him, it's not a date.

And then a second time.

No, it is a date!

And then a third time?

Darla frowned. "Three blinks? What the heck is that supposed to mean? The only choices are yes, no . . . or," her smile returned, "aha, your vote is a *maybe*. Well, so is mine."

Then she noticed Mary Ann's casserole dish, which she'd forgotten was still sitting on the counter near the register.

"Green bean casserole, not exactly my favorite," she admitted. "Guess you were right on the money with this one, too. But I don't want to hurt Mary Ann's feelings." Then, remembering Robert's reaction to it, she went on, "However, I think this dish would make a nice little welcome-to-the-new-apartment meal for Robert tonight. What do you say?"

Hamlet stared back at her with unblinking emerald eyes for a long moment.

And then he winked.

Truth can be deadlier than fiction . . .

ELLERY ADAMS

The Last Word

A BOOKS BY THE BAY MYSTERY

Olivia Limoges and the Bayside Book Writers are excited about Oyster Bay's newest resident: bestselling novelist Nick Plumley, who's come to work on his next book. But when Olivia stops by Plumley's rental she finds that he's been strangled to death. Her instincts tell her that something from the past came back to haunt him, but she never expects that the investigation could spell doom for one of her dearest friends . . .

**"Visit Oyster Bay and you'll long
to return again and again."**

—Lorna Barrett, *New York Times* bestselling author

facebook.com/TheCrimeSceneBooks

penguin.com